After You've Gone

Also by the author:

In the Fall
Lost Nation
A Peculiar Grace

After You've Gone

Jeffrey Lent

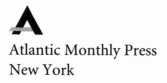

Atlantic Monthly Press
New York

Published simultaneously in Canada
Printed in the United States of America

FIRST EDITION

ISBN-10: 0-87113-894-8
ISBN-13: 978-0-87113-894-1

Atlantic Monthly Press
an imprint of Grove/Atlantic, Inc.
841 Broadway
New York, NY 10003

Distributed by Publishers Group West

www.groveatlantic.com

09 10 11 12 13   10 9 8 7 6 5 4 3 2 1

Marion, Esther, Clara

One

*I*f love had a language, he'd realized it would be this, not words or gestures but the mellifluous richness he'd heard that summer evening, anchored between the pair of violins and the bass. The musician seated with his cello tucked between his knees, bent in concentration and intensity of focus that swept and fled, stroked and drew upon the man, instrument and bow.

Henry recalled the warm room, an upper story of the Civic Club and how he'd sat next to Olivia, their moist hands clamped as if she knew his unease. During his years at Brown and then Yale he'd had opportunities to hear music performed and dismissed those out of hand. He was otherwise busy, and music was for him an unfathomable abstract for other people. So it was in Elmira the summer of 1891, soon after their marriage, that his introduction came. He remembered this string quartet, not gifted amateurs but dispatched from somewhere to here, by unknown hands and purse strings. The program a mystery, but for all the ample virtuosity of the two violin players, the settled heart-rhythm of the bass, what flowed out to him that evening was the lovely dulcet balance, as pure as the hand in his, of the cello.

The essence of life; those long drawn notes or swift arpeggios of that love both ardent and calm beside him. He was transported.

In the pale green evening—the day lengthening in a slowed leveling toward its inevitable night—he and Olivia had left the reception

1

and strolled hand in hand along the height of land above the valley of the Chemung, the grand homes of her childhood, the summer shade of big elms and sycamores and shagbarks cooling them. Walking toward their own modest pleasant first home, only two streets down and a bit to the west, closer to the campus, he stumbled over a sudden realization. And was as quickly shy.

"Olivia."

"Yes?"

"Your piano." Referring to the handsome parlor upright that had been moved into the house following their wedding, along with other bequeathed furniture. He'd considered it somewhat like the array of paintings on the walls and potted plants to be only another fixture of this new life.

"Yes?" And heard her own shyness.

"You do play it, don't you?"

"Of course."

"I've never heard you."

She was quiet a bit as they strolled and then said, "You never asked."

"So when do you play?"

"During the day." She paused again and said, "Not as often as I used to."

He knew not to ask why. He said, "Would you play for me?"

"Would you like that?"

"Certainly. Very much."

"I'd thought perhaps you didn't care for it. Since you never mentioned it."

And he had the great gift of young love, to entrust fully and so be trusted and was not wise but passionate when he responded, "I've never truly heard music until this afternoon. And I so do want to hear you."

"Oh." She was alarmed. "I'm very poor compared to those musicians."

He stopped her and swiftly kissed her, careless of passersby. She was blushing when he stepped forth and offered his arm and said, "Everything about you is beyond compare."

So he first sat and listened to her and then as both she and he became more confident and he understood better what she was doing he stood alongside her bench and although his ability to read music was limited to his early training for singing in church he soon was able to turn the pages for her as she worked her way through a much larger repertoire for piano than he'd expected. Not only the popular parlor songs, some few of which she sang in a strong rolling voice, but also not uncomplicated works of Beethoven, Chopin, and Schumann. And so music filled their house in evenings and her flush of pride met his own in this accomplishment and while she played he would rest one hand against the small of her back as he loomed gentle, her page-turner, her husband and lover.

Two

*U*nder a pewter sky of clouds folded in tight waves, the wind at his back, Henry Dorn crossed Nieuwmarkt, near empty this late afternoon almost four years since the signing of the Armistice, some few bicycles steering gingerly around patches of ice passing him as he trudged onward, his greatcoat belted tight and brushed-wool fedora clamping his ears, the canvas case with leather strapping gripped by both hands as the wind caught and tugged it, the cello a kite, a bird captured that the wind would free. His nose and cheeks were bright with cold and his lungs seemed to lodge and trap the air to freeze him from within.

Henry Dorn was fifty-five years old. He'd outlived his father's short span by nearly thirty years. He'd written his mother this past spring just before his departure for Holland but had not been back to Nova Scotia in fifteen years. He loved that gloomy spit of land between St. Mary's Bay and the wild water of Fundy like no other place but some time since had decided he'd not return there. It was a love best kept at a distance.

And then abruptly eighteen months ago the devastating double tragedy which had brought him to this place, this strange city the other side of the world. Or had seemed to at the time. Did this account fully for the essential if unspoken exile? Certainly not but from the youngest age the unpredictability of life had been a constant companion—only for that span of now-lost years had he thought otherwise.

4

Then face into the wind past the Waag and right onto Recht Boomssloot, the canal frozen, the houseboats encased, the trees skeletal traces overhanging the railings and here the wind was cut a little and he was able to carry the burden by the handle, balanced so the case rode alongside him now, the neck forward and up. As if tamed. He snorted.

He hadn't anticipated the cello when he'd signed the lease and so was faced, as he was each Tuesday afternoon, with the narrow steep steps up to the third story—a little effort was all. You got used to these things. And the staircase made possible the tall broad windows at the front, the view and serenity of height that had compelled him that sunstruck day in June when the sparsely appointed two-room apartment offered a graceful alternative to his railway hotel room and her grand suite at the Hotel Krasnapolsky.

The rooms were warm, the steam radiators thumping gently as if to remind of the coal monster in the basement. Out of his coat and hat he sat for a time on the side of the bed and studied the canvas case. His chest still straining. If he had to be trivial, why not a violin?

His sixth Tuesday. Morozov had served him tea, not in the Russian style but some brewing of his own device—likely simply a large kettle steeped throughout the day. Then sat after tuning with him and leaned forward, his hands on his knees and listened as Henry worked his way through *Kummer's Daily Exercises.* Or the 1st. Midway through Morozov stood and turned his back as if he only wanted to listen not see. When the piece was done the teacher, with no expression on his face, came and stood behind him, his right arm coming down and lifting Henry's right hand so the bow was away from the strings and guided the hand, arm, and bow through the air, hovering above the strings, not touching, just movement and then halted, pressed hard as if to say There and stepped away, settled himself and took up his own instrument and bow and played the piece through, slowly but with an even tempo, the bow not at stark right angles but quivering fluidity, not attack and retreat but sudden depths of caress. When done, Morozov looked at him, his face the same.

Morozov spoke an English less flawed than idiosyncratic. "The music," he said, "you cannot force like a dying horse."

Three hours later when the windows showed only reflected light and the cello had warmed through he opened the case and set the sheet music on the small beaten secondhand stand and brought out the instrument. The stand centered under the single electric ceiling fixture. He inserted the tail peg and tightened it and brought the beautiful fragile construction between his spread knees, tipped the bow against each string, tightened the A-string against its flat and without thinking or pausing to consider played the piece through and his right arm flexed as if it were merely an extension of the bow and was following not leading and the final six bars of the little exercise came forth into the room with all the dazzlement and purity of spring light and he sat listening to the final note trail off until all remaining was the echo in his inner ear. He sat so for a long time with no desire to move or even attempt the piece again. It was enough. An exquisite and muted triumph.

Finally he bent for the soft piece of flannel within the case and wiped the cello down. There were beautiful things in the world and there are beautiful periods or times—usually not known until they had passed. And yet throughout his life, there had been those moments when he was forced or found by accident, once again, beauty.

Briefly he considered the small table set just to the side of the large windows that held a gooseneck lamp and his pens, the sheafs of paper, the notebooks. But it was early and he had to go out again. He used to write in the mornings, at break of day but now chose to end the day. Because the writing had changed. It was his, alone. And he liked this.

There was a single gas ring he boiled coffee on mornings. Other than that he did not cook. So he wrapped again in the coat and went down the cramped stairwell and up the street to the end and entered the small single-counter café dimly lit whatever the time of day with old dark wooden walls and a stamped-tin ceiling murky from years of tobacco smoke. He sat on one of the stools and unbelted his coat and ordered the soup without asking what it was—it did not matter—the soup was a meal. With hard bread and a saucer of pickled herring. Three older men were at other stools and each glanced at him and then back to the polished wood beneath their elbows, these three part of a handful he'd come to recognize. The woman behind the bar was friendly in the way of someone who knows she has a new customer she may count on but does not know what to make of. He did not mind this. As every night he spoke Dutch and she responded in English and that was that. Without a thought he used the last hard crust to mop the soup, a brown combination of beans and ham and he did not know what else but the mopping was new to him—something that as a boy he'd have had his knuckles rapped for and as a man had never once considered but here it was the obvious thing to do—to leave anything in the bowl would have been ill-mannered and he knew this simply by observing others. Then he had a single crystal thimble on a long stem of Oude Genever, the clay bottle brought up from where it lay in chipped ice and he sipped this slowly.

It wasn't only the pickled herring but the soups reminded him of his mother's chowders: cod, scallop, haddock—each winter progressing the cubes of potato grew smaller, the fish more dense. By spring they would be down to seed potato and after great hesitation and a murmured discussion with herself, she would go the store owned by her brothers-in-law and purchase a sack of winter-stored fresh potatoes. But not until spring. They were not poor. In fact in Freeport they were wealthy people. But on Digby Neck and the Islands wealth was gained slowly and hard and easily lost, never assummed, never losing sight of the precariousness of everything and if for a moment or a day attention was diverted from that safe penurious grasp there were the God Almighty storms of the Bay to remind. The church was less sanctuary than seat of hope.

The wind had fallen with the dark and he walked slowly back along the canal, the frost in sharp refraction off the lampposts, the windows of the houses throwing warm rectangles of domesticity against the dark.

A woman passed around him, gently bumping as she did and he watched her stride away, wrapped in a scarf and long drawn-tight coat but clearly a slender young woman. He watched until she passed from sight. She did not look back.

That evening he filled his pen and wrote

I am a beginning cellist but shall not be a mediocre student. It is only so long since I was a beginner at anything.

Not true.

There should be time for work. Daydreaming loses its value when it overwhelms. It was Benjamin Franklin who asked, "Dost thou love life? Then take heed how you waste time for time is the stuff of which life is made." Maybe I always misinterpreted his meaning. He certainly wasted time in a plentitude of enjoyments, if my memory serves. How did I miss that? I wonder if Franklin played an instrument? I'm quite sure he enjoyed music. I only now understand his years in Paris. Or think I do. "Ye shall know a man by his works." I'm no longer convinced of that.

Daily I become more fond of Amsterdam. The tumult of infatuation, that heady first blush has passed and so now I proceed renewing the pace of the heart. The local citizenry surely consider me the strange American. But the shopkeepers are grown used to me, friendly in the abrupt way of the Dutch that makes sense to me now.

Write to Mother.

This last entry recurred through the filled pages. When the ink was dry he turned this page atop the stack, facedown, like the others not to be read again.

The apartment with its two small pools of light. Over the writing table and over the music stand and stool. The cello lying on its side, the swells and long neck and scroll of beauty. And the embarrassment only a teacher can know—leave the Kummer exercises for now. Practice the scales. How many variations on this had he himself begged, cajoled, thundered, red-penciled, conferenced over, tapped chalk for emphasis, sotto voce implored against his temper over the years? Countless. Was he a child again? Was all he knew of himself mere assumption? Was there even hope of relearning the world? Just months ago he'd not thought but known so. Now he was less sure. He contemplated the stack of writings.

He rose and turned off the gooseneck. Undressed and folded his trousers over the back of the chair, hung his shirt there and went on sock feet to the bed, sat and removed his socks and slipped into the bed. He reached and pulled the chain and the room and music stand went dark. Sleep far more elusive.

Somewhere in this night, Paris he assumed, was Lydia Pearce.

Whom he'd met on the North Atlantic passage, the unexpected encounter, the flare in an otherwise dark night, at first he'd thought Two lost from others recognizing comradeship. By the time they'd disembarked in Rotterdam and made their way north by train they'd entered into an irresistible but nebulous alliance. She maintained year-round suites at the Grand Hotel Krasnapolsky and for a few short days Henry had settled in a mildly depressing railroad hotel room just off the station but four days later, armed with a tip from the Krasnapolsky's concierge he'd hiked the beguiling and still mysterious network of streets in the old city and found this apartment. On the third floor, spartan and old but filled with light from the four tall windows overlooking the canal, two large rooms and he'd sat with the landlady in her groundfloor chambers for what seemed an unnecessarily long time as she dictated all the conditions as if he were a young man, a student or striving artist not quite to be entrusted with the magnificent rooms. Already, then, there, scheming how he'd bring Lydia here the first time. He was a welcome guest at her suite, even owning a key but she'd been emphatic that he maintain a separate residence.

"I'm already all the scandal I need. Not that I mind adding you to the mix," she smiled. "But I'm not without peculiarities." As if he'd needed to be told that.

The apartment was spotless, the bed linens fresh and starched. Knowing she'd wonder where he'd been that afternoon, even as she'd sent him off—pointing to the stack of correspondence awaiting after her month-long absence. So, freed anyway, he'd wandered the neighborhood and found what he was looking for, stocking the apartment carefully, selectively and all for one purpose.

"So where'd you go?" she'd queried when he arrived back at her suite, the stack of waiting letters disappeared as if spirited away by unknown hands.

"Oh," he'd said, glancing out her windows toward the evening bustle of the Dam. "Walking. I found my way back to the old square, with the weighing house—"

"Nieuwmarkt."

"Why yes. Actually I almost missed it, just crossing the easternmost tip but then went on along the other side, into the old neighborhood over there—"

"Isn't it lovely? I'd planned to take you over there myself. It's one of my favorite parts of the old city."

She was beside him, pressing gently and his arm was about her waist. Feeling delightfully sly and free of guile, he said, "Well let's explore it tomorrow. What do you say?" Turning toward her.

"Absolutely." Her face, heart shaped, subterranean brown eyes, the lock of auburn hair tumbled onto her forehead, her hair cut shorter than was the style but he liked the way it showed her delicate neck, the tautened strain of tendons of her throat when she lifted her face to his, her breath like warm bread upon him.

It was after noon the next day when they set off. Henry's excitement not diminished but growing although he'd said nothing that morning about her suggested excursion. From time to time he fingered the silent key in his trouser pocket.

So off they went, cutting through alleys and side streets, Lydia leading Henry although to onlookers they would've seemed just another couple strolling in the crystalline languor of an early summer afternoon, Henry soon with no clear idea where they were but for the general north-northwest of their bearings, when abruptly she plunged down a side street. The canal here was narrow and domestic and the overhanging trees spread nearly across it, the sun speckling down through the new leaves onto the still-green water, the trees allowed a strip of soil canalside and then the cobbled lane also in shade before the narrow four and five story domiciles of white painted brick with their gabled pitched roofs. Between the cobblestones of the roadway, too narrow but for the smallest of automobiles, and facades of the buildings, lay another small strip of soil, broken by the entrance steps and the ornate iron railings that guided up those three steps. And here they paused, looked at each other and smiled.

It was, all of it, a miracle of small perfections. Each railing was different, with its own twists and spirals, hammered buttons, vined metal stalks and leaves, and at the base of each entry its own flower garden in those smallest of possible plots. Some a profusion of density and blooms, others a single careful pairing of tall and short flowers, some so exotic Henry was sure they'd come from far distant lands. And so they went, Lydia in the blue sleeveless dress coming just below her knees, hand in hand, until one or the other paused without warning so the other was caught up, turned back face to face for the quick kiss and on again. To the next discovery, the next intriguing pairings of metal and flowers that would take Lydia into a squat to breathe close, Henry leaning behind her, his hands on her shoulders, peeking around her head to try and gain the scent also but often as not the scent he sought and found was that which came from her, the faint delicate perfume she dabbed from a vial so small he doubted his own fingers could open it—then her face tipped back to him as she rested the curve of her back against his knees, to know he was seeing what she was.

Squeezing his hand as he squatted beside her, canes of yellow roses the size of his fist rising above diminutive dimples of mounded flowers dark red with white centers, their foliage a green so deep as to be almost black and it was these leaves that allowed the combination of majestic roses and the tiny profusion of blossoms to work, to create a balanced beauty, thoughtful, intentional.

Which was when she stood and said, "Something else I've been meaning to show you but so far every day we've been out I forget about it but recall it later. Don't you have that happen to you?"

He paused a beat. "Of course," he said. "Lead onward." And helping her to her feet she came without effort or signal against him and kissed him again.

They broke out onto Nieuwmarkt faster than he'd expected and the Waag lay almost in front of them and he knew now that without effort he could find the apartment and decided this was again all happening because it had to, because there was no choice.

The square was ringed with cafés with tables set out for the afternoon sun and people sat with hats off and collars loosened against not just the warmth but the slowed draining conviviality of late afternoon. A beer wagon with a four-horse hitch trundled in the shadows on the far western side and ragged streams of cyclists pedaled by. An elderly gentleman walked a brace of small off-white terriers, his past-century mustache the same color as the dogs. Lydia's hand in his had grown warm, damp in the full sun as they worked their way, Henry thinking they were crossing over to the far side and then realizing they were aimed for the faded green and brown canvas canopies just beside the ancient weighing house.

She fell back and leaned against his arm. "The flowers in my rooms?" she said. "This is where they come from. Even in winter they're here, with gas blowers to keep them from freezing. Now of course all the flowers are cut from the fields fresh each morning. But when it's cold you can still get flowers. They have huge hothouses, all over just outside the city. One day we'll ride the tram so you can see them."

"It seems a great deal of work to have flowers in winter."

She stopped then, just feet short of the backside of the canvas stalls and took his elbows. "Flowers, having flowers, is not a luxury. I see them as being both ephemeral and a mark of civility. Which perhaps are the same thing."

"Perhaps you're right. I'd always mostly thought of flowers as decorative."

"They are not." Emphatic not challenging. She led him around to the front of the stalls and said, "Now wait here." And was gone, but not from sight.

Tin buckets filled with flowers of all types, shades and colors lined the fronts of the canvas stalls and in the strained light within he could see tiers of more buckets, more flowers, these likely more delicate against the afternoon sun. But what he was watching, as much as the splendor before him, was the woman in the blue dress pacing back and forth, dipping to look, sometimes raising a finger and one of the vendors would move behind her as if that finger communicated all that was needed. He stood considering this being versed deeply in what lay before her. As she had thus far ever appeared. And it was then, the fleet thought, that he knew he had yet to learn where she lacked command. This with no quickened pulse but only a jab of dread—one day, one way or another, he would learn that place in her. As she would in him. And how they'd muster themselves, each alone again.

She came forth with a trimmed bouquet, wrapped and tied and hugged tight to her chest, almost hiding her, her eyes tracked onto his as if he were a beacon.

"Look," she proclaimed, her excitement rippling.

And he did, leaning close, parsing the clutched tight crush and he thought perhaps some were some sort of dark sunflower but the rest were strange as life to him. "They're magnificent," he said.

And then she was laughing. "Oh God," she choked out. "Fifteen cents. Can you imagine? I get carried away. So carried away. I wanted to show you this but now what? Henry, what in the world am I going to do with them?"

And he looked again at the flowers and slowly said, "You know, perhaps I have an idea."

"And what would that be?"

He touched her laced fingers and gently took the flowers from her. "Come along," he said. "I'll show you."

He found the apartment easily and led her up the stairs, Lydia following silently and stood in the ill-furnished but attractive old rooms as she inspected, standing a long time by the tall windows. Finally she turned and said, "I like it. It's just right for you, I think."

Henry was going through the scantily stocked cupboards and found a pair of old jars to fill with water for the flowers.

"I love the windows," she went on. "So peaceful. But it's not the Dam. I love the bustle there. When I look down, I feel I'm at the center of the world. But those jars? Do you intend to steal my flowers?"

"I'd thought to offer to take them off your hands. Since you were so overcome and spending so wildly."

"Stop it. A housewarming gift."

"No, no. That'll come later. I'll pay you back."

"You're a terrible man. How did I ever get mixed up with you?"

"I've wondered that myself." She had pulled apart the oversized bouquet and was dividing the stems between the two jars and she glanced at him quickly, for a moment her face perched on a serious question and then she smiled.

She said, "This is a good place you've found, Henry Dorn."

The afternoon before the slender stock of supplies he'd laid in were limited to a bottle of Montrachet and sacks of fresh cherries and strawberries, hard bread and cheese. A block of chocolate dark and dense, wrapped in waxed white paper. They sat on the floor with the food spread between them, the windows heaved up for air and rising neighborhood sounds. A quiet, speckled afternoon.

When most all was gone but the last of the wine she lay back, her head on his lap, stretched out, her shoes kicked off and one ankle up over the other knee so her dress slid down her long thighs and pooled in her lap. She said, "I'm growing rather fond of you." Other than during sex the only admission she'd made. However intimate their conversations they'd yet to speak of themselves as joined.

"Are you sure about that?" He stroked her face, her cheeks and nose and forehead, last running a finger against her lips. He half expected her to nip him then but she didn't.

"It's a bit overwhelming."

"How could it be otherwise and be worth anything at all?"

She reached and took a flower, pulled yellow and black petals loose and let them drift onto the stomach of her blouse. "Yes," she said. And closed her eyes.

After a bit he realized she was asleep. He sat, his legs going to sleep, holding her. Still terrified and with absolutely no other place he wanted to be.

Three months later she was gone. And two months after that he lay, still waiting sleep's restless wandering.

Three

Spring 1921 came early to Elmira so by mid-May the daffodils and tulips were failing and well-placed lilacs were rioting in bloom and the grass greened and men in overalls were out pushing mowers, the spinning blades leaving clippings that for a brief period each afternoon smelled like fresh-cut hay. On a Thursday afternoon in the third week he left his office exactly at six and crossed the campus to the house. Girls hurried past with either downturned heads or quick bright smiles—both gestures reassuring and meaningless at once—they invested more power over their academic and personal futures in him than was true but only he knew that—they must believe otherwise to excel. He gave this little thought that afternoon—he'd made this same walk easily a thousand times. Perhaps closer to five. Mostly he was enjoying the summerdream of the day. Examination week was quieting everything except the twelve hundred anxious brains and then there was the week of steady hoopla and stern pronouncements of graduation and another week of letter writing and meetings with faculty and then he and Olivia would take the train north to summer at the Lake. Both of their daughters would come for visits with their husbands and young families and there were the uncertain weeks when his son Robert would come, most likely checking some girl into a hotel in Watkins Glen where he would spend most of his time from late afternoon on each day, showing up at the cottage mid-morning still hungover when father and son would circle slowly with taut jabs of language and cast eyes within the iron circle of protection erected for her son that Olivia produced. Striding with purpose, breathing the flowered spring air, the truth was simple and long known to him; he loved his three children but struggled with his son and almost always had. There were many reasons for this, starting he supposed from the beginning with the age difference between the boy and his much older sisters although even this was problematic—it seemed to Henry that he and his little man had been close as his own dreams until the frightening bout of whooping cough when the boy was eight. Although even that seemed long ago and unlikely.

Henry was holding his shoulders a bit too tightly as he walked toward dinner with his wife. And perhaps his son. There was no telling. And as frustrating as this was he knew, as he approached the tennis courts and heard the thock of a ball and saw the two young students, done with their examinations or taking a much needed break, calves flashing below their skirts, the red clay softened with the evening sun, that once he rounded the courts and passed the small clump of Lombardy poplars and his own house came into view, knew if his son was lounging on the porch or steps for the last of the sun— Henry could see him, in his golfing knickers and argyle stockings, a sweater tied over his shoulders or if it was a harder day the young man would be wearing his puttees and uniform, the swagger stick cane drifting through his fingers like a baton, even then, Robert would toss back his whiteblond hair and smile at his father and Henry's own surge would leap for a moment as his face broke to smile. How close they'd come to losing him.

It was almost as if he'd had two families. The girls born little more than a year apart, Alice first within a year of marriage and Polly fourteen months later—Polly tall like her father and willowy even yet with her young daughter, fiery, determined, even and easily pugnacious while Alice remained ever his firstborn with a game cock to her eye and mind that kept her nimble. Alice was a reader and would argue books with her father. And while she made no overt claim to peacemaker she alone could turn a conversation without anyone realizing she'd just done so. Even after almost ten years he missed her presence in his house and looked forward, most of all, to the few weeks or month she and her family would be at the Lake.

On the other side of the balance sheet were the four hundred young women he loosed upon the world each spring, each imbued with everything he'd worked his life for. For which purpose his life seemed designed. Even as undoubtedly some of these girls would lose within months or years what they had gained. He could not change the world.

It was a beautiful day. A fine afternoon for tennis. Healthy bodies. Shadows stretching but the air still warm. He looked forward to shirtsleeves over his meal. He could now smell pork roasting, the smell of food from the house still hidden, mixing with the new-mown grass—the same campus workmen who were mowing earlier that week had taken down the storm windows and doors and fitted the screens. He was a breakfast and supper man. Lunch was light, always, even in winter. Midday food clouded the mind. And the evening meal was supper. Dinner was on Sunday, the early afternoon roast joint after chapel or church and then a short nap. He would stay up late that one night of the week, composing the next week's study plans when the rest of the house was already asleep. It made perfect sense to him—the day of rest being over but for sleep.

He rounded the clump of poplars, their slender intertwined branches flecked with delicate new green and for a moment he was in their shadow and the coolness of the spring earth enveloped him and then he left the broad walkway and crossed the front lawn, up the brick walk to his house. He'd thought Olivia might be waiting him on the porch as she often did these new days but the porch was empty. He went up and in, stopping in the front hall to leaf through the mail on the telephone table and, after a moment waiting for her to hear him, he called out her name, somehow already knowing, feeling the emptiness of the house. He draped his jacket over the stair rail and loosened his tie and collar with one hand as he walked down the hall, passing the dining room already set for three and into the kitchen. The note on the table was from the housekeeper Irma, addressed to Olivia, the time noted in the upper right corner, 5:15, the quiet remonstrance of invaluable help who knew she was. The roast should come out at six-thirty and rest before being carved. It didn't matter that this was old routine—what mattered was the mistress of the house had not been there in person to thank Irma for her day.

Henry took a tumbler from the cupboard and shaved ice from the block in the icebox that stood next to the new refrigerator, went into the dining room to the cupboard built into the wall along the china cabinets, dug his wallet from his rear pocket and slipped out the small key, opened the cupboard and poured a hearty splash of rye over the ice, relocked the cupboard and replaced the key in his wallet.

Robert did quite well managing with bootleg whisky or bathtub gin.

It had not always been that way.

He carried his drink through the kitchen and out the back door where he wasn't surprised to find the Dodge sedan in place under the hickory tree and no sign of Robert's two-seat roadster. He took the first sip of his drink and went back inside, walking through the house and up the stairs, passing their bedroom with open door, the high bed made up neatly and the blinds up to let in the afternoon warmth, a pleasant room of dark wood and carpet, bedclothes, and wallpaper all varying shades of ambers. Down the hall past closed bedroom doors, the empty ones and Robert's childhood room reclaimed these four years and at the end into the small room he used as his home office, the ceiling pitched to accommodate the attic stairs. He'd have preferred to sit on the front porch for this end of day libation but even with the respectful distance according himself and his home those days were gone now, save for the comfortable nest of privacy at the lake cottages.

Henry had taken the Temperance Pledge at the age of ten in the Freeport Baptist Church and silently renounced it five years later but the message was taken and held—even in the occasional raucous parties during the summer he was the measure of thoughtful restraint.

Which didn't preclude him from enjoying his rye over ice before dinner. Or wine on festive occasions. And it hadn't been the laws of prohibition that now held that restraint in even greater check. As he told himself not for the first time that he could serve as example for no one who refused to see him as such. But still. He would do what he could.

He sat at the small rolltop desk and wrote a short note to his mother, took a checkbook from the drawer and filled out the monthly check, addressed the envelope, his script as fine and even as the ruler-snap on his knuckles all those years ago had enforced, sealed the envelope and set it aside. From the window here he could see the poplars and the tennis courts—the game had ended.

He swallowed the last of the whisky-water and stood to pull his watch from his vest pocket when he heard the car crunch in over the gravel behind the house. Whatever jaunt Robert had enlisted his mother in had come to an end. Well and good and it would remain so. Henry was determined to be pleasant over dinner. Most times he was successful and the times he was not he always knew he'd lost whatever battle was being fought. Because it was a battle without winners.

He was halfway down the upstairs hall when the front doorbell rang. He'd expected to hear their voices and the slap of the kitchen screen door the other end of the house. And realized the automobile had been far too quiet to be the roadster. He set his empty glass on a side table and called "Coming," as he made for the stairs and then the door below opened, no one bothering to ring the bell a second time and he cleared the second floor just in time to see his father-in-law Doyle Franks and longtime family friend and physician Emery Westmore let themselves in and stand looking up at him, the men side by side, faces tightly drawn and silent.

Stricken, Henry thought.

Doyle said, "I can't bear this." Then pulled a handkerchief from his breast pocket and performed some ancient ablution across his features, not blowing his nose or dabbing his eyes but something both more and less vague. Raising a screen for an unbearable moment.

Henry arrested on the fourth step.

Emery Westmore revolved his hat in his hands by the brim, crown out, shielding his belly. He said, "They were motoring back on the Horseheads Road and there was a truck on that curve just before the Erie tracks." He glanced down and said, "I'm sorry, Henry."

And a world was gone, not changed but gone and he was already lost and sinking within when some stolen voice, something borrowed or brought up, the rasp of a timorous breast-broken crow. "What are you telling me."

Later, so much later, he wandered through the house turning off all the lights except for one low reading lamp in the parlor with its frosted globe and tasseled shade to sit within a roar of silence pounding blood vessels in his ears—his very heart—and the mantle clock chimed one and he realized it was already the next day, the day after their deaths. Never mind sleep and rising in the dawn which he doubted would happen anyway. Last thing he'd turned off the scorched coffee in the percolator on the stove and realized someone, perhaps Irma, perhaps Olivia's mother Mary, or any one of the faculty wives or friends who had drifted through the house as the news spread and those self-elected who came within their rights—someone had removed the roast from the oven and placed the covered pan in the refrigerator. Alice and her family had already boarded the overnight from Chicago and he'd managed to convince not Polly but her husband Jack to wait for dawn to set out on the drive from Utica and so sat in his parlor with the date to be carved already behind him and the gaping void already drawing before him but for these hours, at least these hours now, alone and silent within the emptiness of what appeared to be a fully occupied home.

He would, he thought, in time forgive himself even as he was already forgiven for his ugly outburst as Emery Westmore described the accident where it appeared the waiting truck had blocked view of the signal lights just beyond the curve and so also the rushing freight train as Robert swept around the truck as if there was no possible reason for it to be halted there or perhaps he simply thought it was going very slowly but the whistle from the engines pulling the hundred coal hoppers had long before been swallowed by the wind as the little roadster piled head-on into and then under the massive twisting steel.

"He was drunk, wasn't he? On top of the goddamned morphine. Drunk and doped and driving his own mother and going too fast, isn't that it? Damn it, Emery, tell the truth."

But there was no truth to tell. After lunch Robert had made it most of the way through a round of golf at the Club and then wheezing and gimping had quit but his partner Fuzzy Chickering had sworn neither of them had been drinking. This, Henry knew could be true or not but even as he spat his viciousness he recoiled before it. For much as she loved her son and as she'd admitted to Henry after a single hushed late-night quarrel, also loved riding in the fast two-seater, Olivia would not have been persuaded, even on such a lovely day, if Robert was listing more than usual. In ways she worried about him more than Henry did but her indulgences were not foolish. Most likely, he knew, she was thinking the bracing motor car ride would be a tonic delightful with the afternoon, a better way for her son to fill that time than most others.

But now in the darkly hushed house there was no anger. Henry sitting alone accepted that in ways that would not last, that the days ahead would change and alter and fully reveal themselves to him but for the moment he was essentially numb to the death of his son. Not from anger and certainly not from having given up on him but a far more complex process of grief and relief, reconciliation and guilt, that extended back to the day in the spring of 1916 when the letter arrived, mailed from New York on the afternoon Robert was to board the steamer for France, already a member of the American Field Service Ambulance Corps, the letter timed so when it arrived he was already days at sea and far from their reach. As if they'd truly had any. Plucked, Henry thought, with the other young romantics eager for a war they were missing and no doubt aware of their status as the elite of American youth—the best and brightest and so already special and thus indomitable. The shrapnel and the gas seemed to end the war for him until he did come home and the war was evident in a long grip, in ways at first uncountable and then over the past four years ever more clear and leaving all three of them helpless within a seemingly endless reach.

He sat with his hands on his knees trying to sort his mind which was not ratcheting along but felt thickened as if it were the slush of a thawed pond. If this was grief he did not understand it. Nor was it the grace of faith for while he silently ran through the usual passages of condolence and strength they were vacant words more cloudy and vague than he already felt but neither was it a crisis of faith but simply God along with much else had left the house. He told himself it was the shock, the suddenness of it but even this did not explain the sluggish leaden mind. Was he thus? His true self? In a trite huff Robert had once called him a shell of an intellectual wrapped in a husk of self-importance and Henry had not risen to that juvenile jab but walked out of the room although the barb of the words had stayed with him. Not truth but that his son should see him such. Where was grief? He did not know.

Hours ago briefly alone in the kitchen with the doctor, Henry had refused the sedative offered, not able to explain he already felt sedated, only saying there had been too much of that stuff around the house anyway.

Westmore studied him and then said, "If anything, Henry, there might've been a split second when they realized what was about to happen. But the rest of it was too fast and absolute. Neither of them felt a thing."

"Am I to find solace in that?"

Westmore raised an eyebrow. "Few are so lucky in death. You know that."

"But," Henry stopped. Then quietly, as if guilty he said, "I would've liked the chance to have talked to her."

The doctor nodded. "You think so now. But such scenes are rarely as gratifying as we imagine. And usually a culmination of weeks or months of suffering. And the patient," he corrected himself, "the dying person is not always in sound mind. My own mother as she lay dying was such. I bent to kiss her cheek, thinking she was sleeping and told her that I loved her. At which she opened her eyes, raised herself onto the pillows and told me she had no idea what that meant anymore. And sank back and died. What she left me with."

Henry was quiet a moment. Then said, "Thank you."

But now this night, this morning belonged to Olivia.

He turned off the parlor light and went up through the house in the dark where he sat on the far side of the bed, his side, looking out the window upon the silent dimly lit campus, his hands spread palms down on the tightly stretched counterpane that just this morning her hands had snapped tight and tucked. They might have a housekeeper but Olivia made their own bed. As he became aware of the faint violet sachet scent of the room, so long present he wasn't sure when he'd last noted it and now recognized as long as it lasted it would be the scent of her. Then he was enveloped by the combination of absence and fullness within the house and placing his elbows on his knees sat with his face in his hands. Ephemerally he thought he heard her voice and then did not—as he tried to recall it, to raise it into the ear of memory it was maddeningly just out of reach, not even an echo so much as an audible glimmer—the tone and pitch he knew but could find no words, even direct memories of actual conversations were rendered in his own interior tongue. How could this happen so quickly? They knew each other so well. And then, the revelation of death—all this was now gone, the day-to-day gauge of himself against her, against that knowledge she had of him, was gone. And with that, a trembling uncertainty. What had he missed? What essential core of her had always been tucked back, withheld? It was true of us all, he knew this. It was how we live. And so, there is always that promise of one more fraction of knowing, one bit more slipped through one to the other. Now gone. She would recede, was receding already into the multiple beings of memory that belonged not to her but the people who knew her. He might have first claim but there were some no doubt who would think they knew her better. He'd seen and known this before—in fact it had been part of his life since his own youth. And he wavered under this, for with it came a short memory from the summer before at the Lake Cottage when he had arrived by train and walked down from the Lakemont platform and so entered the cottage with no one knowing he'd arrived and stood for a moment in the entryway; looking out the window at his two oldest grandchildren, cousins, playing on the grass that went down to the small incessant flap of wavelets against the smoothed shale shore and from down the hall overheard his daughter Polly speaking. Immediately afterward he broke it by reaching behind and pulling the screen door sharply shut because he did not want to, did not need to hear anymore of it. But still the tone and emphasis were unmistakable. As was the target of the comment.

"You're a saint, Mother. No, don't argue with me. Don't defend."

Polly's voice was clear as if in the same room. Was this then part of the expenditure of dying? If he'd paused, waited to hear Olivia's response he knew it would be no more clear than his earlier attempts, but he knew at least something of what she would've said, regardless of whatever set Polly off.

"I'm no more a saint than you, Polly."

Or some such.

They'd eaten breakfast together. Robert was not yet up. There had been no argument, no discussion, nothing memorable. Perhaps they'd

25

spoken of the coming summer reunion with the girls at the lake or that could've been the day before. She'd been wearing the yellow dress with the small blue flowers, he was sure of that. He'd read the morning paper when his plate was pushed aside, over his last cup of coffee. He'd kissed her goodbye but only the perfunctory buss of morning departure. So much lost, there. And yet. What would they have done otherwise if somehow they'd known? Emery had been right—it had been a fine lovely day for both of them right up until it tore like a sheet of paper. A far better day to die than to have someone die. A smile with no pleasure crossed his face and he was lonely again—only Olivia would've understood this wry humor upon himself. Only Olivia.

Earlier, but not much, after all had left but Doyle and Mary, Mary had come and taken him with a stern grip upon his arms, her eyes a red welter, looking up at him, an older different version of her daughter. "I was just recalling the two of you meeting. That first time. At the station to go down to the Lake. You were the new professor of English and we were all surprised by their choosing such a young man for the job. But even before you came up the word was out about you, did you know that? Now, who was it? I forget. Who was it that brought you up that summer? I can't recall. And you were so sincere and polite and in such a bad suit. There wasn't room in the carriage for you and we promised to send it back up but you said No, that you'd follow us down and we all thought that strange but endearing, a bit of a lark. And you didn't follow but loped right alongside the carriage down the hill, right beside me keeping pace all the way. Commenting on the beauty of everything we passed but all the time your eyes on Olivia. And we all knew. Maybe you didn't realize it but the rest of us did. And there was a dance the girls got together that very first night and arranged it so there was no one but you to take her . . ."

And Henry held his again-weeping mother-in-law, his head over her shoulder as he patted her back, his eyes off across the years, thinking she'd gotten it wrong—he'd glimpsed Olivia two days before that day and hadn't even known who she was but knew all he needed to.

In a long white dress tucked tight below her bosom, some sort of dairy-maid round cap trying and failing to hold her full dark chestnut hair that in sunlight took on hues of wildflower honey, her face turned away from him in a crowd of other young women but time to time her chin dipped toward him as she'd known too.

He stood in the dark room, only enough light from the window so the furniture were dark bulks although it could've been pitch night and not mattered but he made his way to the damask lace over her bureau top and lifted from among the scant bottles and single sandalwood box, the silver handled and backed hairbrush and gently pulled free one of the longer hairs there and left the room, wrapping the hair around his finger, over his wedding band as he went along the upstairs hall and stopped before Robert's door. Where he lost his grip on the hair and felt it slip like air from his fingers.

Then he leaned his head, his forehead, against the shut door of his dead son, slowly bringing his hands up to press with his forehead against the door. To keep him in place. To remain upright.

As he finally wept.

Four

*H*is uncles George and Fred, known collectively as the Dorn Brothers owned the best wharf, a store for marine supplies and other sundries, a shipbuilding yard, an ice house, coal supply and salt yard, three coastal schooners and interests in half-a-dozen fishing boats, as well as a red Highland ox and cart. The summer Henry was ten he was hired to deliver coal to the homes in Freeport and galleys of the fishing boats. Despite lye soap and the hard hot water his fingernails always held black half moons—a brand of his work. When fall came it was dark by the time school was out but he worked an hour and a half, sometimes two but the deliveries were staggered at his mother's demand so he was not out too late. And by November of that year he had earned fifteen dollars, enough for his mother Euphemia to take his measurements and send off mail order for his first suit with long pants. To this time he had only worn rough trousers to work in but short pants for school and church and the rare dress-up events. His excitement was tremendous, as the work had proclaimed him a man and now he would have the clothes to announce it. Light mail—letters—came down the Neck from Digby by stage which was ferried across Petite Passage onto Long Island but heavier objects—household furnishings, boat fittings, store goods, parcels—came up the coast from Yarmouth twice weekly and arrived between four and six o'clock in the evening depending on the weather. He met that boat seven times before a package wrapped in brown paper and tied with rough twine was handed down to him. The post-mark was a Boston mail-order firm and this seemed doubly propi-tious since that city held a great mystery for him and he ran home and tried the suit on and it fit, he thought, most handsomely. He barely slept that night and next morning dressed again in the suit to wear to school, only to be sent back upstairs to change into his old school clothes. The suit would have to wait for Sunday service. His mother was firm as ever and while he changed he already saw the advantage—his step into manhood would be witnessed not simply by his class-mates and teacher but by all the adults in the community in a solemn quiet way—the way it should be. He was a boy who long since had learned to read well past his mother's terse commands and simple tales of example. So he hung the suit carefully to wait the four days.

Two nights later the stovepipe of contention between his mother and stepfather began to burn off an accumulation of creosote while all were sleeping, the thin tin soon a ragged lace of black stitching failing before the orange fire raging inside and so collapsed, leaving four feet of open space between the parlor stove and the chimney which had already also caught fire and the tatters of pipe brought the fire down onto the carpet and against the wall and the flames shot high from the stove and by the time the smoke had filled the down-stairs and was seeping up and the chimney was roaring it was all that could be done to get everyone out, the children and their mother and stepfather. The big pump was hauled around the bay but the water was a gesture and nothing more. By dawn the house was smoking rubble, except for the chimney, which stood blackened and mighty.

And Henry stood with the rest in his nightclothes with a wild wailing crying and when his mother finally came and knelt and drew him close, her youngest son, and held him as he racked against her and held him until he was only snuffling and choking, stroking his hair until he blurted, "My suit. My beautiful suit."

Euphemia, still kneeling, slapped his face. The only time he could remember her doing so, ever. Then she said, and this he would always remember, "We've lost two homes in six years. And you snuffle over nonsense. If I should ever see you in long pants it will be when you are out of my house and none of my doing." Then she stood and left him. His sisters watched this but said nothing. He stood alone. After a time his stepfather, Charles Morrell, whom Henry and the rest of his siblings all called Mr. Morrell, came and stood by the boy, setting a hand on his shoulder but was wordless. Even at that age Henry knew this gesture was not simply about him—early that fall his stepfather had wanted to replace the pipe and Euphemia had thumped it twice and declared it sound enough for one more year. Even then when a new fire was laid you could see fire through the joints of the pipe. Until they sealed over with the creosote that would destroy it all. It was an argument badly won.

After a moment his Uncle George appeared from behind and wrapped his own wool coat around the boy and said, "Your feet are blue. Come. There's nothing to be done here."

They walked silently for a bit, Henry thinking. He needed clothes for school. Denim serge pants, canvas fishing pants—it did not matter to him. His Uncle George would want to outfit him without cost—kicking his feet against the lumped frozen sand of the road he knew this already, guessed that all the family would be offered such. But the humiliation of his mother's blunt words and slap had been seen by far more than his sisters and Mr. Morrell. There would be no handouts taken, not by him. And much coal to deliver that winter and spring just to pay for those clothes. But he would be in school that day.

George gently said, "Gil's a fishing?"

"With Captain Titus."

"Simon Titus is a good man, a good captain."

"Gilbert's a good hand."

Beside him George nodded. "He is."

Henry said, "Gil's the lucky one tonight."

They went on silent.

The coat for a man fell around Henry like a dense robe and he wrapped himself tight against the wind coming up the bay from the wild hungry water of the Bay of Fundy. The meager winter sun was not up yet but it was mere light anyway, there was no warmth to it as if it had died or flared out to an ember, a shadow of a sun. They passed the field of salting racks and were out along the other arm of St. Mary's Bay, away from the town. Here was the wharf with the schooners, and the boatyards and the store, the piers of fishing boats, the shacks built on stilts for lobster traps and sail-lofts and netting-works—the world of men. The store windows were lit. It opened at three in the morning for the fishermen and Henry, walking toward it, knew his Uncle had seen the house burning from there and helped haul the pump. And so the boy walked toward the dawn-quiet store and resolved to ask the question that his mother had refused the once he'd asked her. The question Gil had beaten him with a strange vigor in his only other attempt. But he would ask Uncle George. And George would tell him. Something at least. Not because of the fire. But because the boy knew it was time.

The interior was a sensory assault after the brittle salt air—the new rubber smell of fishing boots and vulcanized overalls and coats and gloves, the faint-straw odor of the great spools of hempen rope, the stringent ribbons of kerosene, raw plug tobacco and old cigar smoke and like everywhere else along this side of the bay the constant underbelly of fish. Rows of lanterns hung overhead alongside gaffs, long fish knives, scaling pliers, and high along one rafter an old whaling harpoon—not for sale. There were shelves of rough clothes and racks of wool coats, blankets, mittens. A crate of flares. A stack of new varnished oars for the dories. One small shelf of food—canned peaches and pears, sacks of onions and potatoes. On the counter glass crocks half the size of him filled with pickled eggs. A smaller jar of hard licorice drops.

Uncle George took his place up behind the counter in his plain suit with vest and his heavy white mustache and thick hair that rolled back from his high forehead as if his earlier days had blown it there forever. The man watched the boy and the boy watched the man.

Uncle George said, "Your mother—" and stopped.

Henry said, "Just because she argued the pipe was sound doesn't mean Mr. Morrell had to leave it like that."

His uncle studied him. He said, "Well. Charlie Morrell is a good man. And it was far more than Euphemia Moore he took on when she brought the lot of you back."

Henry said, "She was a Dorn then."

George Dorn nodded. "In a sense. A manner of speaking. But she was born a Moore and will remain one. It's the stubbornness of a woman raised below what she regards as her rightful place. But you're here for clothes. Pick out what you need."

"I'm not after glad-rags. But I can't go to school in my nightshirt." And opened the loaned coat and worked his way out of it and folded it and set it aside. His uncle came around the counter and looked him up and down.

He said, "You'll look more like you're ready for the boats. But you'll be warm enough. We'll start with socks for them blue feet and long underwear and work up from there. How does that sound?"

Henry said, "I'll work it off."

His uncle reached and rubbed the boy's head. "I'd not charge for a tragedy such as this. You'll need to be earning money anyway, not working off debt."

"No."

"Suppose I was to refuse you, then?"

The boy stood silent.

George did not wait. But went about gathering the odd assortment of clothing he had in the smallest of men's sizes. As he did he talked, almost as if to himself.

"The difference between a gift and a debt can be large or small and it's not always easy to see the difference twixt the two so what we'll do is simple and that's I'll charge you cost for the clothes, which is a gift but allows you the debt. I lose nothing that way but my profit and you gain something which is pride so we both come out ahead and that is the end of that argument. And you'll need not one but two sets of everything or else you'll be in school each day layered in coal dust and your mother would be up the Neck buying you what you don't want her to buy. As it is she'll have to keep ahead of the wash but that's not my worry. She might not admit or remember but it won't be the first time a Moore has reddened their hands with hard soap. At the moment her mind's upon where the lot of you'll be living."

Henry was dressing. He was very cold. He said, "I guess there's Mr. Morrell's old house."

"The Morrell house is rough. Men are funny. They can do most anything they set their minds to but I've seen it before—they just let a place run down. Still, I'd imagine you're right and that's where you'll end up. At least for the winter. But I'll bet you a dime come spring Euphemia rebuilds right there on that burned-out lot."

Henry was nearly dressed. The denim pants were long and he rolled them up and the shirt was short at the wrists but he was used to that. The coat was heavy red and black checked wool and came far down the backs of his hands. He said, "Uncle George?"

"What is it?"

Henry heard the caution as if his uncle knew there was a shift in their particular wind. But he forged forward. "What happened to my father?"

George glanced toward the window. To see if anyone else was approaching. To gather his thoughts. Then turned back to the boy and said, "Why you already know. Certainly you remember. He took the whole lot of you down to the Boston States when you were just a little boy and wasn't there but close to two years when he took sick and died and your mother buried him and brought all of you back up here. Where you belonged."

Henry said, "No. What really happened?"

His uncle studied him a long moment. And part of that moment was the first time Henry could pinpoint for sure that the world of adults was less certain, more tenuous, strained, and daily in struggle toward events unknown—the future.

George said, "Even dressed warm as anyone out on the Banks you're still shivering. Do you drink coffee?"

"No sir."

"Well, it's a good morning to start. Come back and sit. You might be late for school."

"I guess," Henry said. "I've got as good an excuse this morning as I'll ever have."

George poured coffee into two white and black speckled enameled cups and lightened both with condensed milk from a tin and went around behind the counter, Henry following. There was an angled clerk's desk with a wall rack of numbered and lettered cubicles against the wall behind the desk. The desktop was a fury of paper, from long legal forms to slips of paper torn from brown bags, stacks of letters rubber-banded together and a pad of paper with the Dorn Brothers letterhead, a can of pencils and a set of pens and inkpots and George sat there, swiveled around and indicated the other chair, which once had a woven rush seat but the rush was gone so a piece of plank was nailed over the seat. Henry sat and his uncle handed him the coffee. The boy sipped and was transported—the sublime flavor and warmth running down into him and so one of life's long loves began for him.

"It's good," he said.

His uncle did not respond. He chewed one corner of his mustache, small persistent nippings of thought. Then ran his tongue around his lips, drank from his cup and said, "Your father was the youngest of us boys. He was different, some would say strange." He paused then and scowled at his nephew. "You asked me and I'm going to tell you. What you make of it's your business. But it stays between the two of us, do you understand that?"

Braver then he felt, Henry said, "Yes sir."

George thought a bit and then went on. "They say he never belonged in this place but then I don't know the place he would have
belonged. There are men, and he was one of them, who aren't of their
time. Or perhaps any time, as any place. He dwelt inside himself. He
couldn't absorb the everyday, it bored him, and frustrated him I think
as well. Yet when left to himself he became nervous, unsettled, almost
flopping. When he was like that there was a look in his eye like a
skinned fish. I couldn't tell you more than that what it was like to be
Samuel Dorn but I wouldn't want to know either. Whatever, it wasn't
comfortable, nor easy to be around. I think perhaps where he failed
was his mind could not invest in what was before him but he lacked
the resources to do with it what he might have. You must recall, all
he had was six grades and that spotty. He weren't much older than
you when he went to work on the boats but that didn't last the year.
It wasn't that he was slight, like you; he was but there are plenty men
lean and tough. It was that he would stand in the midst of hauling
nets or be gazing off toward the black clouds working up upon the
crew frantic to get the work done and in ahead of the squall or storm
or gale—some days you never know what it'll be until it's upon you.
But he would watch it as if studying how it unfolded. Which is a unusual mind and some rare intelligence I dare say myself but not the
sort of hand you want working alongside you. Like I said, it wasn't
even that first season and there were no captains who would have him.

"So Fred and I put him to clerk in the store and he was a fair hand
at that. Still a daydreamer but there's time enough for that and he was
sharp with figures and Fred and I were still younger fellows, at least
than we are now and so I went back to running one of the packet
schooners, which as a young man I loved nothing better. Then he met
your mother and we thought There, Euphemia Moore is just the one
to buckle him down. And for a time it worked well. Fred and I came
near making him a partner after Gil and Lucy had come along. He
seemed well settled. Then, I swear it wasn't maybe a week before we
were going to sit down with him but he came and asked for a six

month leave from the store. Six months off! And the season just starting. We tried to talk him out of it but he was determined. He'd saved
enough to live on. And they had the house—it had been our grandparents's and was conferred as a wedding gift. I guess maybe then we
all knew he would need at least that much help.

"Now, I make him sound something like an idiot or a ne'er do
well but he weren't either one. He had a gift and it was considerable.
He could draw. And he made paintings too, landscapes, the sea, scenes
from fishing, all of what he knew. He had no training at all but I saw
a many of them and he had a gift there. But, even more so than that
was his drawings in pencil or pen. He'd go down along the Bay at low
tide and find some thing or another. A piece of driftwood. Even just
a scrap of kelp. Scallop shells for the love of God! But he'd take it home
and sketch that thing out in the finest lines you ever saw and right
there on that piece of paper was the most everyday thing we'd all
stepped on a thousand times and it was not just beautiful. I mean the
drawing was not just beautiful in being accurate. But he had a way of
bringing it onto the page where you recognized it immediately, the
detail incredible to see but it was more than that. It was as if he discerned the perfection in those things and rendered them for us to
understand as well. It's hard to explain. You could set a scallop shell
next to his drawing of one and it was the drawing that made you suck
your wind in. As if he saw the design of the Lord in these simple things.
Or the Lord allowed him so the rest of us might pause over them
as well."

"What happened to them? The drawings? The paintings too?"

"Wait. You did the asking. I do the telling. So he took the six
months and then six more and then six more. During that time you
were born. Euphemia never complained, at least to any of us and never
ran a charge account neither, but she bought precious little. They had
a garden like everyone of course and she and Gilbert would scallop
in the bay and dig clams too. They had a cow. Nobody was starving
but it wasn't a flourishing neither.

"Then Sam came to me and wanted a mortgage on the house. To buy passage for the whole family to Boston. He had these two huge folders he'd made of box-cardboard himself and he showed me some of the work he'd done and said he'd been in contact with a man in the States who thought the pictures was good enough to earn a living with. Now, your father was not the type that some stroke of luck like that he'd be worked up about. No. He was quiet and serious and, God's Truth, I thought Maybe this is what he needs. Maybe this is where he's truly to fit in this life. So I refused the mortgage but gave him passage and told him there was always return available and if he should end up back here we'd work out repayment at that time. It was the closest I could come to telling him I thought it was the right thing. But I think he knew.

"Now this part is thin. Your mother could tell you more but she won't. All I really know is things went well enough, maybe not setting the woods on fire like he'd hoped but they were doing well enough so after the first year they were able to buy a little house somewhere outside of Boston. Newton, I think the town's called. So yes, you all went down there. And Eva was born there. What none of us knew was your father had the tuberculosis. I guess he hid it well enough, although your mother must have known. That secret I don't hold against her, it was between the two of them. And some people, most in fact, live years with it. But your father died of it on a single afternoon and evening. A great hemorrhage of blood that would not stop, that could not be stopped. What I do not, can not and never will, forgive your mother for was the first I heard was a telegram saying he was dead and buried and she and you children were returning. Why she waited so long I'll never know. Why she buried him there when it would have been simple to put him on ice and bring him home I'll never know. I try and give the benefit of doubt—she likely was not thinking straight at such a time.

"But there's a little more you need to know. A pair of stories your father heard from your grandfather who had heard them from his great-grandfather who lived to the wondrous and likely horrible old age of one hundred six. The first is the family came up from the States after the American Rebellion, good solid loyalists. But they had been there, down in New York before it was New York, when it was New Amsterdam for nigh two hundred years before they came up here. That fascinated him. When he was a lad he would go round pestering all the old people for stories back to those days. Which never went far enough back to suit him. Because, you see, along with that first Dorn to come first to Yarmouth then Digby then down the Neck to Freeport there also came another story. Or the legend of a story. The ghost of one. But that same old great-grandfather, Abraham Dorn, or rather van Doorn as the family was known then, had this old glimmer of a tale that the first one of the family to leave Holland and settle in New Amsterdam did so because of some trouble behind him. Something he wanted hidden. Time's done its work there. But your father, those two stories, they were a haunt to him. I think because a part of him thought that if he could only somehow follow it all back he would know something, comprehend something missing from him. Now, I can't explain just why I think this, but it seems to me there was a connection between that urge and his striving to make those beautiful pictures."

"So what did happen to the pictures?"

George was quiet a moment and when he spoke his voice was quieter also. "I guess there's a plenty somewhere down in the States. If he was making a living at it."

"All of them?"

"I believe," George said. "I believe before she returned with you children, your mother destroyed what was left of them."

"Why would she do that?"

George looked at his nephew. Locked in a drawer under the desk he sat at were half a dozen of the early drawings. But he would not mention this. It was not the right time, certainly not the right day. He spoke slowly. "I imagine, they were too painful for her to keep.

Please, do not mention them to her. Certainly not today. And if you get it into your head to talk to her about all this do me one favor."

"Yes sir?"

"Come talk to me first."

Henry studied his Uncle. Then he stood from the hard seat. "I'm late for school. I'll be by after to deliver coal."

"Perhaps tonight you should help your family in their new dwelling, be it Morrell's or somewhere else."

"They've enough hands. And people count on me. Thank you, Uncle George."

"You were ready to know. Now, pay attention in school."

A smile flashed, a bit of joke between them—Henry was ahead a grade for his age. "I'll try."

"Did you like the coffee?"

"I did. Afternoons, it would warm me before I set out with the coal."

George nodded. "Just don't tell your mother. She'll think it'll stunt your growth. But no fear of that, eh boy?"

"No sir."

Five

Next to the gas-ring was a glazed bowl of tough-skinned oranges from Spain that when broken open revealed a pulp crimson in color and a flavor vibrantly tart that shrank to sweetness as it was chewed. In the morning after his coffee he would eat one of these fruits and stale bread bought the day before with chipped hard butter he kept on his window ledge. The apartment was always cold in the morning although the pipes continued their sporadic hissing and thumping and he could only guess that the furnace and boiler were stoked on some schedule discerned by the landlady who clearly believed there was virtue to be attained starting the day this way. Henry understood well enough coal heating to know there was no money saved in the process—what was cold took more fuel to warm than to maintain warm. In his younger years, those not so far passed, he would've sought the woman out and tried to explain this but now he accepted it as it was and so did not spend his mornings reading or practicing the cello or brooding melancholic but peered from the windows to gauge the weather and dressed to his best guess and went out onto the streets to walk the morning away. He walked mostly the great loops of streets of the old town that lay within the ring of the Amstel and the canals that ran up toward the open water of the Het Ij, separated from the rest of the old city by Prins Hendrikkade and the Centraal Station, but he avoided that end—the Station held no allure and suggested a folly he refused to consider. So he walked. Over the weeks extending his way beyond the main thoroughfares and obvious shopping jostle of Kalverstraat and learned the beauty of those small pinched alleys with their implausible nooked shops of uncertain and oft confusing array of goods. A room perhaps ten feet square would hold a pair of marble topped end tables, a brass spittoon, a collection of chipped porcelain dolls and three or four old leather folios. With an American cigar store Indian standing watch over these precious items. Or the used bookstore with its small bins of British and American editions of classics and outdated popular fictions. A woman sat behind one of the tables reading a magazine. She wore her hair in a tight practical bun—the hair of a woman who had just entered middle age. Her facial structure was strong and, when he was out again on the narrow pedestrian way, his feet bumping against raised cobbles he realized she was a beautiful woman who had someway given up on her own beauty. A husband and mob of children he guessed. More so, some heaving disappointment in her life. But then he was prone to seek that in others, these days.

It was in this way early in the fall, when the weather was still alternating with warmth of summer and the chill rain that was just-not freezing, that he found the cello. Which he did not know he was looking for until it appeared.

It was not that innocent. The cello was not found in one of those hob-gob shops but an emporium devoted to used instruments he entered deliberately, although he thought he was browsing. But had held a quiet but deliberate affection for this instrument ever since hearing one played for the first time more than a quarter century before. Of course there had been music in the house, first Olivia and then both girls playing the piano and then the gramophones. But until now, or not even yet, the idea just dawning, taking shape, he'd never considered attempting such a thing himself. Although through years of listening to music both in performance and recordings, it had been the cello that drew him. And now he stood before one, available, his for an acceptable sum. The cello was upright in a stand, polished to catch and hold all available light in its buffed contours and he walked straight to it and stood looking down upon it. He turned away and took up a clarinet from its velvet-lined case and turned it about in his hands but only as a pause, as the truth of his consideration was coming over him. He then went to the bins of sheet music and thumbed through and was about to leave the store when he turned and looked again at the cello. And his reaction was again direct and immediate but this time twofold in a combination that was embarrassing and emboldening at once—his mind heard the lovely soft notes ranging like a voice in a room just beyond his knowing but not locked, beckoning even. He turned away and went out and walked hard around the block and was sweating in a damp misting rain when he returned without pause through the door and bought the thing.

In that first week he twice took it out and with tentative fingers attempted to find notes but the gut strings were old and impossible to tune even if he'd been sure of the tuning. Which he was not. It was clear he needed a teacher but he had no idea how to find one beyond the obvious return to the shop where the cello was acquired and inquire there but his pride was up—the young clerk who'd sold it to him had been swift, almost rude with the transaction. But one morning purchasing the *International Herald Tribune* for the news in English, without forethought at all he asked the proprietor if, by chance, he happened to know of a cello or violin teacher. Who looked up from reading the English headlines upside down from the paper laid on the counter and said, "You want the Russian."

"Yes?"

The man nodded confirmation. "Oude Hoogstraat. Past the brewery but before the fish market. Yes?"

"Yes." Henry knew the street, or had passed it and could find it again. The rest of the directions were vague but interesting. But if it took two or three days that was fine. He was learning the city at a pace he liked. Also, a fish market could not be that difficult to locate.

And neither was the brewery. Outside both were carts and resting horses, barrels and huge woven square baskets, and from both
strong odors. Approaching he could see the workers around the carts
but it was the fish he smelled first. And for the briefest of moments
trembled as if approaching his mother's house but also considered
the single drawing matted and framed that was the sole decoration
on his apartment wall, an ink study his father had made of a basket
of cod that Uncle George had given him the night before he was to
board the Boston-bound schooner for the rest of his life. Then, coming closer, mingling in an elaborate overlay came the smell of stale
beer and the more pungent odors of malt and roasting grain. He
paused, moving aside to let a beer wagon pass by and standing so spied
between the wide doors of the two businesses a boarded-up storefront
with a single dark brown door set into the center and above that but
still on street level a pair of filthy windows. He stood considering this
for some time. If this was the right place, and it had to be, what sort
of man would choose to live here? No walls would be thick enough
to mute the jumble and roar of sound nor cut the odors. He knew
fish—regardless of how much they might wash down the floors and
the processing rooms and the cobbles out front the smell was perma-
nent. The business might cease but for years the ghosts of fish would
swim the air. And it seemed brewing was a vein similar. A musician,
a teacher, would be a man of some refinement. He came close to turning away, to begin the search again when the answer came to him. A
very poor man of refinement. He'd once been one himself.

He knocked and waited. If there was sound of any sort within it
was lost under the commercial din. More beer wagons rolled behind
him. He knocked again. After a bit he decided that perhaps it was
either truly the wrong address or the Russian was out, thinking he
himself would be if he lived here. Perhaps it was quieter at night. And
like anyone else the Russian would leave to shop, buy newspapers,
pick up laundry. Henry was about to turn when the door opened. Six

inches. A small alert face, bald above but with the idea of hair blown back just out of sight. Smacked tight mouth.

In his rudimentary Dutch, Henry asked if he was the music teacher Morozov.

The man swept Henry up and down and said, "You are English?"

"American."

"American?" The suspicion was tangible, far beyond the barely propped door and tone of voice but as if the man had his own competing odor of fear to slip turtlelike within the fish and beer odors.

Henry said, "I'm a retired professor. Not of music. But I've purchased a cello. I would like to learn to play it."

"A cello? Who sent you?"

Henry told him.

"You play another instrument then? A piano perhaps?"

"My wife and daughters all played the piano. I've never learned an instrument."

The Russian leaned a little more, glancing up and down the street. Henry was not sure what he was looking for. Or how many things he was looking for. The man turned his eyes back up. Pale eyes of a blue gray. His face was heavily creased and worn as if a frown of concern had been stamped there years ago.

The Russian said, "This wife. These daughters. Where are they?"

And for the shortest of moments Henry took offense. He was there for music lessons, not interrogation. But he simply said, "My wife died almost two years ago. My daughters are grown with families of their own. I'm alone."

The man now also paused but did not take his eyes away. He said, his voice a tone softer, "So you have a cello."

Henry said nothing.

The man nodded. Then, without opening the door or extending a hand, said, "I'm Dmitri Morozov. Next Tuesday at two in the afternoon. Twelve guilders."

"My name is Henry Dorn. What should I bring?"

"Dorn? A Dutch name." The suspicion was back.

"Yes," he said. " But a long time ago. Three hundred years."

A pause. Then, "Three hundred years. A long time to come home."

Henry said, "It feels that way. Now that I'm here."

"Three hundred years. The cello is not new?"

"No."

"Buy new strings. And then we will see what you have."

"Very well, then. Next Tuesday at two."

But the Russian had already shut the door. And Henry Dorn who had spent his adult life with teachers and professors of every stripe, type and disposition thought this might turn out to be that rare event. A singular being. At the least, his shoes slipping through the fish overwash on the cobbles, a mind framed and informed by a culture he'd studied but never encountered in an actual person. As he walked, contemplating this it occurred to him he was lonely. And because of this, or more truly to spite the loneliness he hiked on through the streets until he came upon the store where he'd found the cello and with something like his former self firmly and politely requested a new set of strings, a tuning fork and glancing upon it a sturdy secondhand music stand. He bought no sheet music because that would be Morozov's job. To tell him how and with what to proceed. Then walked directly home and took the delicate gut strings from their paper envelopes and began to learn. The strings were obvious by size but the key was the envelopes, labeled from largest to finest. C,D,G and A. He removed the old strings one at a time so he might study how they were put in place and one at a time restrung the instrument. Then sat and did his best to tune the cello. It was not quite right, but close. There was satisfaction. Small to some perhaps.

He went out for his supper and returned and the fall dusk was settling in, the windows holding an array of light from the sky, water, and buildings in a multiple of glimpses and reflections extraordinary and radiant. He sat and watched the last bit of day lingering and lengthening—not a draining of dusk into dark like home. Odd word, he thought. Home.

He stood and turned on the gooseneck lamp on his writing table and tipped the metal neck so the flood of light went up the wall and went and studied the drawing of the basket of cod for a short time. But he knew it so well he could see it always and nothing new was revealed tonight. Out loud he said, "You ask too much."

The third evening together on the crossing, Lydia Pearce had ended a discussion of particular frustration for them both by asking, "Henry, what do you want?"

He had not been able to tell her.

Olivia would have known. And that, perhaps, was the problem. Not that Lydia did not know but somehow he suspected his dear wife was still too close. Perhaps her spirit in his memory and sense of honor. Or perhaps he was frightened of this young woman who so strangely resembled everything he'd spent his life's work upon.

Six

O God whose mercies can not be numbered.
   The deaths of his wife and son produced a series of stunned blurred relentless days and nights leading toward the double funeral after which Henry felt battered and marooned as upon a pinnacle of loosely stacked roofing slates, the rush of people suddenly receded, the press of which he'd ridden in perverse energy that while it was occurring seemed what life would now be like, until it was done and he was utterly alone.

He will swallow up death in victory.

A sullen morning with low wet woolen skies above the tower of Trinity Episcopal Church, the early promise of May abated for several days. Henry upright and rigid with a daughter either side of him, flanked by granddaughters and alert sons-in-law. The other front pew held Doyle and Mary and Olivia's bachelor brother Quincy and the two aunts and Mary's mother, a collapsed crimped woman in a wicker wheelchair.

The two coffins under their palls.

Like as the hart desireth the water-brooks

So longeth my soul after Thee O God.

The nave filled behind them, the scent of damp wool and undoubtedly compassionate small dashes of perfume sifting in waves. The lilies of resurrection flanking the alter. His chest constricted, his hands squeezed by his daughters, Polly weeping silently but for the shudders against him.

Raised in incorruption.

The rising and singing and sitting again. Henry did not sing. The prayers. He kept his eyes open upon the two caskets, his hands now furious as if his fingers would rend and shatter themselves.

And now shall he lift up mine head

Above mine enemies around me.

Incongruous, somewhere in the ranks of pews behind him sat four young veterans of the American Field Service as well as their officer, the same man who'd recruited Robert from Cornell. Met the evening before at the vigil, the man who for five years Henry had entertained the possibility of meeting and the words he might say—words sucked out of him, gone. Perhaps it was the moment, as likely the presence of the other young men, ambulance drivers. The words in that letter late autumn of 1916:

> *Robert, alone with the other drivers, is an honorable man in a place utterly shorn of honor & humanity. None envisioned what they'd encountered, few quailed. Robert wasn't fearless, we all work in great fear. But the work must be done. His wounds are such that I speak with great confidence of his recovery. I shall, I swear upon my soul, return your son to you whole. Most sincerely, diddly-do.*

Six months later with sunken cheeks and skin like wax Robert hobbled off the train on crutches, his rasping wheeze from the effort accentuating his appearance that stopped Henry even as Olivia rushed forward, Robert's head raised then a bit over his mother's shoulder to meet his father's eye, a solemn cold appraisal as if battle had already been joined. Or joined again. The morphine still a secret but not for long, Robert caring less about the crushed tops of the glass ampoules, the syringe rinsed with alcohol and rubber tourniquet left on the glass shelf below the medicine cabinet in the bathroom. Home a month and the wicked little roadster appeared. I was a volunteer, Robert explained to his father, but I still got paid. And now? And now what? Olivia long into more nights than Henry could recall, listening, talking, responding, defending. Time, she'd said. Over and over. Time and patience. Cajoling. Excusing was what Henry thought but knew better than to say. And did not need to because Robert felt it from his father as a current, a pulsation. Blown off the motorcycle with its sidecar carrying a French officer from a dressing station outside of Verdun, back, back toward the lines and the field hospital, the mortar Robert said heard as a sudden shriek and the Frenchman was pulped, the machine destroyed, Robert some time in the mud before the regular ambulance convoys tried again after the shelling, the mist of gas already dissipated, the gas actually missed, unrecorded, no one aware of it during that empty hour, a sudden change of breeze sweeping it over him as his lungs gasped for air against the blood seeping from his leg. The gas only realized days later in the hospital outside Chantilly. He was fortunate, all the nurses told him. One night after Olivia was in bed Robert had come in late smelling most clearly of sex and gin and sat with his father and told him this, adding the nurses took a special interest in reviving all of his functions at which Henry rose silent and left the room.

In my father's house are many mansions.

The night the past autumn of early dark when he sat with crossed legs and folded arms as for the first and only time in their marriage Olivia stood before him in the house otherwise empty, her eyes glistening wet with rage and held tears and spoke in a deadly chill voice just hours after the final shouting between father and son. You. I'll no longer stand for you to blame Robert or myself. I was never outside my bounds as mother. You think I coddle him but I don't. It's some blameless place in your own mind you've cultivated for years and years—it's your own poison Henry. How did he fail you? When? Better to ask yourself how you failed him and still do. You assail him at every opportunity. This anger, this vitriol Henry. When he was missing and then word came of his wounds, I listened to you and remained silent, thinking this is what a father does, this is how he copes, how he expresses his own fears. Even as we huddled together and I knew your fear as real as mine there was that anger of yours seeping through. It felt like contamination. I prayed, Henry. I prayed to spare him and prayed for your understanding and each prayer as heartfelt and heavy upon me as the other. And here he is returned to us. Not what he was but then, what was he, to you? When was he ever enough, just Robert? What do you know of what he should be? Henry, tell me. When I see you unable to extend a portion of the compassion and hope that you give to all these young women but not your own son? Oh you put a roof over his head, you allow him meals, you ask nothing from him. Except every moment for him to be otherwise. From what exactly, Henry? From yourself? Is that all you have to offer a son? Henry, he loves and admires you, but he is not you and never will be. Can't you allow him that? Can't you see he's lived and seen things we can't begin to comprehend? The vitality has been sucked from him and each day you remind him of that. I'm sorry to say this Henry but you've disappointed me. At his age, would you have done what he did? And if not, Henry, why not? Why not . . .

Grant to all who mourn a sure confidence in thy fatherly care, that, casting all their grief on thee, they may know the consolation of thy love. *Amen.*

For the first time in his career he skipped all the graduation festivities and the commencement itself, excused graciously by those few he chose to offer his intentions to, and then, those days alone and silent in his small upstairs office in the house, increasingly aware that his absence was noted almost certainly exclusively by himself, save for the three students who expected him to present their special commendations and who certainly were no less delighted by whoever stood in for him, their thoughts far away from their missing professor.

Then there was only the summer pall of an empty campus.

Alice and Polly returned in early July and cleared their mother's intimates from the house; clothing, coats, handbags, the entire drawer of white gloves, things of that nature and, without seeking his advice or consent, divided up her jewelry which he only realized after they'd departed and which made him a little angry—he would have liked the bittersweet activity of going through the pieces and recalling what they marked and where they came from and designating not only his daughters but his granddaughters but it was not worth fussing about. It was possible the girls knew best anyway. And he had the only thing that mattered—the wedding band of slender but premium gold, the twin of which was with her in the ground. It had taken him three years to pay off those simple rings.

He decided against the full six weeks at the Lake and only went for the last week of July and the first of August, not so much a decision as understanding how much of it he could stand this year. Two days before he took the train up, he sat at his desk and penned his letter of resignation to be effective immediately following the commencement exercise of 1922. Which he hand delivered to Fred Singleton, his closest friend on the board of trustees the same afternoon he wrote it. And stood in the hot July parlor with a glass of iced tea while Fred was courteously considerate and so the protest disguised as praise was short and perfunctory.

He had to catch a noon train for Lakemont. It was more of the same strangeness. This departure had always been overseen by Olivia amid days filled with trunks in the front hall and detailed arrangements with the housekeeper.

Instead he packed a single suitcase, the sort he'd take if traveling for three or four days to lecture somewhere. By nine o'clock in the morning he was done and all that remained was the twenty minute taxi ride to the station. He returned to his desk and wrote a letter to the Holland American Line, requesting schedules and fares for New York to Rotterdam the following May. This, like almost everything

51

else accomplished that summer was not so much thought through as simply one more cog in the wheel of sequence he was upon. It was not such a grand plan but something he'd intended to do for a long time and quite clearly he'd have to do something once that resignation took effect. For within that damning sluggish grief he'd known he couldn't remain as he was, as he had been. And the fact remained— his house, his home for many years, where his children had grown up, where Olivia had overseen their passage into the world and where once he'd thought they'd enjoy some years of peaceful solitude, had never become that, and never would. And come July of next year some other man, some other family would come to occupy it. Already, that not-quite year looming seemed more than he might bear. He thought, hoped, once the students returned in September his work would save him. It always had.

He had alerted no one of his arrival. So no one would meet him at the station. This was fine. He'd walk down. He'd done it before. That simple dirt road down through the vineyards toward the shoreline trees and drop of land that led to the spit where the cottages lay out of sight was one of perhaps three places on this earth where he felt his soul left its footprints.

His suitcase bumped his leg and the handle was wet in his hand so he switched sides and examined the day. Stretching both sides ran the long rows of grapevines on their wire supports, now in midsummer heavy with dark large leaves hiding the bunches of green grapes, the hedgerows between the vineyards filled with the sluggish summer afternoon birdsong, the woodchuck he saw yearly eating the clover planted between the rows of vines suddenly standing upright to look at him. He whistled a sharp note and the chuck was gone underground. Below lay Seneca Lake with a small fleet of sailboats working under a northwest breeze and also the occasional wake of a motor speedboat, which he did not like but he couldn't hear it up here and he'd learned to live with them as with much else.

Across the lake a hillside identical to the one he was descending rose evenly above the shore. Gentle, these lakes were. People spoke of Seneca with pride; the coldest, the deepest, the most dangerous of mood. He never argued but wore a secret smile. No Bay of Fundy, this. Even in winter.

The Grotto they called it, although the name had probably been attached to the place before any of them came along. Like a number of other narrow stream-ravines that broke the farmland on that southwestern side of Seneca Lake—centuries of water running downhill through the limestone and shale ledges had rendered this restricted tight gulch of slender streams and deep pools and waterfalls either broad or long braided drops, all down to the lake. What made this one distinctive was the small several acre delta that had formed at the shoreline. And the half dozen substantial cottages, one of which had been Doyle and Mary Franks's wedding gift to their daughter and son-in-law many years before.

Henry walked down knowing that this also was a particular occasion. Certainly gone was the plan to retire here—he could not imagine the long winters without Olivia although not so long ago the idea of that solitude had appealed—the two of them alone with lazy tucked-in days just reading or conversing, listening to the phonograph or taking the daily strolls that were more hike than walk. Not that he would sell the cottage. It would remain as it was now, and over the years become even more so: The summer retreat of his daughters and their families. And all would grow there and flourish in those long never-ending all too short summers of childhood and come to love and know this place as their grandmother had and perhaps one day, one of his daughters or one of their children in a future he could not imagine might gain age and serenity and choose this place as a final home. He hoped so. But it would not be him.

All were there save for Alice's husband Philip who Henry liked because he was an awkward sincere man older than his years, a lawyer in Chicago who would only get away to join them for the first two weeks of August.

The two weeks passed with more ease than he'd expected. His daughters with little effort that he knew disguised great coordination retained the summer routine that had endured, existed from their own childhoods—breakfast was a great meeting of the family and the food was almost afterthought to the planning of the day's activities. Lunch was either catch-as-catch can or immense picnics spread on blankets on the lawn. The children would stay in the water until they were blue and prickled with gooseflesh, teeth chattering. Some evenings dinner was eaten as a group—other times Henry would dine with the Westmores or the Pyles, and as always accepted an invitation to dine with Joseph Jensen and family—the local farmers at the top of the hill who owned the vineyards and by long-standing agreement kept watch over the cluster of cottages during the winter although the Pyles often spent Christmas here. The hole left by Olivia and Robert was within and around all these things but once there, Henry could not have imagined not coming, because the hole was communal, hovering over all the adults and Henry realized this was part of the letting go—part of receding into memory—his wife and son were owned part and parcel by all these people, surely not only by him alone.

But it was with his granddaughters that the summer regained some measure of its old glow, and new as well as he more so than before saw the perpetuity of the generations.

The girls were tentative with him at first and he understood this— he stood closest to the mystery of death, the fearful everlasting absence of their grandmother and remote uncle but it was this very hesitation of theirs that pressed him from the shell of mourning back toward life. Early morning when the sun was just up on the still water, he would take the old rowboat, dark green with oars hand-smooth with age, and the two sisters and their cousin aboard to poke along the dents and small coves of the shoreline, the sun warmly lighting this east-facing shoreline in etched detail and they would follow the mallard hen and her three ducklings from a short distance and the girls would bring bread to break and toss as the ducks bobbed alongside, the nervous mother back some few feet until the crumbs began to float and then she would streak in and grab one up. Or round the point where there was a great leaning willow and they would glide with the oars up through the long slender drapes of soft leaves and the girls would break tender tips free and fashion garlands for their hair or, as the water stayed calm he'd row out a bit into the lake, where the bottom began to drop but was still in sight and drift again, all leaning quiet against the rail gazing down into the water for fish, not interested in the fry and minnows or even the flash of a pumpkinseed sunfish but waiting for the green trout shadow to dislodge from its own drift and flash off and whoever spotted it would cry out and even if no other saw the fish the cry was never questioned and it was as if they had actually caught the fish.

Afternoons, when parents mysteriously wanted to waste this precious summer with naps he would take them up into the lower reaches of the gorge where they would pull apart the loose shale looking for fossils, mostly minute shells no larger than one of their own thumbnails but true as a scallop in design, there in the rock as if yesterday and he would wonder if his father had ever seen such a thing and what he would make of it. The youngest girl, Polly's daughter Kate, always trying to catch up to her cousins Gretchen and Patty even though only a single year separated each of them, became adept at catching the small green frogs that lived about the smaller pools of the gorge and Henry named her Frogcatcher and told them all tales of the great Seven Nations of the Iroquois who for hundreds of years had lived along this vast belt of wondrous rich land and lakes. Leaving for the time being the closer tale of Sullivan's march through that country of theirs, burning and destroying all villages and crops and stores of seed and leaving mostly the old people and women and children for the bitter winter of starvation ahead of them but content for now to let his grandchildren envision this place as it was now but with a different people and a different way of life than the one these children knew. So they might foresee, however briefly, other possibilities in life. And also find, with great excitement a small stone overhang where years of fires had smudged dark with soot soaked deep into the rock. He saw no reason to tell them this could be simply the summer campfires of their own families for the last half-century—let them believe those other people had been here. As he knew was true. Every year men working the vineyards found flint arrowheads and Joseph Jensen had a collection not only of these simple artifacts but several exquisite spear points, grinding stones, fishing weights, even a horn tool for cleaning hides. He hiked up the hill one drizzly day and called on Jensen and with the boldness of grief asked for and received three small but perfect arrowheads. Bird points, Jensen called them. And the next time the three girls went up with their Grandfather to search for fossils and catch frogs and salamanders he carefully seeded two of the points as they went and then proceeded to find the third. Which sent them all looking, scouring the ground on hands and knees but it was Kate who actually found one of the other points and so very slowly Henry had to discover the final one so each child had one. And a charming thing happened—the oldest girl Gretchen insisted they keep looking until they found one for Grandfather. Henry went along with this as long as he could and then, not so very much feigning exhaustion, declared he was done and perhaps another day they might find one for him. He was seated on a rock by the lower pool where the water threaded down in a long fifteen foot drop from above. It was warm and time for all to go back to the cottage and, for the children at least, the lovely long afternoon in the lake and on the diving raft buoyed fifty yards out in the deep water. And Kate, bold before her older cousins, came forward and handed her bird point to Henry and said, "Grandfather, you keep this. We'll find another one. I know I will. I found this." And Henry sat silent for only a moment, watching the deep serious face of the five year old, not in the least expecting this but knew the grace to accept the gift.

Evenings, the long summer twilights, he and Doyle went fly fishing for the big brown and rainbow trout found in the pockets below the cliff faces rising straight from the water. Drifting. Casting. It had been Doyle all those years ago who had taught the young man from Nova Scotia this sport that was more art than harvest and it had taken Henry some years to accept the slippery difference and even longer to embrace it. The trout were fine to eat although to his mind, never once spoken aloud, inferior to the firm dense white flesh of saltwater fish. But the sport was delicate and easily ruined by a bad cast and so over those years he had come to appreciate it. Occasionally they would go further out into the Lake and take turns rowing a steady rhythm while the other sat at the stern of the rowboat with the large spindle of a Seth Green rig—essentially an oversized fishing reel that needed no rod—and with heavy weights and live minnows on the hooks to troll the deep waters for lake trout; some true monsters of fish, at least for these waters. But the work at the oars was hard, the pace had to be steady and so these attempts had grown shorter in duration over the years. Henry was twenty-three years younger than Doyle and could still row a strong quadrant of the Lake, watching the bent back of the man whom he loved as no other. Those evenings were quiet, even this year. Only once did Doyle rest his rod across the gunwales, the oars shipped as they drifted and Doyle gazed off at the placid green evening water. Henry knew they were done fishing and so broke his own rod down and waited. Finally Doyle said, "She was the light of my life."

Henry would not diminish this statement by adding that she was his, as well. Instead he waited a time and then quietly said, "I feel as if I failed Robbie."

Doyle looked at him then. He shook his head. "You didn't."

They floated, Henry gazing down into the still water, the murky reflection of himself, wavering, oddly accurate. Not for the first time recalling his folly, his bitter self-certainty, pushing his son, too hard, too late. The choices made, never to be undone. Never to be forgiven.

Then he reversed his position on the seat, slipped the oars into the locks and rowed them home.

It was his daughter, Alice, who would speak to him. He knew this and knew also she'd pick her own time. Which came three mornings before he was due to leave. Breakfast was cleared away and Philip and Jack were joining Doyle and Quincy to get the big motor cruiser the *Mary Nan* out and take the children for a long expedition down the lake to the park in Watkins Glen where they would picnic on hot dogs and ice cream the vendors sold there. This was an annual event and one Henry had no desire to take part in—let the fathers herd the children. Doyle's only job was to drive the boat and eat an ice cream cone. So he sat on the green lawn in a white wooden chair and watched the big boat slowly back from the boathouse with all crew aboard and turn in a slow throb of engine backwash and then head out into the lake. A jolly roger flying aft.

The chair was one of several scattered around the lawn but there was already one pulled close. He tried to recall the afternoon before but couldn't remember which two had been in conference or simple conversation—likely just parents talking while watching the children in and about the water. But was not surprised when Alice appeared with a tray and twin cups of coffee. She set the saucers on the wide chair arms and laid the tray in the grass, a swiftness of movement about her that she'd had since childhood, a gracefulness that was purely from her mother. She settled easily into the chair and watched the boat going down the lake, the pulse of the big engine already distant.

"Dad?"

"Alice?"

"What're your plans after next spring?" She set her coffee down. "You couldn't expect to just resign and not have the word out, probably before you were even on the train up here."

He was quiet a time. Then said, "Perhaps that's reason enough."

"Whatever does that mean?"

"It means nothing. As for my plans, they're in flux at the moment. Be assured I'll inform you first thing when I know myself."

"No need to be testy."

"I didn't intend to be. Actually, you and Polly should discuss between yourselves what you would like from the house. I'll keep some of it, so I'll have the final vote, at least while I'm still alive. But I'll have to move and have no need for a house that large."

"I talked with Philip—"

"No," he said. "Perhaps in those let us hope distant years when I grow feeble but us Dorns are strong stock. Look at your grandmother Euphemia. Seventy-nine years old and still ferocious about living alone, although she claims she'd have to take in boarders if I didn't send her a check once a month. But the last thing a young family needs is a geezer rambling around the house in his robe and slippers grumbling about the children making noise and interrupting his reading."

She smiled. "Is that what you plan for yourself?"

"No. I think I'll take a year off. I may do some traveling. But, although I couldn't see myself staying on at the College, or even Elmira without your mother, doesn't mean I'll dry up and hide away. I imagine there's a college or two that might welcome me. I might even be able to arrange to be a perpetual visiting scholar—the sort of thing where I'd teach a course or a lecture series each semester and not much more than that. Chaucer most likely. It would be such joy to immerse myself in the *Tales*. Without other distractions."

"An itinerant academic pilgrim lecturing on the ultimate pilgrims." She smiled at him and then went on with the bit he'd tried to slip by. "Where would you travel? Back to Nova Scotia?"

He sighed. "I should I suppose. But no, I don't think I'll go back up there. Mother and I do best with our letters; face to face we just joust with each other and it's exhausting. If it'd been her that had the education she would've made a fine attorney. Or judge by now. So, to truly answer your question, No, I'm not sure where I'll go."

She smiled swiftly. "You'll tell me when you know?"

"Of course."

"Dad?" A change of tone.

"What is it, Squirrel?"

She leaned to put her empty cup and saucer on the tray in the grass. She said, "I was pregnant at the funerals. But in June I lost that baby."

"Alice, I'm sorry."

She stood. "I wasn't sure if I should tell you. It was such a terrible spring," she said, her face smooth but set.

He was up too. "You should always tell me, Alice. Anything you need to."

"I'd planned to name that baby after either Mother or Robbie." As she spoke she walked toward the wall above the rocky beach and he went alongside her. "Now, when we try again, I don't know what to do. I don't know if the baby I lost was a boy or girl—they either couldn't or wouldn't tell me. It was not quite three months. So," she turned and faced him, "when there's a new one would it take something away to use whichever name fits? Is it awful of me to ask you this, to tell you this?"

"No, Squirrel. And you'll know the right name when that new baby does come."

She was quiet a long time, both side by side looking out upon the water. A breeze was up and the first of the sailboats were appearing. Then she said, "When I was growing up and you and Mother took such great pains, made such effort to show Polly and myself and Robbie the beauties of life, the music and literature, art, but also the simpler beauties of the patterns of the fields and vineyards of good farming, the wonders in the woods. All those things. Was it, is it, because you truly believe in the primacy of beauty in life? Or was it simply to fill our childhoods with something to look back upon, perhaps even to gain strength from, when we discovered how ugly and precarious and delicate life truly is?"

He waited a bit until she turned to him. Very quiet, he said, "Perhaps both."

She reached and took his hand. They stood that way. It was quiet with all the children gone and for long moments all they heard was the small plash of wavelets against the shore.

Finally Alice said, "When Robbie was so sick with the whooping cough. I was so scared he was going to die. But I was also angry. It seemed like you and Mother had forgotten about Polly and me. I was a teenager but—"

Quietly he said, "Of course you felt that way. It's nothing to feel guilty of."

"Did you think he was going to die? I know Mother did."

He paused. "It was very strange, Alice. I certainly knew he might. But because of things, the need I felt for everyone, perhaps my own fear as well, I refused to allow it into my head. At the time I felt as if perhaps my certainty that he'd pull through was what was needed in order for him to do so. Sometimes that's all a parent can do."

She waited a moment. Then said, "I worry about my girls. All the time. And you know what?"

"You always will. It never stops."

She smiled then fully upon him. Such a magnetic woman, he thought. Such a lovely daughter.

That night he sat longer than usual with the other men on the boathouse roof and drank rye and water. In a silent brooding respected by the others. What comes before looming as large as what comes after.

The final evening he spent with his children and grandchildren, eating a dinner of boned leg of lamb roasted over a hot fire of split hickory and new potatoes and sweet corn, hand-cranked ice cream studded with the halves of oxheart cherries for dessert and then sat on the sunporch with lights burning both sides of the couch with three little girls piled in against him while he told them the tale of Robin Hood and his band of Merry Men, or rather an abridged version thick on adventure, but for the sake of the three girls and his own pleasure, heavily tilted toward the presence and activities of the Maid Marian whom, in his telling at least, was an easy equal to Robin of Sherlock. And why not? The legends aside, it was clear to him that no man could have held such an odd group of fellows together without a woman of equal strength advising and forecasting. If his story was skewed to his own beliefs that was fine—what story was not? He talked on even when the eldest Gretchen was sleeping also, the children slumped and curled into each other like so many puppies and he the vast magnet that swooped them down toward that sleep, his words that lulled them. When he grew quiet he sat for almost half an hour watching them, the sweet breath of them commingling with the freshened air through the screens. In the dining room behind him, one step up, he heard his daughters and their husbands talking quietly. And so he sat with the spillage of children over him until Polly and Alice came together quiet on tiptoe into the room and spoke back in whispers for their husbands and the children were lifted within the deep rubbery sleep of childhood and carried from the room and upstairs.

Then, while those parents were occupied, he slipped from the house. Knowing his daughters would like him there after the girls were abed but he was not yet done. There was a solitary undertaking before him. Creeping quietly he stepped into the rowboat, undid the mooring rope and using an oar as push pole went down the channel and out into the lake. It was a clear night, early August with no wind. He rowed straight out into the Lake until he was far from shore but could still see the clumps of lighted windows of the cottages. Once out he shipped the oars—the boat would drift with the slight current but not far. He pulled his feet from under the seat and stretched his legs and then leaned back so his head rested on his arms wedged across the bow. It was comfortable enough. It was only moments before a star fell against the void. And soon another. The Perseid meteors. He could not begin to count them and did not wish to. Anymore than he could recall the number of times he and Olivia had made this silent journey of summer. Many years ago they had brought the children with them but they were too young and the spectacle not sufficient to be wakened and bundled and brought out onto the water. Olivia had suggested that they wait a few more years but Henry had said No—the children had seen it and would rediscover the summer wonder on their own or not. So it became theirs alone. The two of them. Each year. Now uncountable. It wasn't a matter of doing the math or not. The years were uncountable. So he lay as long as he could and watched the dome overhead and caught the streaks as he could. When he became stiff and sore and slightly cold he still waited. Finally a single burning bit of star flared—no more brilliant or outstanding than the others but out loud he said, "Oh my sweet heart." Then, rocking the boat, forced himself upright and got the oars into the water and rowed for shore. Tears running free and soundless down his face. His shoulders and back ached. His heart a dangerous unreliable engine.

The next morning he took the train back to Elmira. It was a humid hot day. A dense sky of mackerel clouds. It would soon rain. By the time the train came into Elmira station the windows were streaked and fogged. He went onto the platform and found a cab and sat with his suitcase between his knees, dreading the house. Although he knew Irma had been in each day to check things and open or close windows and screens as the weather demanded. And the icebox would be full and there would be something, a cold roast chicken he guessed, awaiting him. But still, with all this, the house was closed up. A place he no longer lived but would survive in for less than a year. He could manage that. But dreaded it.

On the small hall table next to the telephone stand the two weeks of mail waited him, divided into three piles: magazines, personal letters and bills. Atop it all was a thick large brown envelope with the prominent return address of the Holland America Line. His name and address in a handsome copperplate hand. He took it up and held it. Then set it down. First thing was to take care of the house, open his other mail. See about supper.

Seven

Of that first sojourn to the Boston States, to Massachusetts, Henry had almost no memory. There was, he thought, a wooden yellow duck with red wings on wheels so when he pulled it about by a string the wings went round and round. Black shutters against gray clapboards. Sheep in a field past an apple tree in bloom—this was vivid, the sound of the sheep, the bright spring grass, the white and red blossoms and a drift of sweet scent. Of his father there was only a recalled presence; a looming figure, huge hands and a gentle voice but no images to fit this—only the sense of those things having existed. Of the death and burial, even the return to Nova Scotia he remembered nothing. His mother had two photographs of his father but he'd seen them only a couple of times as a boy and they could have been anyone. Years later, when he and Olivia brought Alice and Polly to visit, Olivia pregnant with Robert and sick for the voyage and much of the time they were there, and Charles Morrell dead a year, Henry prevailed on his mother and Euphemia sat for a time in the soft chair with knitted throws over the arms and back and he waited with his request out in the air between them and finally she rose up groaning to ascend the stairs and some good while later— he'd almost decided she'd refused him and was napping—she returned and handed them to him. Both clearly taken at the same studio on the same day. A front view and a profile both from the waist up. His father's dark hair long and swept back behind his ears, his face sporting a trimmed beard and a mustache, both fashionable at the time, but it was the features, the eyes and nose and chin and mouth that Henry wanted to study. And the hands, which were a disappointment because in the front view they were folded in his lap and the side view out of sight altogether. The man in the photographs was at least ten, perhaps twelve years younger than the son now studying them. There was a likeness, he supposed. Although his father more clearly resembled his firstborn, Gilbert who had been lost in a storm off Grand Manan when the boat struck a shoal and foundered and sank with all hands six years ago. Henry was alone with his mother. The girls were out playing with Island cousins and Olivia was napping.

"Mother," he said, holding the photographs. "Tell me."

"Tell you what?" Her voice charged already. She put him in mind of a solitary lightbulb that would not burn out but was the only source of light it knew.

Gently he said, "Of Father. Of Father and you."

She worried a yarn unraveling from her sweater, studying it. He half expected her to rise and seek a darning needle. But she said, "There is little to tell. I was just a girl, sixteen years old when I met him. Pregnant with Gil before the year was out and married. He was charming and as you can see a devil of a handsome man but he didn't know a dime from a dollar. I learned that too late. He was a dreamer, Henry. His head in the clouds as they used to say. We managed just barely and with more help from your uncle George than I expect I'll ever know. Then he died and left me in a strange land with young children and a newborn. It was not an easy time for me."

Henry waited but it seemed she was done. After a bit he said, "But he had a talent. Isn't that right? Weren't things, before he got sick, starting to work out for him? Down there to Boston?"

She was quiet a while. Then said, "Henry. You're an educated man. Something I once hoped for myself, if you didn't know."

Now he was the one quiet.

She went on, "But you've done well. Better than I expected when you slipped out of here if you must know the truth. Take that as you will—I'm proud enough of you. But you must have learned this, all those years at University, all those degrees, all the people you've met and worked with. In a place like Freeport your father stood out. But talent, in any way but I'm talking here of the talent of the artist is not an uncommon thing. At least the number of people who think they have it. Henry, listen to me: He was good at what he did, Sam was. But he was not brilliant with it. He saw the layers of things and rendered them beautifully. And that work suited his temperament. But it was not enough—do you understand what I'm saying? Now, if he'd lived he might well have made a sufficient living at it—he was well started. But he never would have achieved the greatness he felt was in him. Because it was not. And I could not tell him so. It was one of the hardest times in my life, standing so firm behind him when I recognized that ultimately he would fail, that at some point he would realize and accept that. Until he died I always thought when that time came we'd come home and he'd be able to clerk for Fred and George and make a living for us and still paint and draw—that work was something he would never have abandoned, never set aside as the folly of youth. I knew him well enough to know that. In truth, part of me was waiting him to realize it himself so we could get on with things. But then he died—" She stopped.

"Mother, what?"

She rubbed her hands across her eyes. "I'm a stupid old woman sometimes. I know Fred never forgave me for not bringing him home, for burying him there. But when he died. Oh Henry. When he died I was just plain angry at him. I see now, looking back, it was the only way I could get through it all. Good God, Eva was at my breast and we were two months behind not just on the house payments but everything else—bills piling up at the butchers and mercantiles for God's sake. There was nothing in this world that would let me contact George for help. I settled with the bank and paid off the bills and buried him right there and came home. Actually he was buried first and that was one more debt to take care of—I was terrified to try to keep him and bring him home, terrified that one or more of us had the tubercular already. I was a young woman still." She looked up at him and then away again. "I did what had to be done."

"I know you did, Mother."

From outside came the cries of little girls playing. Henry distinctly heard one say "I will never play with you again." Moments later the screams of the game resumed. He studied his mother who had her hands in her lap and was gazing somewhere off into the floral wallpaper.

Softly he said, "May I keep these?"

Her eyes bolted to him. "Why?"

"Well. I'd like them for the girls someday."

Euphemia stood. "No," she said, crossing and taking them from him. "He was my husband." She went into the hall and he heard her trying to tread quiet up the stairs to not disturb Olivia. He never saw the photographs again.

Later that evening, after Olivia and the girls were asleep he slipped out of the house and wandered down round the cove to the store where as if both were expecting each other, George sat on the storefront bench, the dark building backlit by the night sky. Henry sat beside him and for a time they were both quiet, content to simply be in each other's company.

George said, "Those are fine little girls you have. That Polly, she's a pistol. I offered em both sour balls out of the jar and she looked at the red one I gave her and asked could she have lime. Reminds me a bit of your mother. I told her lime was my favorite too. She said Does that mean you get em all to yourself? I said Nope and gave her two." He grinned at Henry. "Reminds me a bit of you, too."

Not needing to ask how so, Henry said, "Tell me something."

"If I can."

"Talking to Mother today, about my father. When he took all of us down to Boston. Something in how she phrased things made me think maybe you supported that idea a good bit more than Uncle Fred."

"Oh I'd say twas about even," George said. He stood and looked off at the dimly ringed lights around the cove. "You recall how when you came back that first summer of your university? How miserable you were? You recall what I told you?"

Henry stood beside him. "How some people left a place because they never were meant to be anything but born there, so they'd know enough to leave."

George nodded. "Samuel Dorn was the same way. Despite what your mother might've thought. Or Fred, for that matter. Well, now, it's late, isn't it?"

"And I haven't been back since."

"That's not a bad thing. The way I see it."

"Not others, though."

"There's always them love to second guess another man." George stepped down off the porch. Henry followed and together in silence they walked up the cove. At Euphemia's house they paused, the shell road crackly white in the starlight. Henry put out his hand and George took it, a tight stout shake.

"It's been good to see you."

"You best get inside. You know your mother's waiting up for you. As Fred waits up for me. He's odd that way. But some of us need someone to worry over."

"He worries over you?"

George paused and said, "He's my brother." Then went on, his broad back crossed by suspenders, black against the pale of his denim shirt. Henry watched him until he passed around the head of the cove and out of sight behind the Temperance Hall toward the house on the hillside with its single windowlight.

It was the next to last time Henry went back to Nova Scotia.

Eight

*I*n early June 1922 three days following commencement Henry Dorn had a quiet dinner alone with Doyle and Mary Franks and spent the night with them. The campus house had been emptied of his belongings which were in storage in the Franks's attic. All he was responsible for now were the pair of cumbersome steamer trunks. Early next morning Doyle accompanied him to the station where he boarded a train for New York. If their parting was subdued it was merely an extension of the mood over and within Henry and so therefore his friends and the academic community the past few weeks.

The worst moment had not been the anniversary of the deaths, which was a peculiarly quiet afternoon of gentle spring rain, the day so long anticipated that its arrival brought no sudden thrust of grief but rather was almost consolation—in that year he'd passed all number of possible anniversaries that were unmarked and this was another he was helpless against, and the world went on raining—but had come unexpectedly just days before commencement when he was clearing what effects remained of his office, moving a last few volumes from a shelf to a cardboard carton when of a sudden he paused and turned, went to the open window and leaned there, his shirtsleeves rolled to his elbows, his hands on the burnished oak sill as he looked out over the leafing campus, a version of a view that had been his for many years, as a dull bubbled panic rose and clutched within his chest. Below in the mild afternoon as always students in pairs or small groups, some hurrying alone, crossed from the library outward toward the other buildings and those same buildings seemed some way blurred, as if he couldn't quite bring focus upon them and he realized this was a manifestation of the dullness within him throughout this last year, the sense of the automaton, the layers of words issuing from his throat as he tapped his pointer along the chalkboard or red-penciled papers or sat through individual conferences, a dullness so complete that once, over a small dinner gathering Emery Westmore had seemingly abruptly asked if he was all right and Henry had paused, looking at him a long moment before replying that he was fine. But now this afternoon what he'd been both denying and awaiting came together and the slender pile of his life came down upon him. As he realized the memory he was fast becoming was merely a larger extension of the memory of himself that went out every year, locked within those young women who had endured and acknowledged and, no doubt, some few admired, but nevertheless he was little more than that for most—a memory. Perhaps at least an induction for some into a life enriched by their understanding that language and the constructions made from language were the underpinnings of all human endeavor, be it fine or folly, but in brute honesty, for most he was already a vapor, a recession within those lives. And now, so shortly, he would become memory to all this, and this life also would become remembrance to him. The bulwark of a life. And even as he leaned thus his vision cleared and he could smell, as the year before, the freshly mown new grass and the maudlin shroud lifted. Or at least parted. He could see his way out.

Ten days later he disembarked at Penn Station and porter and trunks in tow hailed a cab and set off for the pier and the *Veendam II.* Which was to sail from New York harbor that night for Rotterdam. He'd booked passage first class the summer before after a week of misgiving—there was a difference between comfort and opulence and never in his life had he confused the two, never lusted after the frivolous. But it had been this very thing that sparked the decision—if he was to do something momentous once again in his life then let it be at an appropriate level of comfort. Once he'd wired the money for the ticket he woke and realized his justifications were merely old habit—the boat crossing offered what he had never once had—the anonymity of bearing—all else would be mystery to his fellow passengers. If there was vanity in this he decided it was a thimbleful. He had no intention of passing himself off as anything other than what he was. And finally there was enough of Nova Scotia left within him to recognize that this gesture of decadence was not the beginning of some irresponsible draining of funds but only a once-in-a-life experience, a journey of dreams.

Nevertheless his stateroom was near overwhelming and once his trunks were delivered he fled it for the upper promenade and stood there, in a light tweed against the water breeze as the liner was moved down the harbor at dusk, the array of lights of the city spreading on all sides and the heaving island of Manhattan was reduced to the columns of buildings against a blue twilight sky and ever so slowly they made their way out of the harbor, passing Lady Liberty and he gazed upon her and then back at the land now a glow of lights and recalled that for upwards of one hundred and fifty years his people had made their homes here, had in fact owned much of what he could see although even if he'd known the precise tracts he could not point them out. It did not matter. That ancestor, Abraham van Doorn who fled the fledged experiment for the brutal safety of British Canada, had, like most men in most times made the best guess he could and acted upon it. Henry doubted this migration had less to do with the new ideas and ideals of the American experiment than it did with the now unknown losses he might have undergone through the Revolution, or, conversely or in concordance, the gains offered by the Crown. In any event, Henry thought, the Lady growing smaller and the land now a mere smudge of light in the sky, it was not possible to say the man had made a mistake. The generations evolve from such actions but that does not mean there is a right or wrong to be guessed or arrived at. If that long-ago Abraham had not made his choice, would there even be this man leaning against the rail as the liner came churning smoothly onto the open ocean and the tugs peeled away and retreated back into the night? Was he inevitable or simply the end result of this man meeting this woman and procreating and thus on downward through the years? As well ask if accident is design or design, accident. And to what difference? Our fathers who art in heaven might know. But do the dead care?

He was the last to know. He was also the last to leave the deck and retreat, not as others did down the long broad stairs that opened at the bottom like a fan, flanked by huge potted palms and the dining room but back to his stateroom. He was not hungry. He was in a curious state. He might as well have been that seventeen year-old boy going south all those years ago. Leaving behind all he knew.

A short time passed. Perhaps an hour. There was a knock at his door. When he opened it there was a steward in immaculate whites, holding at shoulder height a large oval tray. Henry surveyed the man and waited. The steward was not put off by this silence but spoke.

"I beg pardon, sir. The Captain couldn't help but notice you did not attend dinner this evening. And while you may ring at any time for whatever you might like, he thought perhaps you would require refreshment. May I?"

Henry was embarrassed he had kept this man with his burden standing and so stepped aside and said, "Why thank you. And the Captain as well. I forgot dinner altogether with the excitement of departure."

The steward entered and set the tray on the table, the three serving platters all covered with domed lids. At one end of the tray was a bottle of champagne, in ice but uncorked. The steward ran his hand in the air over the bottle and said, "It's pre-war Clicquot. A lovely vintage and we're in international waters. There is no prohibition here. Please, sir, enjoy yourself. And if I may, my experience is that passengers who eat the first day are less likely to suffer if we should encounter rougher waters later in the crossing."

Henry said, "I've sailed in smaller ships in far worse conditions than we'll encounter on this island of steel and turbines. But thank you." And began to dig into his pocket but the steward had bowed his head to reveal a finely greased part in his hair and a small thinning spot on the top of his head and then retreated through the door. Leaving Henry with a frayed dollar in his hand and a sense that he already was in debt to the man.

He ate the oysters on the half-shell and the lobster in cream sauce over rice and fine flaked rolls. The champagne was superb.

In his pajamas he stood a final time before his porthole, more truly a window, and gazed upon the water. Silver tipped as far as he could see. Then pulled the soft heavy cloth over the window and felt his way in the dark and lay upon the bed. He was exhausted. On the bed it seemed to him that he could feel not only the faint thrum of the engines but beneath that also the depths and wild currents, the brutal unforgiving discriminating ocean beneath. It was everything he wanted.

In the morning the dining room was little more than an oversized version of the better hotel dining rooms he'd been in and out of over his years of academic travel. But the soft boiled egg was hot and perfect and the toast was hot and perfect. Then he toured the promenade of outer decks, passing people stretched in wicker lounges tucked with light blankets against the sea breeze and a group of women performing calisthenics and a net-enclosed tennis court and beyond that the swimming pool, all these things promised in the promotional materials he'd received the summer before but now, once faced with them, striking him as mildly improbable. They were at sea for God's sake. But then, what would these landlocked people expect to do for the days of crossing? He went as far forward as possible and stood gazing out at the ocean. This boat held no resemblance to those he had known in his youth—those were working boats, all of a piece with the ocean, sometimes too much so. But this was merely a behemoth of comfort designed to convey people from land to land with a minimum of understanding that they were even at sea. Except for the water stretching in a vast circle that seemed at the horizon to actually dip downward. And the high fleets of clouds. The water below was nearly abstract—the tips of waves soundless white feathers. He turned his back on the sea and faced again the humanity of the ship. For that, he realized, was what it was. Barring disaster this vessel was merely a slow moving bridge. The small ships and fishing boats of his youth were bicycles on a cowpath compared to this locomotive on near silent tracks.

Although there was no mistaking the salt-density of the air, the wind ruffling and thickening his hair as he stood. With a rueful smile he reminded himself he had made this choice. He had not, for instance, taken passage on a tramp steamer, as Robert had done off for the war. For a moment he wondered why not. But that was the feat of an eighteen-year old. He was, he had to admit, where he was supposed to be.

A woman in the tight knee-length and sleeveless calisthenics outfit suddenly came upon him, loping in a steady slapping of bare feet. She was beaded with perspiration and her short almost-copper hair was at angle from her head, pushed from her eyes back as he watched. She glanced at him as she passed but the glance was empty as if she were looking toward some far distance greater even than the horizon. He leaned against a lifeboat up on its trucks and pulleys and watched her go. The suit fit snugly and her body was clear to him as she went away. He felt his mouth tug down. The girls at Elmira were required to wear skirted athletic outfits. And then he held paired thoughts—he was not responsible for anyone anymore and, more clearly, intriguingly, how had he missed the very simple and obvious equation that if women were to be truly equal to men, not simply to vote or have education or pursue careers, why did he expect that they would not also embrace the sensual, the beauty of form, the elevation of body as part of those rights? After all, women were made the way they were for reasons. And his ideas, up until that very moment had been cast in the eye of men—that women were to be attractive to attract, that their beauty was primarily for the sake of men, that they should not flaunt or simply enjoy this as a part and measure of their lives. Women, if they ever had been and he knew they had not, had ceased to be the statues of virtue that the men of his generation and the ones before him had cast them to be. It was a bad analogy but one in the circumstance he could not avoid: Men were the great vessels that passed over an ocean as if it were only there to be passed over; women were the scrappy schooners of his childhood, not only down in the trough of the waves but riding up to the tips and sloughing down again. It was a hair's-breadth of truth and he recognized it as such. Yet truth by a hair is better than layered cushioned falsehoods of comfort.

It was only when his shoulder grew sore from leaning against the chocks of the lifeboat that he realized he was waiting to see if she would pass again.

She did not and it took a prolonged moment to realize how long he had waited to see if she would. When he descended again into the dining room it was near empty and the waiters were cleaning and resetting tables for dinner but he found the steward from the night before and without pretense palmed a bill to him and asked if he might have an apple and a pair of hard rolls for his lunch. The man looked at him and Henry knew the steward was trying to determine if that was what this man before him really wanted or if he should offer late luncheon. Henry said, "I don't mean to interfere with your duties. But a light lunch has long been a habit of mine." And so shortly, with apple and rolls wrapped in a linen napkin he retreated to his stateroom after a pause to pick up an assortment of New York weeklies. After eating and exhausting most of the meager contents of the papers, he took a long hot bath. For the simple reason that he imagined he was the first Dorn ever to have a hot bath at sea and then rested on his bed. There was an excitement within that he had not truly known since he was a youth. His body was aging, his brain was full of facts, information, ideas, arcane baubles and brilliance, all this overlaid and scored with the experience of living but still there remained a simple truth—his essence might be informed but was not changed.

Also, he could not rid himself of the image of the young woman of the late morning. It was not lurid—she was not a child, not a student, not an innocent off for her tour of Europe. That was clear from the radiation of self-possession that trailed her. Or preceded her. He could not say. Except that he lay on his bed and conjured her over and again. This conjure not erotic and he could not say if this was a function purely of his own mind or a portion of her radiance. As if she dared him reduce her so.

Open ocean in June the afternoon went on forever. At his usual dinner hour he rose and washed and dressed carefully, made three very slow measured revolutions of the promenade and went down to dinner.

He requested and was seated at a small table well off to the side, declining an invitation to dine at the captain's table—a vast slab on a dais surrounded by several other solitaires as well as couples in evening wear and the captain in a brilliant uniform, the table heavy with crystal and floral arrangements and altogether too much forced cheer—Henry had been at too many of those tables, regardless of the circumstances, to voluntarily place himself there. He had grown used to eating alone.

He was waiting his soup when he looked sideways and saw her escorted by the steward across the room, her own face turned in profile as she spoke with the steward and then not so much as if she felt his eyes but as if she had been directed toward him all along turned her head just enough to meet his modest gaze. Henry made a slight nod and looked down to his table, moving a bread plate a quarter inch. All the while aware of her progress. There were three other tables for two lined under the same archway as his own. A waiter slipped in from behind and placed the soup before him. A tomato bisque. A favorite food and this version pretty to look at with strands of shredded basil in the center of the bowl.

He reached for his soup spoon and stopped. She had also stopped, unmoving, a dozen feet from his table. The steward escorting her for a moment seemed to be in the process of catching up. She was looking directly at Henry. Now he returned her gaze.

She was in a black sheath dress with bare arms, a lace white shawl providing sufficient decorum. The dress seemed to square her upper body but as it fell became overwhelmingly feminine with the low waist that then radiated in simple pleats to her knees. There was certainly nothing staid about this dress and yet it was purely elegant, lacking the popular overt sexuality of the outfits many young women recently favored. Although even as he took it in he understood perhaps it was less the dress that stated this than the woman wearing it.

She turned and spoke to the steward and, alone, came to his table.

"Good evening," he stood, his tone carefully neutral, not inviting but pleasant.

"You're the man beside the lifeboat earlier." Then having delicately and deftly pinpointed her awareness of his watching her she went on. "I'm Lydia Pearce. And despite how it might appear not forward and also not as young as you might think. And in a minute I'm going to be sitting one table away from you where we can both eat our dinners in peace and quiet. Which is preferable to being in a party of baboons but lacks the pleasantry of company and conversation, which, at least to my mind, enhances any meal. Except breakfast which I always eat alone—"

Almost a puppet of manners he said, "I'm Henry Dorn. And I might be rusty but some pleasantry over dinner would be welcome."

And like a man she held out her hand and said "I'm pleased to meet you Henry Dorn."

But when he did reach and take her hand it was nothing like shaking hands with a man and the thoughts twinned I've not been touched like this in longer than I can remember and Be wary. He said, "Let's try it, shall we?"

And started around the table to seat her even as the steward did the same but she only pulled out her chair and sat and looked up at both with a crinkle of amusement as if to ask what these two men were doing colliding around her. She looked at the steward and said, "Please, Perrier Brut and oysters." She glanced at Henry and then back. "A dozen please. With horseradish."

Then they were alone. She was looking directly at him. His hands were in his lap, folding gently into his napkin. Then she laughed and said, "Please. Eat your soup. Cold soup is dreadful. Although you'd probably enjoy sharing the oysters more. Do you like oysters?"

"I do," he said.

"Leave the soup then," she said. "Oysters should be eaten only with champagne."

He cocked his head but only smiled.

"Now," she went on. "Let me see. You're married but traveling alone. Your shirt isn't stuffed but you have a certain bearing about you. Certainly not in business. But this is your first trip abroad and for some reason you're not quite sure what exactly it is you're up to. How'm I doing?"

"My wife died a little more than a year ago."

Her eyes flicked down, then up again. "I'm sorry."

"It's not for you to be sorry about. I still wear the ring for reasons both private and obvious. I'm a retired professor of English and making a foolhardy trip to Holland where my ancestors came from three hundred years ago."

She said, "You know what I hate, Henry Dorn?"

"What's that?"

"Obfuscation."

He tipped his head in agreement. And then said, "But isn't that how we all try ourselves out with strangers? To see how much we should reveal and how much to withhold?"

"That's the convention. But to what purpose? To save ourselves? And from what?"

"Well," he said. "Sometimes a potential disaster. Or embarrassment. For instance, you already know a good deal more of me than I do of you."

"Perhaps." She lifted her eyebrows and smiled. "But we do have to start somewhere, don't we? Look, here's the food."

The soup was removed. The platter of oysters resting on their shells suddenly made the table very small. The glasses were filled and then Lydia Pearce turned her face up to the waiter and rattled out a lengthy listing in French which Henry was only in part able to follow and then she turned back to him and said, "I ordered for both of us. Does that offend you?"

"Of course," he said.

She smiled and said, "Remind me to ask you again when we're done." She took up an oyster and sucked it from the shell, her tongue a quick pink scoop. All the while with her eyes on him. Such eyes he thought. So full of laughter and enjoyment, pure pleasure at what she was doing. But within her laughter a quality otherwise—she was not laughing at him, nor at herself for imposing upon him and winning that imposition but most clearly laughter just that—a delight of life as if everything around her was arrayed for her pleasure and yet he sensed in other circumstances her displeasure could be acute. He thought. And thought then of Olivia and what she would have made of all this—the woman, the food, the wine and sadly how he wished she were here. And drank again from the flute and ate another oyster. And looked at the young woman who it seemed now had been seeking him and said, "So, Lydia Pearce. Who are you?"

She was busy with the oysters. She looked up at him and said, "Company over dinner, Henry Dorn." Then, knowing this was near abrupt she did not retreat, and he supposed she never had nor would, but reached swiftly and covered a hand with one of hers and said, "Perhaps that's a story for later. Or not. It's fair to say I'm more than most men ascribe to me and less than others do. And that's enough for now." She took her hand away, reaching for another oyster and between touching the oyster shell and raising it, flared a smile that was not intended to flatter or tease but a gesture of friendship, even comradely concern.

The food began to arrive, in multiples of small servings, not much more than mouthfuls. Lobes of foie gras seared in butter, sweetbreads with morels, quail in a nest of puff pastry, miniature ham and asparagus tarts and finally crème brulee, each with time between to sip their filled wine glasses and chat, which they did.

"What a wonderful way to eat."

"You've never had French food?"

"No. Yes, I mean. But never like this. The portions . . ."

"Are you one of those men who needs a great slab of meat bleeding off the sides of your plate?"

He smiled. "I'm capable of it. But no, this is delightful."

"I'll tell you a secret." She smiled back and leaned forward, her wineglass extended up between them. "I can eat like a horse, myself. And sometimes do. I love nothing more than to consume an entire rack of lamb. When the occasion calls for that. But this, this is just what I wanted, tonight. Lots of bits of delicious things. I'm full of energy tonight. What about you?"

He studied her a moment and then said, "Did you have something in mind?"

She pulled back. Then she said, "I always have plans. Even if I'm making them up as I go along. At the moment I'm thinking of a long stroll about the promenade."

"Would you care for company?"

"I'd be delighted. But I don't care for that glassed-in section that keeps you from the sun and breeze."

He arched his eyebrows. "That's for the old people. I prefer the forecastle deck myself."

She studied him again, her dark eyes sparkling. He thought, My God, who is this? She said, "Why don't we meet there in ten minutes?"

Old people indeed, he thought. He smiled again and said, "By the lifeboats?"

Later, on the deck, strolling with the other after-dinner walkers, the sun huge, hovering, not moving, spilling the waters surrounding the boat with gold. The liner was suddenly small. The sun sank a little, sucking into itself, growing a muted scarlet. The air changed, not cooling but thickening.

And so it began.

Nine

The summer he was eleven a new minister had arrived on the Islands. A man from Halifax, a big-city Baptist with modern ideas and sermons more pointed to the everyday than the great wheel of angst and sulfur of the previous reverend. It had been the summer Henry joined the Bible Study Group and took the Temperance Pledge. For a time he thought he had heard the Call and walked about his work with the stories and his own quaking homilies and sermons ringing his head. There were times, delivering coal, that he was silent but there was a siren of voice in his head—a stream of words racing faster than he could keep up with and he was suffused with the Word of the Lord. Then came the Sunday in late September when he along with the rest of the swollen congregation filed into the church and took their seats. The stoves were not yet lit and the room was cold and Henry thought that right; comfort caused one to drift from the Word. But the ten o'clock hour came and passed and there was a quiet undertone drifting as neighbor leaned to speak with neighbor. Then the door of the church opened and all eyes turned to the vestibule but it was Henry's Uncle Fred Dorn who strode up the aisle and stood upon the platform before the lectern and waited for the organist behind him to notice his presence and allow a final chord to die away. Then Fred leaned forward and with both hands lifted spoke.

He said, "Last night the Reverend Lewes took passage on the packet boat to Yarmouth. A little after midnight with his single trunk. I asked if it was an emergency of some kind and he answered No, that he was leaving. Stealing away in the middle of the night, I asked? What crime have you committed we should know of? He asserted there was none. But he could not face you all to explain. Explain what, I inquired. It was the strangest thing. That man stood looking down at his shoes for the longest time and then said I have to go, the air is too heavy for me to breathe here. I said The air? He was quiet again, still not looking up. Aye, was what he told his shoes. The air."

Laura Crocker was a brash-mouthed twelve year old who caught Henry off guard and thrashed him in the school yard, not a difficult thing to do as he was not only unprepared but wouldn't fight back and so lay with the breath blown out of him as she sat astride his chest, her knees pinning his upper arms to the ground, her high buckled boots digging into his sides, the frenzy of attack having stirred her long skirts sufficiently so her petticoats and bloomers were a frothy mass inches from his face. She smelled of rosewater and the thick ropes of flaxen curls had escaped their band and cascaded down over her heaving chest and framed her bright serious eyes and the full red bow of her mouth. She rocked against his chest, studying him.

"What'd you do that for?"

"Because I wanted to. Because I could." She pushed a final time against him, then stood and stepped away. "Smarty-pants."

He scrambled up, smacking the dirt and shell bits from his long pants. A group of younger boys had lingered but left when Henry turned toward them with his fists up—he might be a scholar but he was quick and hard-muscled from his years of delivering coal. Laura and her three girlfriends were already partway down the road passing the Community Hall, heading on their afternoon loop around the forks of the bay. He stood watching them go, that mass of hair down her back, a smudge on the lower back of her skirts. Then he ran his hand through his short-cut brush of hair and picked up his book-satchel and headed home to change to workclothes.

He'd seen her knees, white-shining, cupped, round. Whiter than her bleached and starched underclothes.

The only thing to do was ignore her. Which over the next months he tried mightily to do. At first it seemed she'd dismissed the episode as well as any further notice of him also but then, time to time when he felt most secure within the business of school or the more difficult thus less likely to be witnessed glimpses at church, he caught her looking back at him. Or waiting for his eye. At Christmastime he returned late one dark evening after work to find a small box of fudge had been delivered for the family. He endured the sly comments from his sisters but nevertheless later was able to retrieve from the trash her holiday tag, wanting it for the gorgeous flowing rendering of her name. He hid this in his secondhand copy of *Robinson Crusoe* which only prompted fantasies of being stranded by shipwreck with Laura rescued by him, the two of them under palm trees, on white sand eating coconuts and swimming in clear blue warm waters. Naked, he thought although the few actual dreams this produced were maddening as she always seemed sheathed in some version of white underclothing. Her hair underwater like sun-made kelp.

The next summer everything changed. School was out a week when Uncle George met him at the coal shed, the little ox and summer cart already gone along with the day's sheaf of delivery notices and bills. Henry was out of a job. The work had gone to a Titus from Brier Island, a man Henry knew only by story—the winter past the man had lost a hand caught in the mighty blocks lifting the thousand foot, four hundred hook longline with its full catch of cod and haddock. No longer any good for the boats. George told him to go up to the office to see Fred.

Henry's sister's fiancé, Nelson Thurber, was behind the counter in the mercantile as he had been now for over a year. He nodded as if Henry was expected and indicated with his head the rear office, where

Henry was headed anyway. Nelson and Lucy were to marry shortly and life at home had been wretched by Henry's reckoning for several months.

Fred pushed up his visor and sucked the pencil tip a moment and then told the silent waiting boy, "Part of the time you'll help Nelson. Most of the time you'll be working with me. Not so much sitting in here although there'll be enough of that. Mostly though you'll be my legs, ears and mouth when and where I tell you to."

"But I enjoy the coal route," he said. "I know all those people. What they need and when. And I like going back and forth between the houses and the boats."

"Are you arguing with me?"

"No sir."

"Look at it this way. What you know of the families and the boats, that's key to everything else they need and use. Almost all of which, one way or t'other, flows through Dorn Brothers. Need I clarify?"

"No sir."

"Tomorrow morning. Seven sharp. You've saved money?"

Silence was answer enough.

Fred said, "You'll be wanting more long pants and white shirts. You're too young for a vest or suit coat—the men would think you've airs. Have your mother measure the trousers long so they can be let out as needs."

A month later Lucy married Nelson Thurber. After some argument Gil prevailed and walked his sister to the alter. It was a grand affair. Someone—not Euphemia and certainly not Nelson's family—had rented the Community Hall for the feasting and merriment after the ceremony. Henry suspected his Uncle George. There was no dancing but two fiddle players, a man playing a snare drum strapped to his waist and the Hall's regular pianist provided a flow of reels, jigs, laments, ballads and airs even as the guests, the whole village and many from up-Island and crossed over from Brier Island, sat to the heavy laden tables spread with the best borrowed from everyone possible linens and lace. Although festive, most of the music one way or another was born of the sea and the toll it exacted. Weddings, Henry decided, were strange affairs, as likely to produce tears as laughter and no telling one moment to the next who would erupt with any possible combination. The food was grand—chowders thick with lobster or clams or fish, cod tongues baked in cream, platters of cod, haddock and pollock cooked every conceivable way, bowls of fresh summer vegetables and, most delicious of all, an entire pig roasted two days and nights in a pit attended by a select group of men who wouldn't let Henry or any other of the curious youngsters come close.

Outside the hall there was a furtive but distinct path that led behind the building, in fact to the grove where the now cooling hog pit was. Henry, coming and going, didn't venture there but kept a careful eye and more than once saw his new brother-in-law slip around the green clapboard corner into the clump of forlorn crabapples. Once, Uncle George as well. It was a simple route to escape to as the Hall had the necessaries set off to the other side, some distance apart and so it was no great feat to leave and enter the Hall as needed. A hedge of battered salt-bitten roses separated the men's from the ladies'. And so, just before the great three-tiered cake was to be cut, the ranks of pies and puddings and other, lesser cakes, the tubs of hand-cranked ice cream thick with strawberries or handfuls of black walnuts, the crocks of lemonade and birch and root beers waiting on side tables, Henry excused himself for the third or fourth time and stood a moment in the dazzling heat and light, his body and mind already off-kilter from the combination of ceremony and rich food, then coming from the dank spidery outhouse into the spangling day once again, his fingers working to align stubborn buttons to his flies, peering down to try to determine where he'd gone wrong when she spoke.

"Have you lost something there?"

In a brand new yellow frock with lace at the shoulders and long tight white sleeves, heavy braids wrapped crownlike about her head as a sun-bedecked halo, her pink cheeks, eyes glistening as if merriment held there, one hand raised, extended slightly toward him. He hastened the button.

"Hullo Laura. You hadn't ought to be over to this side. You'll catch the devil, your mother hears of it."

"My stars and garters! You haven't been back there after that rum with the others, have you? Mother's inside not missing a bit of it all, weeping away as if twas me instead of your sister. Besides, Nelson's little brother Raymond just come round that corner and tried to give me a squeeze and steal a kiss."

"He better not try."

She brought her face closer to his, the floral scent stronger than he recalled. She said, "I kicked him in the shin."

He nodded.

She said, "You're not a rough fella, are you Henry?"

"I can blow the flukes right off Ray Thurber's anchor, I took the mind to."

She shook her head. Then said, "Do you think I'm pretty, Henry?"

"Fishheads," he said. "Plenty girls are pretty, Laura. You, you're beautiful."

"Fishheads, yourself," she said. "Then why don't you ask me to walk out with you some Saturday afternoon?"

He kicked one shined leather toe against the white of the crushed shell road. "My mother'd say I was too young for that."

Laura Crocker leaned in quick and kissed him, her lips soft warm surprise that ran through him. She pulled away before he understood what she was doing and said, "I couldn't care less what your mother thinks. We're plenty old enough."

He met her eyes, his face fired. "I'd be happy if I could buy you a root beer next Saturday evening."

She studied him a bit and said, "I'd like that. I like root beer. But say, Henry? Have you been up above the Pas of an evening to look out for the whales this summer?"

At the moment, other than working for his uncles, no one had any other plans for him. Except clearly Laura Crocker and while not sure exactly what her ideas might be, he expected he'd enjoy learning them as they were disclosed.

Until the winter weeknight two years later after he closed the mercantile himself and walked home through a dense freezing fog and steady drizzle to find his mother, uncles George and Fred, the Reverend Critten, and head of the Freeport School, Master Haines, balancing tea and waiting for him in the moist warm parlor. Where he sat in silence and gathering excitement as they laid out his future already discussed and long-agreed upon. But it was still a full two and a half years distant and his immediate focus was upon his slightly lessened duties within the family enterprise, duties he now knew so well he could discharge them within the reduced time, and the additional studies were nothing more than what he desired.

Uncle Fred finished. "If it was all my doing, I'd say it will be fine and well and then you'd be able to return and put all that to even better use, right here. And you keep that in mind."

The Reverend attempted the last word of the night. "Your mind is quick for business, you've already demonstrated that. But it's for other things it's meant. Which does not preclude you from considering seminary following a university education. The Word remains the most exalted purpose we can set ourselves to. But only you, Henry, perhaps with the Lord's intervention, will be able to determine that." He rose and the other men with him. "There are multitudes of righteous paths, gentlemen. Let us go forth into the night bearing that in mind."

"And a righteous rough night it is," said George. Who had been the man with the least to say that evening. Although whenever Henry turned toward him George's eyes were full, hard and quizzed upon him.

Alone in the kitchen with his mother as she washed, dried and put away in the high cupboard the good china, he'd felt tall, rough and clumsy, too large for the room. Then she turned, dish towel in hand

and her hidden eyes revealed red, she stepped and gathered him tight and said, "The world calls you, does it? The world called your father but he alone heard it." She stepped back and held him by his upper arms and shook him and suddenly louder, angry it seemed, "You must eat it, Henry. As good breakfast oats. Make it nourish you. It shan't eat you. Remember that."

That evening no mention was made of Laura Crocker. And Henry, with that great gulf of time before him, also did not think of her.

For many reasons all practical these new plans were held close and yet in any small place even small changes are noted and considered. Fewer hours around the docks and processing plant and cannery, among the drying and salting racks, additional texts at school and quiet but observable solitary meetings with Master Haines and the other teachers, the inevitable if subdued shift in Henry's carriage of himself, the long hours given over to more reading than usual.

Next summer a high mid-June evening he was seated with Laura in their usual place, high up in the bracken and blueberries and stunted cedars overlooking Petite Pas toward Brier Island, below the light-house the dark spruce on the sheer side of that island dark and oily appearing in the long lengthening sun—a huge lemon-drop far out in the Gulf of Maine. Side by side, her legs folded under her, their upper arms touching as they leaned against each other. Some puffins worked along the steep shoreline rocks.

She dug into a pocket and brought out a small cork-stoppered clear bottle. "My brother brought this back from Saint John. It's mild, a sort of mint tonic." She pulled the cork with her teeth and sipped and passed it to him. He held it and looked at it and back to her. The red tip of her tongue ran over her lips. She said, "Go ahead. It's nothing, you'll see. I've had it before." Her eyes snapping and laughing at him, taking him right back to when she first sat on his chest, pinning him to the ground. A different ground this, but she had him pinned. He lifted it and sipped. It was thicker than he'd expected and far smoother. Easy, really.

Quickly he kissed her and said, "Oh, that's sweet."

They passed it back and forth and kissed between sips, their mouths growing moister, sticky, a wet wild peppermint shade of evening over them. And then she said, "It's been months since you were like this. Truly."

"Laura—"

"Hush now." This time when their mouths met she slowly gathered him to her and settled back against the sweet spinning earth.

Later with the first of summer stars over them, his fingers idly twining the reaches of her hair, she said, "So you're going then?"

"I don't know," he said, looking off.

"What in the world," she said. "Are you scared all the sudden?" She was quiet a moment and then said, "It was me, I wouldn't think twice."

Now he looked at her. "I really don't know."

"Yes, you do."

"Laura." Letting it trail off. She heard his plaint clearly and stood quickly in the deep dusk.

"You'd better pray, Henry Dorn. Because I won't wait for you. Not even so long as tomorrow."

Dazed all ways and bolt upright he walked her home where she refused his mouth and he stood wavering a bit in the dark watching as she let herself in. Then he walked the long road back around the Cove, passing his house, his mother's house, he told himself and kept going, all the way down past the drying racks, the cod turned skinside up for the night and morning fog, on past the store where he was not sure but thought there might be a light burning in the back office and on from there past the canning shed and the docks with the hoists and gutting sheds, along the string of docks with the tied-up boats all the way to the end to the deep-water wharf where a single fishing schooner and one of the coastal freight boats tucked and rocked against their bumpers and he stood out at the end of that wide wharf, feeling the gentle motion of the boats as the relentless tide moved them, here where the broad sweep of Brier Light swept the passage and fled then into the fog-shroud of Fundy, stood there with the flood of brine and salt and fish strong up into his nose as he tried to make sense of where he was and what all of this life around and upon and before him could possibly mean.

Walking finally back up the wharves and past the dark buildings he saw the figure of a man deep in the porch of the mercantile. Fred Dorn. Henry paused ever so slightly to be hailed and when he was not he walked on.

Laura Crocker ignored him for the remainder of the summer, although he felt her eyes, and her eyes through other girls upon him also. It was a silent, fraught time. But when school resumed that fall it was clear to him that she carried no baby. As the autumn went on he attempted to regain at least a bit of their old familiarity. Henry thinking it was too small a place for her to react so. Laura saw it differently.

In late summer 1882 at the age of seventeen he went south to Boston on one of the Dorn's coastal schooners where he took the train to Rhode Island and began his undergraduate education at Brown University, paid for by his uncles and a modest academic stipend with severe standards. In one of his two trunks, protected with a rough folio of box board was the drawing of the cod basket his father had made and Uncle George had given him days before departure. It would be several years before he could afford to have it even modestly framed, but from that time on was never out of his hands or sight.

So off he went. Equally split with terror and excitement. He recognized the vastness of the opportunity and mostly had little doubt of his abilities. He also had his own secret plan. To spend his weekends and holidays tracking down what he could of what remained of his father. If it was nothing more than finding that grave in Newton, perhaps recognizing the house. But he was confident also he could find some of the drawings, the paintings he'd only heard of. Things like that, beautiful things, did not disappear from the face of the earth but lasted. It was only a question of being dogged, not giving up, asking the right questions enough times to enough people and he would find them. Only to see them. It was all he wanted or expected. After all, someone would own them. And he now had his own.

As with most such ventures this scheme proved not only daunting but impossible. The single name of a dealer his mother had been willing or able to recall had turned out to be an emporium of home furnishings in Boston, the owner from his father's days long since dead and the walls dotted with undistinguished land and seascapes and scenes of homely comfort, most in great heavy gilt frames worth more, he reckoned, than the daubings they held, interspersed with free-standing ionic columns meant to support potted plants, elephant-foot umbrella stands, coatracks of unlikely and hideous construction. Adding to, or perhaps crushing upon this disappointment was the realization he had neither the time nor funds to travel from Providence to Boston as his brain was strangled by the magnificent critical expectations of his masters.

But still, in early October when this apparently temperate climate seemed bathed in a glow of light and snapping colors, one Sunday he bought a round-trip ticket to Newton. Departing at dawn, the ride, even with stops, took less than three hours. At the station he received directions to the town cemetery and not only found his father's grave but had ample time to sit before it in a curious state of emotion that was grim and overwhelming at once. When the bells in the church summoned morning service he had seen enough of the plain white stone so he rose and went inside and sat through the service. The homily was on The Manna and the Grain, which inspired him and he left the church feeling a sense of accomplishment as well as meditation— that old plan was not his and now was the time to make his own. He had wanted to talk with the minister about the grave of his father but felt unrooted and without manly explanation for his appearance there. He thought At least I've seen it. I can always come back once things get sorted out.

Ten

The first week of November there were three days of harsh cold rain that on the third night turned to ice. Dawn brought a brief clear sky, the sharp bright of cold, the streets and trees and railings thickly glassed and he didn't venture out but made coffee on the gas ring and shivered in his heaviest sweater. By midday the sky rolled low again and great saucers of snow crested down, the oversized flakes appearing to arrive in jumbled layers and by late afternoon as the light was failing there was sufficient snow that he began to see people moving about on the street below, wrapped against the weather, walking with care for the ice still under the snow. The flakes had receded in size but not density and he knew the temperature was dropping and so he pulled on his overcoat and rubber galoshes and went out. He had laundry to pick up and had for days been meaning to return to the secondhand bookstore in the alley off Kalverstraat but both these were on the far side of the old town and too great a trudge for this day. Even his daily trip to the newsstand and the bakery would be put off. He was after a hearty meal and then back to his apartment, hoping the coal furnace would be thumping up steam into his single radiator.

The canal had filled during the day with a soft slush that as he walked along he could see was already firming, the surface catching and holding the crystals of falling snow as the air froze them and he guessed if this cold continued the boats would be locked in for the winter. Then from one of the houseboats saw what he'd missed before —a jutting length of stovepipe and sweeps of dark coal smoke. Passing by he was at the right level to glance down into the lit quarters and was greeted by the upturned face of a middle-aged man. Henry didn't stop so much as pause in his stride and the man below him was similarly arrested, as if both had been caught peering into a privacy otherwise ignored. The man was in the rough clothes of a laborer, his face heavily creased, longish hair pomaded back. For the moment their eyes caught it seemed there was some warble of recognition before the man turned away from the porthole window and Henry also was gone, moving beyond.

Back in his apartment, fed but not cheered, he'd retrieved his own bottle of Genever from the ledge next to his butter jar and poured a small measure into a glass and sat in the dark by the large windows, illumination sufficient to his mind coming from the streetlamps and lit windows across the canal, all muted now with the still-falling snow and having lost the refraction of the enveloped water below.

An apparition. Slowly moving through the thickening snow the color of butter from the dimmed lamps. A man, head wrapped in a scarf with a broken-crowned hat pulled over it, his greatcoat buttoned tight, progressing in cautious even lurches, a crutch under one arm and no leg below the coat on that side of him. Henry pulled back from the window, then realizing he couldn't be seen even if the man were to look up which didn't seem plausible, he moved forward again and watched the slow progress until the man was cut from sight by the window casement.

Someone who had to get from one place to another, impediment aside. Henry was impressed by the great care the man took, also the near-savage prodding ahead with the crutch for purchase to be trusted, not truly slow as much as a series of quick jerked explorations before swinging his body along. Progress made.

Henry sank back, his eyes raising toward the dimly lighted rectangles of windows across the canal. There are any number of ways to lose a limb. Countless, no doubt. And the Dutch had not been in the war. Although that wasn't to say the man was necessarily Dutch or that nationality prevented him from volunteering. He might've been drunk and slipped under a cable car. But there was something familiar, something of great fatigue to the man that spoke of more than arduous movement along an icy street.

Robert had been home a year when Henry was near literally carried home across campus in an oddly buoyant and pacific state of mind that seemed to come from nowhere although it was a pleasant enough early autumn afternoon. And so into the house where he found his son alone, leaning back in an upholstered chair, a glass of iced mint tea on a coaster beside him and Henry had, after changing into more casual trousers, shirt and boat shoes, his mood intact, settled down across from him. The softened features and somnolent morphine eyes Henry had grown used to didn't bother him this afternoon. Or he chose to ignore them, overtaken by his mood and what felt to be an opportunity. He sat across from his son, his legs spread, elbows on spread knees, hands clasped before him, leaning slightly forward.

"Can you tell me, Robbie," he'd said. "What I can do?" Not even knowing he was going to ask until he did and once out, knowing, certain, it was the heretofore unseen bridge both needed.

Robert blinked, straightened a bit and after a moment of what appeared to be deep thought said, "No."

And Henry, Henry who a week ago, six months ago, would've lost his temper at the rudeness of the response, simply said, "Are you sure you don't want to try?"

Then a long silence. The gentle rasp of his son's lungs working.

"Early on when we were mostly still waiting and the front was only something we heard about—" Henry had to lean a bit closer to hear his son who was not looking at him but out toward some unknown spot on the wall—"one of the Brit flyboys took me up for a joyride. It was a sunny, clear day and the guns were muffled but steady, the big guns, and I could see the smoke from them and then we were over a different land than anything I'd ever seen and the guns were below us and even up there in the sky we could feel them and down below the steady orange flashes and then the puffs of smoke that obscured the land which was otherwise without color, just a mass of brown and burning black, here and there small white scars that I later learned were the remains of trees and there were places where the whole earth seemed to be moving, writhing, and I realized those were men, masses of men moving and shells falling among them and they seemed to move more quickly, those, just for a few moments and then another shell would go off and it was the same thing and I wasn't even sure if we'd crossed the lines or not and I realized that it didn't matter. We circled back to the aerodrome next to where the ambulance service was training. Where we finished our training and were broken up into teams and sent forward. And like I'd seen everything was brown and blasted and most everything else and people, the troops, were dug down into the ground except the guns and what was left of the roads. Some brick or plaster bits of walls where once something had stood—a house a barn a church—mostly it was hard to tell. And men both living and dead, their bodies ripped open. Every way you can imagine and plenty more you can't . . ." He drifted off into a silence not looking at his father and Henry felt as if he was holding his breath and then in the very same near monotone voice Robert went on, "When I was a kid, just seven or eight I'd lie in the backyard and watch an ant's nest, you know those little brown ants that're everywhere—the ones that show up in the kitchen at the cottage every summer—anyway I'd lie there and study them, just watch them rushing all about, in and out of their little holes in the ground, the little mounds of fine sand they made and wonder about how many of them there could be and how deep into the ground their nest went and things like that, imaging sometimes that the nest was big, huge, that it took up the whole yard but we just couldn't see it. And those little piles they came out of were all over the yard too, if you looked so I wondered was it all one big nest connected or maybe a bunch of little ones and how did they decide where one stopped and another began because I never saw any of them fighting, just rushing in and out, sometimes holding something, worrying it like a dog, something so small I couldn't see what it was. And once I got bored watching them so I poured some water real slow down into the nest and that sealed up, washed away all the holes. But pretty soon, bit by bit, the holes opened up again as the ants came back out while the ones caught outside were just running around frantic, and then pretty soon it was like nothing had happened . . ."

He stopped and looked at his father. "Except it was men. Everything was dirty and brown, all shades of brown. Except the insides of men. That was red. A lot of red. Splintered bones. White and blue guts. But mostly red."

Robert hitched himself upright, his face the sallow color it became when he was in pain, or when he needed the morphine—Henry no longer knew which ruled which and wasn't sure his son did. Robert took up his neat whiplash walking stick and came around the chair so he was passing his father and said, "So you see. There's thousands like me. Or worse. We're the lucky ones. Don't you think?"

The snow was still falling and Henry rose a bit stiffly from his window seat and in the mild dark made his way to the sink and rinsed out his glass and set it upside down on the dishtowel to dry. He got ready for bed and lowered himself down in, the sheets and blankets cold but warming quickly around his pajamas. On his back with an extra pillow under his head he lay watching the faint play of light from the windows on the ceiling. And again and always, that later final brutal confrontation with Robert known only to the two of them, now Henry's alone, always linked. High spirits in a roadster on a fine spring day. An accident.

After Lydia had told him she was leaving and where she was going he'd once suggested going with her, even as he knew he was fully half the reason she was leaving. And she'd bluntly said, "You don't want

to go to Paris, Henry. You know that. You don't want to see the countryside and you certainly don't want to see the men there. It's a city
full of broken men, Henry."

He had no idea if she was still there. Although he absolutely trusted
Paris had been her destination. Lydia was capable of many things but
lying was not one of them. If anything, he thought, she was too directly
honest.

How alone a person lives.

Eleven

*I*t was the summer that wouldn't end. Through July and August at the lake cottage the heat was noticed but truly only as August came on and the usual cooling nights didn't occur and the dripping sleeplessness of July continued. Henry or Dick Pyle made daily trips up the hill to Lakemont for blocks of ice for the iceboxes but even that was novelty—both men that same spring had purchased their first automobiles, Dick a Maxwell Runabout and Henry a Dodge Touring Car, and so each excursion was loaded down with children and more than a few of the adults. There were frequent late afternoon thunderstorms so drought was no worry. It was only when September came and they returned to Elmira that the fierce lock of heat was deeply felt. Back in classrooms, all of them, Robert in grade school, both girls at Elmira Free Academy and Henry sweating in his office and the classrooms of Tripp Hall. And just then, when they could've served some cooling purpose the afternoon thunderstorms abated and instead sluggish humid air seemed to rise steaming from the cobbles each morning. The Lyceum Theatre was handing out free paper fans to customers. Olivia and the housegirl of the time did all their baking and roasting in the mornings and many evenings they took picnic suppers to Eldridge Park, hoping for a breeze off the river—a practice Olivia disliked, considering the park a place for summer gatherings and uncomfortable with Henry in shirtsleeves in public for dinner, however informal the setting and regardless of how those around them were dressed.

But on the first Saturday of fall, the day dawned as steamy, still and hot as ever and at the breakfast table Henry surveyed his already wilted and short-tempered females and announced, "I've got it! We'll take the trolley out to Reeds Landing and rent a pair of canoes, take along sandwiches or we can even stop at that place, you know, the one past Clinton Island along the river—I've heard they have wonderful chicken—and just make a day of it. Get out of all this."

Robbie beamed and said, "Can we take Bobo?" The year-old collie who even then sat alert beside the boy for either crumbs or unwanted food to be slipped down to him.

"Well, Robbie. I don't know. How do you think he'd take to a canoe?"

"He likes the rowboat just fine."

"Henry—" Olivia began, less than keen, uncertain.

Polly interrupted, "Father. Have you lost your mind? We'd roast like ducks out there on the river."

"Why don't we drive up to the lake?" Alice. "So the cottage is shut for the winter, but the drive wouldn't be so bad and at least when we got there we could cool off in the water."

"All the damned dust," said Polly, who was trying such things out.

"You will not—" Henry began.

"Oh leave her be," Olivia said. "I can't bear the thought of it myself."

Alice snapped, "It was just an idea. I'll end up at the sanitarium if I have to spend another day—"

"Mother, please," Henry said. "Polly, I won't have you talking like that in this house or any other. And if I hear about you and your friends being rude again at the Red Jacket Ice Cream Parlor—"

"I've got it," Robbie cried. "The water toboggan past Fritch's Bridge! That's what we need to do."

"Oh God," Polly said under her breath, rolling her eyes.

Henry and Olivia were looking at each other. At the same moment they lifted their eyebrows. A suppressed smile fled over Olivia, gone before any of the children might catch it. Robbie's enthusiasm was too great to argue with. Alice was holding the tip of her tongue between her lips, an unconscious habit that, Henry had learned long since meant the idea, however novel, held attraction for her. So he rose from the table and smacked his hands together and said, "Robert, my boy, you're a genius. Now, before all the rest of Elmira gets the same idea. Bathing suits, towels, a change of clothes—" he glanced at Olivia, "And unless I'm wrong they also serve a variety of foods that should satisfy all of us." He pulled out his pocket watch and finished. "In ten minutes I want everyone back down in the front hall with whatever you think you might need. Let's get cracking."

They rode the electric trolley west along the bank of the Chemung River, early enough so the trolley cars weren't yet full but clearly plenty of other people had dawned with the same idea. There was a small clot of girls Alice and Polly knew and when they shifted seats to be closer to their friends Olivia glanced at Henry and he let it go. Robbie sat between his parents and between his legs on a short leather leash Bobo sat quietly, watching the surroundings. A boy's dog—he'd been introduced and subjected to pretty much anything a boy could think of.

PROPER SWIMMING ATTIRE REQUIRED—CLEAN BOILED SUITS TO LET IN ALL SIZES read the sign above the ticket counter. The steps up to the water toboggan rose seventy feet in broad easy stairways with high handrails and at the top was a railed platform. The toboggan itself was a smoothed wooden shoot that dropped down and out swiftly before extending in a gradual decrease over the river, plopping the usually screaming descender into the depths midriver, where a number of fellows in rowboats hung lazy in the current for those unwilling or unable to swim back to shore. Under a grove of riverside sycamores were strings of picnic tables as well as concession stands serving up everything from spun cotton candy and ice cream to wieners and fried chicken and all manner of cold drinks. Back away from the river was a low damp spot in a meadow that had been turned into a pond and stocked with bullheads and cane poles could be rented and angle worms purchased as well.

Quickly Bobo figured out how things worked and so every time one of his children climbed toward the platform the dog would wade into the shallows and stand with muzzle upturned, barking as the child came flying down, barking until the child reached the riverbank. Midmorning as the heat truly came on, as well as in the spirit of things, Henry took a few trips down the slide but what he enjoyed most was slowly floating on his back down the lazy current, his body encased in the cool but not cold river, before finally rolling over to breaststroke roughly for shore. The Island boy hadn't learned to swim until he met Olivia and began to spend time at the lake and it had been Mary who'd figured out his reluctance to enter the water was nothing more than fear and so quietly had taken it upon herself to teach him the rudiments of swimming—the young deeply embarrassed man out for early morning sessions with his mother-in-law became proficient more quickly than he might've with any other tutor.

Henry briefly tried to tease Olivia into riding the slide herself but she hushed him by looking with those bold dark eyes and saying, "I'm so enjoying watching the children, dear. And perfectly capable of deciding if I wish to make an ass of myself or not." Smiling. Although she unrolled her stockings in the late morning and hitched up her skirts to wade in the shallows in the shade of the sycamores as Henry went off with Robbie to spend an hour baking by the pond, fruitlessly trying to catch bullheads. Henry guessed the pond water was so warm after the summer that if any of the fish survived they were half-buried in the muddy bottom—something that seemed to him a natural fit for such an ugly inedible fish. Robbie caught nothing but a snagged branch caked with muddy leaves but just as happy for the effort. They walked back to drop off the cane pole side by side, Henry's hand resting easily on his son's knobby shoulder.

They ate a grand lunch of wieners with mustard and sauerkraut, potato salad, late season sweet corn roasted over a bed of coals in charred husks, root beer floats and banana splits for desert. In the afternoon Alice and Polly were finally released to wander within sight with their girlfriends, boys their ages and slightly older swinging close but then away, as much from the swarm of girls and their own shyness as by the presence of parents. It had been the year when Polly, although a year younger and shorter had rounded breasts and despite the woolen stockings beneath the swimming skirt and its heavy though sleeveless top, was a mild torture to Alice with her near invisible bosom and long gangly legs and arms. For a time Henry rented one of the rowboats and with Robbie and Bobo aboard worked along the shaded bank, Henry easy but putting his back and arms into the work. Here or anywhere, he'd never lost his love of boats and could find something good about even the roughest of craft. Then it was too hot and he released Robbie back to the pleasures of the toboggan and the river, trusting now not only the watchers but the boy. He lay up in the shade with Olivia on a soft quilted blanket, cool there in the shade, Olivia in a folding camp chair brought from home, reading; Henry on his side, head propped up on one elbow. Then down on his back with his hands behind his head, dozing in the heat but anchored to the place by the sounds of voices, the screams from the toboggan, the otherwise low buzz of voices all around and beneath that, deep and low as a pulse, the murmur of the river. Just three years before in late spring this river had flooded, washing away not only the toboggan and all the other riverside parks and amusements but flooding the lower streets of Elmira to a depth sufficient that men used canoes and rowboats to navigate among their businesses. A fully loaded train of freight cars had been nudged into place over the railroad bridge that spanned the river, the weight enough to hold the bridge even as the water rose and ruined much of the coal within the cars. The coal from the sheds that served the city, owned by Doyle Franks. As well as a primary stake in the Erie Railroad itself. It was not only a civic gesture, but the bridge held.

Late afternoon, all in the pleasant state of water-and-heat-exhaustion, they rode the trolley back to town and hauled themselves up to the house, where shortly after everyone changed they realized that once again all were famished. Being the weekend the housekeeping girl was off and there was nothing that appealed and so as the early fall revealed itself by the dropping angle of light even as the heat held, they all loaded into the big Dodge for the seven block proud drive downtown where they had dinner in the swank Rathbun House, which rumor claimed was an exact replica, even down to the menu of the Murray Hill Hotel in New York City. True or not, it was a fine meal and they ended the evening once again with ice cream from the Red Jacket. Back at the house, all three children took their turns bathing and were in bed before nine o'clock.

Somewhat later Henry was seated in the parlor with his feet up, a glass of rye over ice mostly idle in his hand when Olivia came through from the bathroom herself, wearing her robe open over a deep blue silk nightgown. She came beside him and leaned down and he lifted his head to kiss her, the soft silk neckline opening to her breasts.

"That," she said, "was an exquisitely perfect day." Patting herself back into place.

"It was pleasant, wasn't it?"

"No. It was more than that. Thank you."

He was silent, took a small sip of his drink, a shaving of ice sliding against his lower lip.

She said, "Be up soon?"

He smiled. "Just moments."

Twelve

*H*enry bought a small paraffin stove, forbidden by his lease, and set it up on a pair of pilfered bricks near his music stand. He had made pleasant gain, if not mastery with the Kummer exercises and had begun working with Josef Merk's etudes, which only impressed him again with his status as beginner. But a plateau of sorts had been reached with the Kummer and so he knew in time the same would happen with the etudes. More importantly, the cello, no longer an abstract cello but the one he labored over daily, had become not merely familiar but extraordinarily comfortable. And comforting. A routine had evolved and like all such was a homely contentment. He would wash his hands. Then take the cello up and buff it with a soft rag. Tighten and rosin the bow. Then perch on the front half of his chair and spread his knees and take the instrument in against him. Pluck the strings and tune. Lightly bow and finger a motley of scales, major and minor, ones that he alternated daily. Some days he would play one or more of the Kummer exercises, others he would delve straight to Merk. A poor session was no longer cause for agony or uncertainty—simply an indication of where he ought to focus. Sometimes this meant retreating and working through an earlier piece that he thought he'd mastered until he played it again and heard the fissures of error. The fingers on his left hand had calluses, hardened pads on his fingertips. He took secret pleasure in them. Sometimes over a bowl of soup or sitting reading he would discover himself rubbing a callused finger against his thumbtip.

On Tuesday shortly after noon he made his way downstairs for the weekly trek to his lesson with Morozov. He did not relish the walk in the cold. Which was enough to get him into his scarf, coat, hat and gloves and down the stairs that he no longer stumbled against and out into the street. The cold a perfection all of its own. A single gull cry pierced the air and seemed a slice of the cold itself. He could smell bread from the bakery across the canal. A blown crumple of newspaper from yesterday lodged against his stoop. Halfway along toward Nieuwmarkt he heard the throaty chants and bullhorn cries of a crowd gathered. He turned onto Nieuwmarkt and paused. The wind was daunting here and the sunlight weak and pitiful against it. The square all the way to the Waag was filled with people. Either the Socialists or the Communists were rallying. He had no desire to get close enough to read the placards and identify which group it might be, listen to the chants or have leaflets thrust upon him. Signs and banners battered and sailed in the wind. The voices through the bullhorns also battered and broken by the same wind. He did not let himself study the crowd, not wanting to be mistaken for displaying interest. The throng seemed to be all men, younger men mostly. In the thin drab brown trousers, waist jackets and round caps of workingmen. Whoever they were, it was too cold to be out. On a workday no less.

He hugged tight away from the square along the shopfronts and cafés and slowly made his way. But not for home. Although the scene before the Waag had unsettled him. He still read the *Herald Tribune* and was beginning to read the Dutch papers as well—his German from years ago as a doctoral candidate at Yale had left him grasping but slowly returned and the connections were made. All Europe it seemed was seething, striving. He did not want to be political—he did not want to know. He'd learned his way around now and while it might make him a few minutes late he had no reason to think this would bother Dmitri Morozov. So he cut back and across and down the narrow way along the Oudeschans, then over past Zuiderkerk and thus around to Oude Hoogstraat. With the cold the huge bay doors of both the fish market and the brewery were closed but the smells were the same as ever, somewhat muted by the draught of fresh chill air. The commingling of the fish and the hops and stale beer had come to signify a place, a singular and special place for him. The Russian had become his touchstone.

He stood knocking on the brown door. The wind funneled neatly down the street and he turtled his head into his shoulders and continued every few minutes to knock. It was not unusual for the Russian to take some time to open the door. Henry understood that this was most likely because the living quarters were vast and the man might be deep within; he did not know for sure because the door opened onto a wide chamber divided from whatever lay behind by thick floor to ceiling drapes of heavy rough fabric and it was here he took his lessons. There was a coal stove, a pair of music stands, two overhead bare lightbulbs and the vat of hot strong tea. A small round table that held the tea and old near-clear bone cups and saucers. And that was all.

So he stood a long time. Every few minutes he would rap upon the door and then wait, his hands in his overcoat pockets, the cello in its case leaned against a beam up the side of the building. He grew cold. He knocked again. The wind was sharp and bit all exposed skin. Finally he opened the bottom buttons of his coat and dug out his pocket watch. It was half past the hour. He knocked once more, long and hard and his knuckles were red and white and when he finished this final tattoo he only paused long enough to press his chapped ear to the cold wood when the door opened. Morozov peered out, the slender fine features above a mouth slightly too thick for his face to be handsome, his balding head uncovered. The door, as the very first time, not opened for admittance but a slender six inches as if he might shoulder it closed any moment. His eyes swept Henry and beyond, up and down. Morozov, finished with his observations, stepped back and swung fully open the door. The two men nodded to each other and Henry stepped inside.

Morozov did not hesitate. "Let your instrument warm. Have tea. Sit."

Henry took the tiny cup and saucer and perched on the chair behind the music stand that he thought of as his. He said, "It's a cold day."

Morozov shrugged. "Every day has good and bad. Sometimes one hidden behind the other."

Henry sipped the sugared creamy tea and considered this unlikely thrust toward the personal. Finally he said, "Beyond your capacity as my instructor of the cello, I'm ignorant of your circumstances. And content to remain so. The reasons you have for making your home in Amsterdam are your own, as are mine." He paused. Dmitri Morozov was standing, holding his saucer in the flat of one palm, his tea untouched.

Morozov said, "How are you finding the progress with the etudes of Merk?"

Henry paused and finished his tea, rose and stepped around the man and set his cup and saucer on the small round table. Without sitting again he said, "Sometimes I feel I'm gaining. Other times not so much."

And Dmitri Morozov smiled at him, the first time he'd seen the man smile. Morozov said, "There is no peril for you coming to me. I have taught children, far too many children, with less ability and much less dedication. As a pupil I hope you remain. My circumstances, as you put it; are not good. Like many other poor fools I welcomed the revolution but with hesitation and such subtlety is noticed. Noted, is the better word. Please, I mean no burden of detail. But I am not of the same sort as the White Russian émigré scum in Paris. I was, finally, allowed to leave Russia. Then when all was ready, belongings sold or bartered, my home long assigned to others, my wife and children packed the single suitcase allowed. All I attempted was the clothes on my back and my instrument. At the station we were told our visas were not good. Some problem with the passports. I am not a fool. I was a musician—I enjoyed the privileges and small pleasures of the artist. The Bolsheviks they hate anybody who has even the smallest smell of the old regime. So, at the station, what is it they want. As ancient as the Flood. They want money. I tried to negotiate and they do that very well. Once they had every last ruble except a gold piece in my shoe they told me that I was free to go. But now, they asked, how to pay for my wife, my children. A son and daughter. I was a fool, thinking I was arranging for all. Not stipulating that at the first. I looked at my wife. She knew of the gold piece. She shook her head. So I offered my cello. It is, you know, you have seen it, very fine. Kindling they called it. One even kicked it. I was trembling. Fear, rage, helpless—all those things. The train was at the platform. It was a cold Moscow night—the steam from the engine covered us all as if predicting. They said Go now or never. I looked at my wife, my son, my daughter. Nadia did not speak out loud but her mouth said Go. I moved to embrace them. My children were crying. The guards, they pushed me back. I almost fell and when I got upright my wife and children had been moved back, away from the platform. A ticket, that stinking passport, pushed into my hand. The train was filling. I stood on tiptoe to see my family and recognized her headscarf. I got hold of my cello and moved toward the train. At the doors I turned and with all my soul bellowed that I would write, that I would find a way for them to join me." Morozov paused.

Somewhere during this telling he had stopped looking at Henry. Now he did. "That was two years ago. I send letters but hear nothing. I have been visited. The Party wants me to come back. You see, I was principal cellist in Moscow Orchestra." He corrected himself. "Moscow State Orchestra. They tell me my wife and children want me to return. They threaten me. They say the Dutch could expel me as a criminal. They say many things. I listen to none of it. I try to listen to none of it. All lies. All lies. It is all they know." He paused and then said, "The mistake they made was letting me go instead of my family. As long as I am here, there is hope. I go back, no hope. You see?"

He stopped. Set his saucer on the table and picked up his cello from its stand and seated himself. He looked at Henry Dorn. "Shall we play?"

Back in his apartment he broke his habit and turned on the gas ring to make coffee. He was too cold to go back out for other fare. Perhaps later.

But still, sipping the coffee which he'd made too strong, he had to wonder about Morozov. Simply as one man concerned for another. That, Henry Dorn believed, was all the politics the world could stand. Or truly needed. The world did not reward idealism—that he knew for certain. The veils of avarice would not be penetrated by simplicity. Massive fruitless wars, utopian revolutions, the befuddling modern world; all depended upon layers of complexity and impenetrable mystery, perpetuating the notions of some brashly confidant self-anointed elect. Sitting now with his cold coffee, beginning to gird himself for the street again and a warm supper, it occurred to him that despite the years of education and despite the temperate considered and resolute approach he brought to teaching and uplifting young women, he was at core formed by his childhood years. A man caught fish and ate and clothed his family or a man did not and depended on his neighbors or starved. A man could recover from a storm-lost boat. But not by sitting and holding his head in his hands. Or ranting at the fisheries' laws and limits that he might blame for forcing him out in that storm in the first place. He built a new boat, was what he did. Or, Henry smiled, learned the cello.

Later he bundled again and went out for his supper. Except for blown trash and a ragged banner wrapped around a single leaning pole there was no reason to think the great cobbled square had ever held such a mass of people, let alone early this afternoon. He ate well and listened to the voices around him, realizing as he did that he was beginning to understand the conversations. There was both gain and loss in this—comprehension brought him back into the world but stole the isolation he now understood had been so attractive.

He had a difficult time sleeping. That damned afternoon coffee. The Genever he'd sipped after his meal had barely made its way through the vat of soup and bread. He lay awake. Not thinking of Lydia. Not at all. He wondered if Dmitri Morozov might be in greater financial distress than he allowed himself to appear. For all he knew he was the Russian's only student. And thought also of the man's family. Which reminded him of his own, his daughters and granddaughters, so largely ignored these past months. He vowed solemnly to write, first thing in the morning.

Still he could not sleep. He recalled Ovid

> *Sleep, thou repose of all things;*
> *Sleep, thou gentlest of deities;*
> *Thou peace of the mind, from which care flies;*
> *Who dost soothe the hearts of men*
> *Wearied with the toils of the day,*
> *And refittest them for labor.*

Perhaps he was not laboring sufficiently.

Thirteen

Very late with no moon and the spread of stars extending in a field not spheroid but flattened and deep, broken only by the looming bulk of the stacks and the ship's bridge behind which he stood on the forecastle of the promenade deck. The ocean near black but for the slight white plume-curls where starlight struck off a cresting bit of wave. Faint beneath his feet in this quiet was the thrum of the great turbines pushing ever closer to Europe, to Holland, to Rotterdam and on to Amsterdam and then he knew not what—this night that destination seemed a vague and unreliable caprice. He'd spent the evening with Lydia Pearce and was in a curious state, exalted, enthralled, most pleasantly exhausted, his body drained of tensions he hadn't even known he was carrying, as well as a faint but palpable smutch of guilt.

Following their dinner and long sunset stroll, the walk itself comfortably peaceful and largely quiet, not of awkwardness but of an ease that at least that evening neither cared to mention, as if for fear speaking might drive it away, her hand slipped lightly into his elbow, a touch lightly tentative as if she knew it alarmed him even as he took pleasure in it—it had been so long it seemed since he'd been touched at all, or perhaps and just as possible the timidity had belonged to her, walking in the gentle heat of the ocean's early summer. There was no discussion or plans made for the morrow but at the end of the evening, after he'd escorted her not to her door but the passageway leading to it, the murmurs exchanged of the pleasure of the evening, after her last goodnight, she'd unexpectedly, just as he was turning away, gently held his lapels as she raised on tiptoe and swiftly kissed him, one cheek and then the other. He'd stood a moment watching her walk away and then went back up on deck for a final turn. Trying to place the kisses, almost chaste but for the swift warmth of her lips. And then found himself reddening, his face hot as a teenager misunderstanding a cue. That kiss was continental, although he only knew this from reading and so forgotten as it happened.

Next morning (this morning by some lights although the man on the dark silence of the ocean couldn't help but correct himself—all he was thinking of, all that had brought him up here sleepless and restless, all of it was already technically yesterday) he'd half-expected to see her at breakfast and when he did not, awash in disappointment and something he chose to call relief, he ate his ham and eggs and then recalled her speaking of private breakfast habits, then also remembering how he'd first seen her. Perhaps other than the pleasure of walking, her calisthenics outfit served another purpose as well. So he went topside and made slow circuits of the boat, casting prudent cautious glances over the varied groups exercising, in a mild horror of being seen and taken as one with a prurient eye and then when he didn't spy her he continued walking, thinking he might simply encounter her again this way. But either their schedules were not coinciding or she wasn't out this morning. The possibility was real that she was avoiding him, having enjoyed their evening but not wanting to encourage further intimacy of contact. He went to his stateroom with a similar mixture of feelings as over breakfast. But when he shut the door he stood a moment and then shook his head like a dog shedding water, thinking he'd come dangerously close to making a fool of himself.

Not without a pang but he settled in and spent the morning reading Virgil's *Georgics,* an old favorite, a book of ancient dreams. Telling himself the immersion in Latin would make easier the transition from the German he knew, to the Dutch that he didn't—a stretch from the Romantic to the Teutonic but at a deep enough level he felt the logic was grounded if not entirely sound. Mostly though it was for the pleasure of reading exactly what he wanted without any other reason whatsoever—the curse of the academic finally lifted. And also, absorbed, sufficient reason to use the wonder of the ship's telephone system to have his midday meal brought to his stateroom, the cream of tomato soup he'd most pleasantly missed the night before, crescent rolls and a perfect pear. And then, against all expectation, he napped.

It was late when he swam up from a dreamless sleep and sat a moment, contemplating Virgil which seemed to rise in remnants alongside the waking as he realized he was not tired so much as drained, a long fever of exhaustion that went back at least to the deaths of Olivia and Robert, possibly even, he thought, since Robert's return from the Great War. Then he was fully awake and realized the dinner hours were already underway as he scrubbed himself and changed and let himself out, no longer groggy but wanting a turn or two about the *Veendam II* to whet his appetite.

He saw her before she saw him. A good distance away, clearly dressed for dinner, her back against the ship's rail, her arms spread along the top cable as if lounging, speaking with a man in tails—overdressed was what Henry thought—and he was turning away, not wanting to interrupt what seemed an obviously private moment when her face turned and caught his and he stopped, the slide of her face from a concentrated anger and quivering poise to one of open relief and pleasure too obvious to ignore. And she waved greeting and called his name and if there ever had been a choice in those few seconds it was gone now. As Henry approached the man turned, the surly handsome face of a younger man, a man who even if he hadn't been so splendidly dressed was clearly one who thought well of himself. A notion Henry revised as he drew closer—this was not a man who gave much thought to himself at all but merely and naturally expected his desires and wishes to be consistent with those who ignited his inter-est. A man of means and little comprehension beyond that. Except the power he felt he owned also.

"Hullo, Lydia," Henry called out.

"Well, there you are!" she sang. "And high time. I was just explaining to Dwight that I actually do have an engagement for dinner even if you are unreliable about time." Dwight was now considering Henry, a fabu-lously fast appraisal that was both amused, angry and dismissive at once. Dwight turned back to Lydia briefly and said, "You can certainly reel them in, can't you?" And then turned and stalked past Henry.

Henry disregarded this and spoke quietly, very close to her. "Are you all right?"

She lifted her hands and pressed them over her face and dropped them. "Would you," she started and faltered. "Would you be so kind as to walk with me a bit?"

"Of course. Here, take my arm."

They were alone on the deck now and she slipped her hand free of his elbow and took his hand in her own, striding with anger and yet bumping against Henry as they went. After a bit he gently said, "It's none of my business but who was that cretin?"

And she laughed and paused then, swinging around to face him. "Just another cretin," she said. "The world is full of them." Then sud-denly serious she said, "It's not easy, Henry, trying to be an inde-pendent woman. Sometimes I feel I've made a true mess of it." Then a smaller less certain grin flashed and she said, "But I continue."

"Well, good for you. And now, correct me if I'm wrong but don't we have a dinner date?"

She studied him. "I wouldn't hold you to that."

He held her eyes with his. "I do wish you would."

She paused, a hesitation. Then she said, "But you did overhear. How I reel men in."

"I wouldn't know about that," he said. "But I'm awfully hungry. So, what do you say?"

This evening they ate well and the wine was good but the food was backdrop since the moment they were seated, thick embossed menus unopened, he glanced over and said, "Last evening you pegged me as a novice traveler. Which I suppose was easy enough to do but it does suggest an obvious observation—"

"I'm an old hand." She smiled.

"I come from seafaring folk and so wouldn't put it quite that way."

"No women on boats. They're bad luck."

Now he smiled. "It depends on the boat."

"Really? Don't you think it'd depend on the woman?"

"Oh, absolutely. Or perhaps both. Men think it takes brawn to haul line but there's many a slip of a boy who does the work as well as any man. Dexterity can be as valuable as brute strength, even in great storms."

A waiter loomed, menus consulted and wine poured. She said, "This is all quite playful but the nautical allusions are dancing close to the comment that fellow Dwight made. Shall we be more direct?"

"I had an old uncle who taught me to disregard the bitter ill manners of rejection long ago. Beyond that Dwight is no concern of mine, unless he's truly pestering you, in which case I'd be happy to thrash him for you."

"You would not."

He looked away and gazed across the expanse of room and then back. "No. I'm afraid that's not my style. But it's tempting, just for the way the idea lit your face."

She smiled. "He's an overgrown boy is all he is. A nuisance and spoiled but if you lifted a hand he'd turn white and run. Like most bullies."

"I imagine," he said, carefully and less playful now. "That being an independent woman has its challenges."

She shrugged. "It's not so much as if I ever made a choice about it."

"Really? Don't you think we all make choices, even if we prefer to believe otherwise?"

Now she was fully serious. "No. Events occur and we are changed. Even if we play an active role in the events, they're never what we predicted or expected. That's what I think."

He watched her neatly slice a piece of deep red beef and lift it to her mouth; Henry suddenly sobered. "Well. There's certainly something to that. My wife died and so here I am. Not an obvious chain of events but nevertheless . . ."

She dabbed her mouth. "I'm sorry. I only meant—"

"Don't apologize. My wife and only son are dead and I'm alive. And so, to some extent, this journey."

Her eyes were troubled, some hooded sorrow. Softly she said, "Do you have other children? Family?"

"Two lovely daughters and three granddaughters, so far."

They were quiet for a bit, eating. The waiter poured more wine. He studied her pensive, troubled face and then gently asked, "Is there something you want to tell me?"

She remained silent, watching her plate.

Henry said, "Miss Pearce? Lydia? My sorrows are a part of me, but not the sum total. Just moments ago we were enjoying a banter quite refreshing. I'm sorry to have broken that." Then it occurred to him. "Or do I have it wrong? Is it Mrs. Pearce?"

She looked at him now. "No, you don't have it wrong. I've been Lydia Pearce since birth and although there was a time I thought otherwise, now I expect to remain so until I die."

"And that would be the story for another time. The near miss, if you'll pardon a pun."

That edged a smile back. "Perhaps another time."

"Well and fair," he said. "So allow me a moment. Here we are having dinner, off to a grand start but with an uncomfortable interlude. Shall we rescue the evening?"

"I'd be delighted to."

"It seems to me," he ventured. "That since I pretty much gummed things up, you suggest which direction we take."

She swirled and sipped wine and said, "It's our second dinner. The customary thing would be to trade stories but we've not done so well with that, have we?"

He also sipped and then said, "If I may hazard an idea, perhaps our misstep was to dig in the too recent past."

She tipped her head a bit and said, "And because you're a man you assume that the childhood and the struggles you endured and the achievements you've gained would be endlessly fascinating to me." The slowly spread full smile that possessed her face was back, mocking herself as much or more than the assumptions.

He laughed. "Not at all. I find you most curious—"

"A bit of an oddity."

"Meant more in the friendly way of one encountering a specimen one always suspected existed but had never yet laid eyes upon. Don't forget—you labeled yourself an independent woman. It's not simply my own conclusion."

"And you want to know?"

"How it all began. This life you lead."

She nodded. "A fair enough question. Although, putting aside as we agreed my most recent unpleasantry, I'd remind you that all such tales have their troubles endured and woes bestowed."

He nodded. "Of course."

"So. A deal?"

"The terms?"

"I'll tell you my little history and you'll avoid unnecessary commiserations."

"Beyond sympathetic noises at appropriate moments?"

She laughed again. "Fair enough. Shall we shake on it?"

"There's no reason to, that I see."

And she paused to study him again. As if he surprised her, which was very possibly true, as he was surprising himself. And the waiter swept in and cleared away dinner and without blinking she ordered lemon tarts and coffee. When the coffee was poured she swiftly dispatched the tart and he recalled her comment the evening before about her ability to tuck into her food, as he broke forkfuls of his own tart slowly, waiting in silence for her.

"Yes," she said. "On with it then. I first came to Europe when I was fifteen. With a governess, a young Englishwoman who'd advertised in the Boston papers. I'd had the idea all my life and can't explain because I honestly don't know where it came from. In any event, I became infatuated with the notion and bothered my parents incessantly until they agreed. Neither had any interest in traveling themselves; my father was consumed with running the business that my great-grandfather had begun, and my mother, while an educated woman, had her circle and place and was comfortable, ensconced I suppose would be more accurate a term. The Englishwoman turned out to be a disaster—far too many ideas of what I should do and where I should go. I ended up enrolling myself in a school in Lausanne just to be rid of her. This didn't completely satisfy my parents, although there was little to be done at such a great distance. They did arrange, through the school, for another chaperone for me, who I had to endure. And there were the obligatory trips home although as it became clear I was determined on my course, those became less frequent. So by the time I was eighteen I'd gained as much education as I wanted but mostly I'd traveled all across Europe, I'd been to Greece and Turkey, spent a wretched month touring the Holy Lands and even made an excursion to Saint Petersburg for the famous White Nights, an experience I'll never forget, for several reasons, and sadly now will most certainly never be able to repeat." She glanced away, then back and went on.

"I fell in love with both Amsterdam and Paris; they seemed to compliment each other. Up until the war I kept a small apartment there and still enjoy going in the autumn but essentially I've made Amsterdam my home. I've a suite at an hotel which satisfies me completely. When I wish to go, I go, with no worries or concerns and when I return, all awaits me just as it was, but maintained and ready for life. And, as now, every few years I do return home. My mother died some years ago and my father holds forth in the house that one day will be mine, although I've no idea what I'll do with it. Otherwise I'm unencumbered and have found that particular choice of life to suit me very well. And that, in rather broad strokes I admit, is Lydia Pearce."

He considered, paused and plunged. "That was a remarkably opaque account of a life."

She lifted her eyebrows. "Should I invite questions?"

"Absolutely. Earlier you mentioned events beyond one's control."

Her tongue slipped moisture to her lips. "I believe that's off the table. Just as you mentioned a lost wife and son."

In even tones of great hidden control he said, "My son Robert was a veteran of the late war who came home with a bum leg, and weak lungs from being gassed, along with a morphine habit. He and my wife died together in an automobile accident. He was at the wheel but there was nothing to indicate it was other than what it was, a tragic miscalculation."

She blinked and said, "I'm so sorry."

"So am I," he said quietly. "Now tell me your story."

She dug in her small shoulder purse and removed her cigarette case and lighted one, not waiting or giving him the chance to light it for her. She blew smoke off away from them and turned back. Calmly but swiftly, almost as if speaking of another, she said, "When I was seventeen in St. Petersburg I fell in love with a young army officer. In retrospect he was ridiculous, very full of himself but of course I didn't see that then. When the usual outcome occurred he disappeared, was, I assume transferred—he was a cavalryman and those men take care of each other. I was fortunate in that my chaperone of the time was a young French woman of progressive views, although she may have only been taking care of herself. In any event I spent the requisite months in a small apartment outside Paris in Neuilly-sur-Seine and then into a Catholic hospital for the birth. I never saw the child—I was told it was adopted into a good family but hindsight allows me to understand it could have been anywhere. I don't even know if it was a boy or girl. Within weeks my chaperone, once she was confidant of my full recovery, also disappeared, having had enough of me, I suppose." She paused to snub out her cigarette. "I went on, as one does. Back for a final year of school, in my case. There were no questions because I'd taken the previous year off to travel to Russia. I was little more than a child myself, although that only explains how I was able to do such a thing so easily. I try not to think of the child—there's no point. Since the revolution I do think of Sergei. I doubt he survived it."

She paused again and Henry suspected she wasn't quite done and waited. Soon she looked up at him and said, "But I hope he did. Long ago I forgave him. I can't imagine what life we might've made together. Even if I'd managed to keep the child, I'd still prefer the life I have."

After a suitable moment he said, "Lydia. I'm truly sorry. I take nothing away by saying you must know, your story is all too sadly common for young women. Society offers little choice."

"There is very little common about me, Henry Dorn." Even with her chin tipped bravely up he still heard the slight quaver. He offered a gentle smile and reached to just touch her hand, then took it away.

He said, "I'm curious. I'm going to Amsterdam for a purpose, even if it's vague and unlikely. And from there possibly to France if I can bear it. But you've said you've come to prefer Amsterdam and I wonder why? What exactly about that city pleases you so much that you make it your base?"

She nodded and smiled at him. "The answer, as most are as you grow older, is simple. Amsterdam is a dynamic exciting city. Paris in winter is far more exciting than Amsterdam but the weather is wretched. I like snow. I like cold bright air. I like the sense of how it brings people together. Even as they remain almost obstinately independent. Perhaps that's it—the Dutch for as long as there have been Dutch have had to work together simply to hold their land together, their nation, literally the soil under their feet. When all are needed, all come. But otherwise, they go along with their own lives. Somewhat like myself. And it's familiar to me. It reminds me of home. The people and the brilliant dazzling winters and the high northern light of summer, as well. The periods between, when things are brown and bare and a sunny clear day is rare, that's when I travel other places." She looked at him. "And not just Paris."

"You're returning now, then. To Amsterdam. From the mysterious unidentified home you speak of."

"Most obviously, wouldn't you say?"

"I grew up in a very small town in Nova Scotia, which I also left as soon as I was able. My family was prosperous there, but only by the standards of the place and it wasn't a prosperity I had any interest in. I made my way in the world and by my own lights did a fair job of it. But since leaving, I've only returned twice. I may go a final time. My mother is still alive and I'd not fail her by not attending her funeral. But otherwise, and even with her in old age, the place holds no interest for me. Although I love it dearly. So I think I understand a bit of what you're saying. Including your love of far northern places. I never left the snow but lived for many years in a place that did not quite have the brilliant light you spoke of and I know so well. It's cheering to hear Amsterdam offers that."

"It does." She was looking down, gently holding her teacup by the rim, twisting it in the ring of its saucer. She said, "It's luck, so much of the time, isn't it, Henry? It was luck that the first Pearce to leave Connecticut and go north to Vermont had the sense and fortune to buy land along the river, where a hearty stream joins the river actually. And on both sides. At first it was only a mill for grinding corn. Then one of those great-greats built a sawmill. But even that was an ordinary sort of luck, what every town had. The real luck wasn't luck at all but foresight and probably a good dose of guile when my great-grandfather realized that water could power more complicated machinery. So within a half-dozen years was employing half the town turning out spindles and other wooden parts for the textile looms in the mills of the rest of New England. And after the Civil War, the whole South as well. They owned everything. Even the forests where the raw logs were cut. For God's sake they owned the railroad spur that for many years had freights moving in and out, day and night. And every building and yard that was even the least connected. I'd say only the farmers didn't work for the Pearces but of course they did. Someone had to feed all those workers. It was a great prosperity and it's allowed me the life I've chosen. And my father is a grand man in the way of grand men in small towns. They hold on, Henry. They hold on and seem to bond even tighter as things begin to slip away. He'll enjoy his life comfortably until he dies. But even if I should keep the house and land, even if I was to do that and return from time to time, I'd be a ghost almost. A memory or reminder, welcome or not, of what we once were. Not that I expect to. I've no interest in living there—I never did. But living in Europe has taught me this if nothing else. All legacies, even empires, ultimately have short lives. As they should."

The table was cleared but for the cold coffee in the bottom of their cups. The room was largely empty as well. Her face bright, a not-quite hidden animation. As if this telling had released, reinvigorated her. "So tell me, Henry? Are you sufficiently enlightened in the matter of Lydia Pearce?"

He smiled. "I know more than I did an hour ago. Although there's a considerable gap, the one we left off the table, as you said."

She pushed a hand light over her hair and said, "Where it still remains. But now, I don't know about you but I'm interested in something a bit lighter. A bit less cerebral."

He cocked his head, amused and amusing. "You have something in mind, I presume?"

"You presume I'd be including you in those plans." The gamine look belied her words.

"Now then," he said. "Let me set one thing straight."

"Yes?"

"I presume nothing regarding Lydia Pearce."

She smiled. "Very smooth. Do you like the new colored music? The jazz?"

Quickly back he said, "I've never had the chance to hear it performed." Withholding that his exposure had been limited to the discs Robert had brought home to play upon the gramophone and as a result had not captivated Henry. But those circumstances were hardly conducive for appreciation. At the moment he'd happily go to a Baptist revival with this woman.

She stood so abruptly he scrambled to rise as well. "I'll tell you what," she said. "Give me half an hour to freshen up and then meet me at the entrance to the Zephyr. The cocktail lounge? You know where it is?"

"I've passed it." He'd come around to her side of the table, one hand needlessly on the back of her empty chair.

"Good. Til then." And again the double kiss, which this time he was swift enough to return.

He strolled rolling back to his own stateroom where he washed up and changed his shirt and then taking his time, suddenly nervous, he went down the spreading stairs and into the lounge where he waited for her, surveying the room as he did, the levels of tables and low lights and beyond that as if a fence the waist-high placards before the orchestra with their name, *The Chocolate Dandies* in flowing script angled across each board. The audience seemed the regular mixture of the ship's passengers, with the exception that the young men and women especially were, in Henry's thinking, spruced right up, the young women to a near-shocking level. And then Lydia was beside him in a just below the knee fringed pale green silk dress with long straps over her shoulders that revealed her breastbone and a wide vee of her bare back and bare arms and she turned her face up, radiant and said, "Did you get a table?" and he shook his head and looked up from where her nipples pressed cleanly against the silk as she took his arm again, the slip of her hand as small and fine as the rest of her and pressed against him, waiting now for him to take the lead.

A young man in black trousers and a white tuxedo shirt with a bow tie and hair slicked close, parted in the middle, brought them drinks and lit the candle on their table. Lydia had no handbag but laid upon the table a long golden case and matching cigarette lighter. She took from the case a long silver and ivory holder, fitted it with a cigarette and Henry was quick enough to take up the lighter and spin the wheel for the small flame, aware that despite the many women in the room more than a few men and some women also were watching her. She was lovely, there was no denying that but so were many other of the women in the room. But there was also a radiance, a luminescence, almost an energy field that surrounded her, that came from her and that she seemed to disregard even as she engaged it fully—he'd only rarely seen women smoke but she did so slowly, as if each drawn breath of wreathed tobacco spilled into her lungs was a satisfaction sensual and complete unto itself.

And she seemed happy to simply sit and observe around her as if Henry's presence was also a force that she settled most comfortably within and demanded nothing of him, as if he too was satisfaction complete. For himself, whisky had never tasted so good and he found himself drinking very slowly, letting each small sip fill his mouth and burst upon his tongue before he swallowed it. And he was struck deeply with the music, at first because it presented an aural shield that precluded conversation, overcome with her presence even as he rose within it. Also at first the music was cacophonous and shrill and very loud as he watched the musicians in their white uniforms, their dark faces shining with sweat from their efforts but there, in their faces and bodies he saw and felt the music and as it flowed from them it dawned upon him that what he was hearing were extravagant and daring versions of popular songs, songs stretched far within themselves and thus reaching toward some invisible boundary that the entire orchestra seemed to comprehend and bounce up against before falling back and it was far different, so very different than the few snatches of this music he'd heard on the Victrola at home—but what he was hearing and those dim reconstructions were most literally the difference between a photograph and a living being. And even as she touched his arm and brought his attention back to her as a song faded in a long tremolo of clarinets, a cornet and the suddenly vibrant strumming of a banjo, he recognized the final necessary connection—at its most essential level the music was no different than the old music of fiddles and accordions and perhaps a drum or guitar or both that he'd heard countless versions of in his youth suddenly not so long ago. Music immediate and physical, sensual and driven—music to dance to, to live to, music that breathed out the fiery force of life.

In a moment between songs she leaned close over the stream of voices, her lips brushing his ear as she asked, "Do you like it?"

He turned his own head, her perfume somehow smelling of the jade of her dress and said, "It's extraordinary. I had no idea."

There came a brief tremolo run of a clarinet. She said, "It's a pity there's no dance floor. It's amazing to dance to."

Sweet Georgia Brown. Even he recognized this. As earlier he'd not recognized until the cornet player sang the lyrics in a breathy lush round voice After You've Gone. But now, for just a moment he felt out of place, felt the age difference between himself and this woman who was pressed close at the small round table. Utterly at a loss to imagine how one might dance to such music. And very glad there was no dance floor. He stole a moment to study her, close as they'd been, her thigh bumping his knee as her foot pattered in a jumping syncopation with the music, smoke haloing her. She was not as young as he'd first thought when he'd spied her at her callisthenic walking. There was also much life, as she'd said, 'off the table'—that implication suddenly rich and welcome. She was younger in years most certainly. Beyond that, he could not say. And then the trombonist stood as if the music pulled him upright from his chair and tipped his horn first about the room as he shot shafts and shimmers of colored notes all sliding into each other and all distinct, the horn rising, rising, until he was playing not to the intricate plaster ceiling moldings but far above, breaking through the ceiling of the lounge and on out through the other layers toward the heavens above and Henry forgot everything else as Lydia's hand gripped his knee, both together rippling and transfixed. Transported. An exuberance utter and pure of gold glassy blue and red splashes and wires connecting everything alive and good, the wealth of life on the earth.

Later, much later a slowed drawn version of Swing Low Sweet Chariot and Lydia leaned close again and said, "It's the last one. Let's go. I don't want to be here when the lights come on."

They walked out hand in hand. Halfway up the broad steps he paused and she turned and came against him and they kissed. And, his hands still on her shoulders, she pulled back and looked at him. Eyes curious, wide, a fast shudder of delight and then she turned and pulled him easily after her until they were again side by side, bumping gently as they made their way, coming to her passageway and without pausing she circled his waist with one arm and he met and matched her, both pulled close to the other, walking wordless. Until she stopped outside a door and dug in her purse for a key and fitted it into the lock without turning it.

"Well, then."

"Yes," he said. "What a charming evening."

"Truly? You enjoyed it?"

"It was extraordinary." She was close, the day's sun and wind on her upturned face. "It was, all of it, far beyond anything I'd expected."

"All of it?"

"Yes." And he leaned and kissed her and her lips were soft, tentative and he pulled back but she followed and the kiss lasted.

"Oh," she said. "My. Well, I suppose—"

"Of course. Goodnight, Lydia. Thank you."

"Yes, goodnight." She paused. "Henry?"

And kissing again, this time the hunger fully out, hands working, her tongue a fireline from his mouth to his groin and she said, "We really have to," and then he said, "Say goodnight," but they didn't stop, even those words painted with nuzzling nibbling lips and then they broke apart. Henry holding her elbows.

He said, "From the first—"

"I know—"

"I couldn't have imagined—"

"It's strange," she said. "Lovely and strange."

"We really must say goodnight."

"Yes," She slipped forward so his hands went up her arms. "We must." As again she was fully against him, their mouths joined and he held her bare back, hands sliding up and down as she also slipped her hands under his jacket and against his shirtback, their kissing now unleashed, leaving aside oxygen and his hands came around and cupped her breasts, her nipples hard pressed heat against his palms and she groaned and leaned harder against him and he twisted his head and choked trembling "We must say . . ." and she mouthed yes against his mouth as one of her hands went to cup him and he reached behind her and turned the key in the lock of her door.

A smutch of guilt. Also a restless racing heart without hope of sleep and no desire for anything except to be where he was, alone under the stars, a crescent moon with the tips pronged up to form a cup or devil's horns just risen over the eastern horizon. Dead ahead. As if they were to hold course and the moon remain where it was they might sail between those tips. And enter where?

The guilt was not about Lydia. Or if so but faintly because she was yet stretched out and around him in ways he could not confine to any simple solution or equation, unable to lock her into any place other than the one she inhabited. Which he only partly knew and somewhat guessed and even less understood beyond the fact that he wanted to gain those things. So was it then the memory, the heart's true fidelity to Olivia? Somewhat, and rightfully so, although even as he stood within this he guessed if she were able she'd only warn Henry to be cautious, knowing his heart as she did. And also knowing and sharing his love, her own, of the physicality of life, of the sensual, the erotic and even the daring thrill of the edge. The only time their lovemaking had not receded but tamped itself had been in the recent years when Robert had returned to them and even then it was not gone, only more cautious then usual. Although nothing ever matched those early years, after their first tentative gropings and joinings had silently frustrated both even as each professed great satisfaction. Then came, three months into their marriage, the autumn afternoon when he returned from his classes to the off-campus house owned by the college for younger less prominent faculty members and, he later realized, much later, that Olivia had lunched with her mother—Henry coming into the house to find her dress crumpled on the floor at the bottom of the stairs, where he paused and studied this in mute alarm before noting partway up the stairs her corset and pantaloons, then, dangling from the top stair the toe and foot section of a silk stocking and he began to make his way up, finding the other stocking next to its mate at the top and looking down the hall, just outside the open bathroom door the garters in a twisted figure-eight and went down to stand in the door and there she was, her still-then long hair bound upon the top of her head, the bubbles of the bath foaming around her, her gaze direct and bold upon him, her arms bare and pink over the edges of the tub trailing water and bubble remnants on the tiles, her heavy high breasts with their puffed straining nipples as a second pair of eyes also direct and bold.

He'd stood a moment, his trousers filling and then said, "Am I interrupting or should I join you?"

"What you should do," she said, "is remove your clothes and then lift me out of here and we'll figure it out from there."

They made it as far as the hall runner outside the bathroom door. The first time. Afterward he'd fallen back after raising himself high enough to look down upon her, both of them gaining back breath and strength in the fall heat. But only moments after he was on his back she pulled up and sat on his chest and, her eyes never leaving his, reached down and opened herself and said, "Touch me. In the daylight, Henry. Touch me now."

Then after his long groan and his fingers reached to explore over and around her own, Olivia not taking her hands away from herself throughout, she suddenly pushed up standing, laughed and called, "Catch me if you can" and was off running down the hall and down the stairs, Henry following as quickly as he could, his penis a bobbing throbbing painful arrow directing the way. He caught her in the parlor, the windows open to the afternoon, catching her up and holding her against his chest for a moment, her body a rounded scoop against him before he threw her gently onto the sofa and they began again, although by the time they finished this time they'd wormed down onto the floor and somehow made their way across the floor up against the bookshelf where she'd rolled out from under him and crawled again on top, her body sliding and working over him, offering him first one and then the other of her breasts as she rocked against him.

She had carpet burns on her knees that lasted a week.

Olivia. Who he learned was round in every way. Not only her compact body throughout her arms and legs, thighs and calves, arms and shoulders and her breasts and buttocks but most magnificently the round clarity of her mind. Once she'd opened herself to him and so also Henry to himself, their physical and erotic life became an entirety between them—something that Henry for a short span couldn't believe any other couple had in just this way. He spent a fair amount of time considering this, watching other couples, young and otherwise for signs of their own secret lives but finally gave it up as beside the point— some might and others not, but none of that mattered. What mattered was the faint burr of sensuality present at almost all times, in all places. Once when he'd forgotten his lunch and she was pregnant with Alice, she'd brought lunch to his office, knocking as anyone else and when summoned, coming in, holding the basket with a blue and white checked cloth over it, looked at him and smiled slowly as she reached behind her and flipped the lock on the door. He was nervous about the pregnancy but she'd already made him flush by explaining Dr. Westmore had assured her normal relations presented no risks and that she was strong, young and healthy and should do as she pleased. And so they did, right there with the faint trip of passing feet and tinkling voices in the hall behind the locked door.

Only the most overt of their lovemaking came to an end with the arrival of children, the girls, when one fine Saturday morning when it was warm enough to keep the windows open at night but cool enough to want a light blanket by morning and so were covered more or less when she'd looked around him to see Alice and the toddler Polly at the open bedroom door and the lock of her arms and her whisper startled him to stillness before Olivia called out, "Well, look who's up bright and early. Go downstairs girls and Mother'll be down in a moment to fix you breakfast. Go on, shoo."

Now the moon was well up, the breeze cooler as the night rolled toward morning. It occurred to him that he might not sleep this night, and while he'd known sleepless nights those were of a different nature but it took no effort to recall the last time he'd felt this sense of being deliciously in way over his head and not caring because the giddiness was not only inescapable but a part of the whole.

Alone on a seemingly tranquil sea he stood gazing out at the morning star and realized that something had just begun with Lydia Pearce, something he could not predict or control but was fully within.

Fourteen

*T*he weather moderated somewhat as November ended and the
following Tuesday was near mild as he made his way with his
instrument to Oude Hoogstraat with ample misgiving and a curiosity that even two years ago he would have thought near sordid—the
temptation to dig beneath the surface of a man clearly in a great distress and possible peril but he told himself Dmitri Morozov had most
likely unburdened himself in a moment of dire need and they'd proceed as usual. Teacher and student. Master and pupil. But the fact
remained that through much of the week past his practicing had been
poor, ill, flat—raw enough in fact that Saturday he'd gone out and
purchased new strings and spent a long pleasant afternoon replacing
them, all the while knowing there was nothing wrong with the old.
But the week had been miserable—he'd had to abandon the Merk
altogether as unplayable and returned to the Kummer exercises and
practiced scales, all the while feeling the entire undertaking was a mild
folly. Finally, he left the instrument be.

    He went out to the American bookstore on Kalverstraat and pawed
through the dusty bins of British, American and Dutch translations and
came away only with an Oxford edition of Keats identical to the one
in storage in Elmira. And he wasn't in the mood for Keats. Monday
afternoon he had picked up his laundry and so had fresh shirts and
underwear. He read the *Herald Tribune* and tried to make sense of
the stories, to find how they applied to his own life. But the news

seemed no news at all but only the grand grave inevitable cycle of human affairs in full motion.

He was out of sorts and attributed it to being almost December and, stubbornly or not, he'd miss Christmas with his daughters and their families. Instead, resolutely waiting in the one place on the wide byzantine world where a woman whom he knew had loved him but had not yet returned. And with no greater indication that she would, only the passing of time to suggest that she would not or could not. Then there was Morozov. Who was as close to a companion as he might find. So it appeared. And that man clearly not willing to open his life much beyond his actual door—that scant perilous entry.

So on the Tuesday following the blunt exposure of personal history so detailed and so abruptly curtailed, Henry came down through the now familiar smells toward the small studio, those scents amplified with the mild weather but also comforting in a way, as if there was, after all, a home in this city. And stood before the brown door and knocked and stood and knocked again and turned his back to look out on the canal where the ice was soaking water up from below, looking more like a gray dirty falling-apart blanket than anything liquid. The spring thaw of salt water on Saint Mary's Bay against the shore of Freeport. An ugly thing, difficult to find promise within.

As had become usual in the cold weather they sat drinking tea while Henry's cello warmed. For the first time the heavy curtains were parted, enough to glimpse an old sprung horsehair day bed with ratty blankets, a wire hung with a handful of clothes and a wooden shipping carton just visible, turned on its side to create a makeshift table beside the daybed, holding a couple of thick volumes and a candlestick on top, rolled socks and underclothing beneath. Whatever else was back there could not be seen but this glimpse was enough to confirm the extreme poverty of the man.

Then an uncomfortable moment as he saw Morozov watching him. He blew on the steaming tea and turned his attention to his teacher.

"I'm beginning to think I'm on a fool's errand." Thinking this was the last thing the man needed to hear.

Morozov said, "What is it? Two months and you're ready to give up? No one learns anything that way. You should know this. A child wants to stop after two weeks. But a man, a man knows true learning is slow. Now, you. You will never be a great cellist, Henry Dorn. But competent? Surely. If the pleasure you seek is your own, then all you lack is patience. And things can surprise you. The world surprises and challenges and I tell you nothing new."

Henry was silent.

The Russian leaned forward, his small belly pressed against his buttoned vest. "So you tell me. What is it that keeps you here in Amsterdam? What is it you're learning? Besides the cello, however badly you may think?"

Henry was quiet. Then said, "I'm not entirely certain, to be honest. I could list many things but what do they really mean? I don't know. I suppose, if there is any one answer to that question, it would be that I'm learning to live alone."

Morozov considered this as one would a grave matter. As one who understood the range of implications. Then he swiftly rose and entered the rear of the small apartment, or more truly the empty storefront that it was, pulling the dusty curtains closed. The unmistakable sounds of a trunk lid squeaking open, papers rummaged and then he reappeared with sheets of musical notation. He placed them on the stand, covering the Merk etudes. Then he sat across from Henry and said, "The heart is the only instrument a man can never master, can maybe never learn. I have received, finally, a letter from Nadia. She is well, she tells me. The children are well. She is teaching in a school, a new school where there never was a school before. In a peasant village, a People's Collective they call it in the middle of nowhere, in Ukraine. It is very different she says than anything she ever saw before or ever imagined. It is, she says, a fine thing, a wonderful thing. It is one big farm. All work together, all eat. There is bread where bread was never certain. There are vegetables and meat, even. They have tractors! It is a good life, she tells me. Healthy, giving vigor to herself and the children." He paused, refilled his tea and gestured toward Henry who shook his head. "There is work for me. Not the grand work I once did but work, she says, that is many ways gratifying. There is, in that little village, as she says there are in all such places, an orchestra for the people. To do such playing is not exalted but only part of life. But imagine, she says, it brings music where before there were only crude peasant songs and ballads, and only at special times. Now there is music in the processing plant, where they can and pickle vegetables, in the dairy, even out in the fields. If it is raining, she says, they put up a canvas to keep the instruments dry. That is the difference, she says. The musicians could very well get wet along with everyone else. But the instruments, they are the precious things."

Henry waited and then softly said, "Are you going to return?"

Morozov took up his bow and rotated it quickly, holding it by the adjusting screw and frog. Then he touched the new sheets of music and said, "These are not so different than the Merk you have been struggling with. But sometimes even a little change can prompt more from you than you thought you were capable of. I do not know. There are more questions than answers. Was that letter all her idea? Are things really as she says? I know her very well, a man and wife, a good wife. I read the letter many, many times, trying to hear her voice, the echo of her voice to hear what she was trying to say behind what she wrote. And I do not know—if there are other words I can't hear them although surely there must be. It can't be all as good as she tells. And then the question why this letter and none before? That is a message I can not miss. But the answer? But what to do." He paused again and looked away, toward what had once been a window but was now boarded over.

Then he turned back and took up his cello. He said, "So a man must decide things as best he can. It is not only my family but my land." He paused and chuckled and said, "Yes, even Ukraine. But there is no haste. Perhaps even less now that I have heard from her. I will write and see what comes. Now please, shall we play?"

Henry was thoughtful, guessing Morozov had no desire or expectation of either Henry's opinion or additional questions. Instead he said, "Am I to go crazy first from Josef Merk and now these new pieces? They don't look less complicated, perhaps more so. Who's the composer?"

Morozov tightened his bow and tapped the horsehair gently against the strings of his cello and then smiled. "I am."

◆

Fifteen

*U*ntil Lydia left he'd known only the area around Nieuwmarkt and the Dam, back and forth from his apartment to her suite at the Krasnapolsky, the small rings of streets and canals that contained the array of restaurants and cafes they frequented, the small almost-hidden club where twice they'd gone late at night, the door painted black as were the walls within, flowing red script on the door Club Jas, and the market stalls, as well as his slowly accumulated knowledge of neighborhood bakeries, butchers, the fruit and vegetable markets, the laundry. The tobacconist where he bought his newspapers. But even then he was aligning himself, his compass wavering then settling onto a steady bearing. The cardinal points had defined and revealed themselves before he was aware of it.

After she left he walked.

Depending on mood and weather several mornings or afternoons each week he'd let himself out into the streets and pick a direction and go, sometimes following a route or area he'd recently discovered and push on beyond the learned realm and extend into new neighborhoods, new streets and new rings of canals. Quickly he'd learned it was impossible to get lost, all the water, all the canals evolved out in half-moons from the Het Ij, the main waterfront beyond the already well-known Central Station and the further east, north or south one went the more concentric those rings became and the streets and neighborhoods were defined by their canals, and with the miles walked measured by his own feet and sense of time he never got lost, although in a few instances he became mildly confused when a smaller street would turn not the way he'd expected but led into a labyrinth of other smaller alleys and courtyards, often allowing him quick snatches of glimpse into back gardens over walls and through gates and only upon occasion did he glance upward to discern the patterns of light and therefore his position according to the shift of day and the time spent and even in those somewhat disoriented moments he always trusted himself and continued on, never backtracking, until suddenly he'd turn a corner and to no great surprise find himself back out on a traveled open street, or come across one of the minor canals that broke through the compass of larger rings as a spoke within a wheel and a quick glance again would determine which way to turn to follow back, back inward toward the city center, toward the old town, toward where Recht Boomssloot joined the Oudeschans, the canal junction where his room waited his return.

Not infrequently on these long strolls he'd grow hungry and alter his route however slightly as if again a compass but of an altogether different sort worked within him and eventually would come upon some type or another of a place to eat a meal and in this way he also learned the city. His sense of direction was keen but not infallible—more than once he'd found an establishment where the food and mood were especially pleasing only to later find himself unable to retrace his route, the restaurant or café seemingly gone, vanished, as he patrolled around and around the neighborhood where he was certain it had been. Twice after such futile efforts he'd abruptly turned onto a familiar street and there it would be but these encounters gave less pleasure even as he again enjoyed the food.

It was a matter of some pride that he could and did navigate so. For navigation it surely was. Or had begun that way.

As a boy, with the rare exceptions of buggy trips up-island to Tiverton or Sandy Cove, everything was oriented to the sea and the sea was oriented only to itself and the stars and sun. So that even a boy walking most familiar ground always knew where he was. This apparently ingrained since before earliest memory. As if navigation was employed by blood, some inner compass complete and steady, locked by not only the sun and moon and the celestial dome and the seasonal round of that dome but also running, coursing throughout him. As if eye and ear were divining some ancient tidal pull, the ebb and flow of waters informing also without apparent need of a sunset or moonrise. And when he left those islands and went south he found himself again in places where the directions of sun and stars and where water lay, first in Providence and then New Haven, paved his way and as much for the pleasure of walking as penury he elected to walk in all but the most ferocious of weather and even then occasionally as some perversity of pride or simply boyish excitement at knowing he could, he walked. His legs were long and strong and it seemed to him made to cover ground and so even during the most drear of winter and the demanding long hours of lectures and studies either in his dormitory room or library or later his own office, while others were waxen and gray, he would hold a flush to his cheeks, not a sudden short bloom of exercise but rather the weathered look of a man who spent his hours out of doors, who labored out of doors. As if upon the sea.

Even at Elmira, even with the horse and then electric trolleys, even after he'd acquired the Dodge automobile, he walked—not only back and forth around the campus to his office and classrooms and other buildings for meetings but many mornings setting out early to walk an hour or more before he was due anywhere, sometimes striding downtown and then along the river and other times depending on the season and his mood simply striking out into one of the adjacent neighborhoods to see what he would see, aware that this was noted and registered as a mild eccentricity but knowing also this marching, this hiking, spoke to the community, offering a visual and routine reminder of the well-being and vitality of the college and the health of the girls thus overseen. Not a few times over the years he'd been shadowed by one of the students on these walks, innocent crushes or at least what he was determined to view as nothing more than that and so he'd allow this for a few circuits and then if the girl failed to lose interest he'd finally pause one morning and wait for her to catch up to him as inevitably they trailed behind and then in the gentlest but firmest of tones he'd inform her she most certainly had work or sleep she needed to be engaged in and not waiting for response but in an even gentler tone would tell her this was his private time, a time when he collected his thoughts and arranged his mind toward the day ahead of him. This was sufficient to remind of the vast difference between them, free of rebuff.

They amused Olivia, or so it seemed. Once she said, "Perhaps I should walk with you. Or one of these days, one of those girls will steal you away."

He'd said, "They are children."

"Not so much as you like to think."

But she did not join him. Or need to.

This continued, deliciously, at the lake, summers. Both Henry and Doyle soon found the habit in common and so in the earliest morn, just dawn, sometimes fog yet draped down against the lake snugged between the rising hillsides, they'd come out and find each other, or Henry would quietly go over and enter the Franks's kitchen and have an unneeded cup of coffee with his father-in-law and then the two would hike the slow road uphill past the treelines and the gorge and then between the vineyards to the top of the ridge and cross the road there to walk down to the Lakemont station where the store was not yet open but the bundle of morning papers had been dropped by the milk train. Sometimes they chatted on the way up; other trips were made in silence. Once at the station one or the other would cut the bundle open with a penknife and each would take a paper, folding it and sticking it into a back pocket before the more leisurely walk back down to breakfast and the events of the day, often planned and out-lined on those walks.

And each, always, left a nickel on the opened bundle for the store-keeper. Never a dime for both, but a pair of nickels. To declare, if only to themselves, that each of them had been there.

And thus he walked Amsterdam as well. With all those years past and all those walks not so much informing him as mute but present company.

Sixteen

Morozov had spoken so deeply, almost out of himself, about his family but what stayed with Henry that night was the Russian's passion also for his homeland, his country. Regardless of what might be occurring. And, after all, some of it might indeed be good, very good. He thought of his own ancestors giving up a fortune around New York because they hadn't trusted a new way of thinking and so ended up amassing more pride than pennies in a place short of both. Henry stood before the framed ink sketch of cod, rendered so many years ago by his father, both of them, father and son, each trying to reach back to that distant yet close land. It offered Henry little pleasure that he'd been served better by his journey out than his father had. None of which explained where he was this night. He turned then and looked out the windows. It was an exquisite night. They all were. His heart ached. Still in the dark but for the slight illumination through the windows, he stepped close and ran his finger over the glass covering his father's drawing.

Dead fish.

His hand fell from there onto the stack of turned sheets of paper. Write to Mother.

Tomorrow.

He went then to the bed and slipped under the covers. Lying on his back. Waiting for sleep. Which refused him, as so often. An hour later he was up and in robe and slippers at his desk with the gooseneck throwing a cone of light. It was late. Even the carnival-light windows had subsided to a muted glory—an extravagant rooster plumped and perched for the night, within the night.

He moistened the nib and turned up a fresh sheet.

> *December 1922*
> *Amsterdam, Holland*

Dear Mother,

I trust First Elmira is continuing its monthly wire of funds in a timely fashion.

As you can see, I've remained in Holland far longer than I originally expected. I apologize for, after all these years, failing in my weekly correspondence. There is no true excuse for this, except to say that I'm in a curious state, yet not one I'm uncomfortable with. And thus, for the time being, I expect to remain at this address as I continue to examine the particular means and methods which brought me here.

For the better part of my adult life I devoted myself to the idea of higher liberal-arts education for women. To free their minds and spirits, to elevate their intellects, and, hopefully, provoke a lifelong appreciation for the beauty of an active striving mind, all the while instilling firm modes of decorum and social grace, believing these principles to be beyond fashion.

Recently, however, I've come to question my central assumption. Which is that an educated woman is a happier and healthier woman, and thus more inclined to flourish in her womanly duties of mother, wife, and helpmate. I've realized my impulse came from believing that much of your unhappiness over the years was the result of being denied this very uplifting opportunity. So I determined to spend my productive years insuring that other women in their youth would gain that exposure that would sustain them in the great trials of motherhood and matrimony.

Now it occurs to me that my failure may have been in assuming a woman would take on these inevitable duties with a lighter heart and quicker mind for having that heart and mind stimulated as I attempted. Or is it possible that I have created generations of young women who will go through life feeling theirs is but a half-measure? Is it not better, in some elemental way, to not know of the possibilities life holds than to know of them and be denied the full measure? Is it not possible that it was myself that offered up that half-measure? I'm not speaking here of the traditional professional roles that a woman may enter into and even flourish in—Elmira had its full share of women with successful careers as teachers or nurses, that sort of thing. But to my knowledge only a small handful attempted postgraduate studies in medicine, a few more perhaps studied to gain advanced degrees to teach at university level (all in colleges for women, I might add).

I fear in my attempt to do good work I might have actually failed, creating a barrage of frustrated young and not so young mothers and housewives. Well, I can hear you say, it is a woman's lot. But as I said, I've come to question that assumption. Perhaps I was simply cowardly in not pushing further, in not demanding that doors be opened to those of particular talent (and there were more than a few) who would have found careers of great reward. I suspect that they still would have made excellent mothers, and as for their husbands, all I can say is that men have always adjusted to the needs and demands of women. I do not declare myself a failure, just more timid than I believed I was. All at a time when my small sphere of influence has been given up. Perhaps this is the way of things. We learn too late the nature of the world, and it carries right along without us.

I imagine this letter will irritate you tremendously, which is not my intent. We never grow too old to learn, do we, Mother? One or two people, perhaps even a single encounter, can upset much long-held presumption.

I'm spending my time learning to play the cello! I will never be more than a mediocre musician but am doing it solely for the pleasure and have no grand illusions of a second career with an orchestra.

Do you recall the old man who had a shack on the Fundy shore up toward Tiverton and lived on fish and scoured the shore for scrap metal which he brought on his back in a basket pack to Freeport to sell as scrap, scrap that was recognized from time to time as not so much abandoned as simply lost? As a boy he was a fearsome sight in his layers of rags and wild mat of hair and beard, and I confess I joined with the other boys in taunting him. As boys will out of fear of something strange. We knew him as Sandy the Jew. Did you ever speak with him? More to the point, what did the people, the adult community, make of him? I'm curious about him because he was clearly washed up by a malevolent wave to that place and yet he stayed, as long as I recalled. I assume he died there. I know not what to make of him, likely because I, too, am washed upon a distant shore. Although there is no malevolence in my particular wave. Still, I have the idea that if it were possible I might enjoy sitting on a boulder across from him outside that shack of wrack and driftwood planks and talk to him.

It doesn't escape me that as a youth, with all of the baggage and false bravado of that age, I essentially left Freeport and indeed, Nova Scotia, behind. As you are all too aware my return trips were few and there were reasons for this, as there always are. However, thinking of the old man Sandy (in truth, perhaps my own age now), I wonder how I failed to such a great degree? What else I missed, not only of the place itself, which had to have been considerable, but of my family there? If I pondered this at all, I must've reassured myself that our correspondence was an adequate and fruitful connection. While I treasure those years of letters, I am yet forced to accept that there were others upon the Island who saw my actions quite differently and must admit that they were more correct than I now wish.

I pray you are healthy,
and remain,
your devoted son.

Without rereading he signed it and dug through the small pile of supplies on his makeshift desk and folded the pages and sealed them in an envelope, wrote that simple eternal address and so was committed to walking out in the morning and posting it. And when he stood he realized it did not matter so much what he'd said but more importantly that he had said it and that the letter was on its way. He knew anything he would have written would have mystified and perhaps alarmed his mother but that he could not help. The letter itself, the physical phenomenon of his mind aimed toward hers after these long months of silence, was enough.

And was suddenly and acutely exhausted. As if he had not so much revealed himself but at least drawn the curtain back a hedge. There was a relief in this. Not the simple relief of finally writing to his mother. But that he had aired himself, even ever so slightly. If he had failed to address the matter of his heart, the letter was an opening, a most simple door within that was beyond closing. Was not, now, even a door. There was no turning back.

He turned off the light and took off his robe and made his way to the bed in the pale light from the windows. He wrapped into the sweet sheets and blanket and realized that it was not a question of turning back. But of going forward. He tried to conjure Lydia but could not and then fell to heavy sleep, the sleep of oceans.

Seventeen

One July evening at a restaurant overlooking the Amstel he was wrestling with, and growing increasingly disinterested in, thick tubes of breaded and fried veal, the mustard sauce over them too thin to be of much help. Lydia was devouring a steak and then abruptly set down her fork. He realized she was watching him and had been for some time—he was drifting melancholic.

"What is it?"

"Nothing," he said. "I seem to have lost my appetite. This isn't agreeing with me." He gestured toward his plate.

"Order something else."

He hesitated and said, "No, I don't believe so. But please. It's pleasure enough to sit with you."

She dabbed her lips with her napkin. "What do you say, shall we walk?"

They strolled along the river canal, the street quieted with the dinner hour. Henry was pensive and she left him be but for her hand slipped in his elbow, a light touch, not possession but companionable. He wanted silence, but not to be alone. He'd been shaken, just after they'd been seated in the restaurant by a sudden glimpse across the room of Olivia at a table with two other women, she the one facing him. That table was a good distance back, and he and Lydia were near the front windows, splashed with light from the river but there she was, plain as day. His first incongruous thought was What are you doing here? He suppressed a desire to rise and approach. Pretending to study the menu, he used the opportunity to shield his eyes from Lydia and study this apparition. Who, realizing his attention, looked up. Her eyebrows lightly frowned as she always did, and then she gave the brief smile that only signaled greeting and nothing more, certainly no invitation and returned to conversation with her friends. Then Olivia began to fade and the stranger emerge but the resemblance was too strong to be cast aside. He'd tried to settle into his meal, the veal a hasty choice with no understanding of what he'd ordered before it arrived, but he couldn't. His hands felt slow, thickened clumsy fingers. Twice more he glanced at the woman. The first time it seemed she was waiting for him, the frown reappearing. The second time she'd shifted her chair enough so she was partly blocked by the backs of her companions.

He and Lydia walked. Among the apparently endless things that bound them, this love of walking, how he'd first seen her on the boat, was an easy and effortless thing to slip into together. Along with silence. Lydia was brightly direct and vocal when she chose to be but was not bothered by silence—in fact he'd already learned she was as comfortable with silence as he was. His silences had always demanded to be sought out—hers were an ingrained part of her.

It was pleasantly cool in the early evening shade thrown by the buildings next to them, the sunlight falling across the canal and lighting the tight high houses opposite. A few men poled boats on the river and twice slow-moving tugs nudged barges slowly past them, upstream, heading inland. A few other couples also strolled hand in hand. Henry was calming as he strode along. Another great pleasure of Lydia was that despite her being near a foot shorter then he was, her legs covered ground easily. He never felt he was pressing her, never felt he should slow his pace or if lost in thought suddenly find himself alone and turn to see her struggling on behind. She was right there with him.

Of course it had not been Olivia. Nor a ghost or some spectral warning. So what then, of this chance resemblance? Only that? Or some greater projection of his mind?

Or both. And not of his mind but of his clamorous thunderous heart. A heart not without its weaknesses, its faults and frailties but nevertheless a true heart. A heart that strived to be true.

He stopped without warning and Lydia stumbled free from her gentle hold of him, caught herself and turned.

He was about to speak when she said, "My God, Henry, are you all right? Your face is dreadfully pale. Do you need to sit down?"

"No," he said and pulled his handkerchief and wiped his brow. "I'm fine, now. I just had a moment, was all."

She was in a pearl evening dress with tiny beads sewn along her cleavage, a rose shawl over her bare shoulders. Her face intent, up-turned. "What sort of moment? You're white as a sheet."

He had to smile. "I imagine I am. In the restaurant there was a woman across the room who looked exactly like Olivia. The resemblance was startling. It was discomfiting, to say the least."

Her face serious, she said, "I'd think so."

"It's never happened to me before. And no, I don't think she was a ghost or anything like that. In fact, once she was aware of a stranger gawking at her she did what most anyone would do and repositioned her chair to be out of my line of sight." He was recovering a bit. "You know, on the one hand it would seem likely that somewhere in the world might be a woman who would strongly resemble her, just given the sheer numbers. And yet I've never in my life met anyone who really looked like anyone else. At least after a moment of study. But then think about it—neither of my daughters look like their mother, although there are bits and pieces, physical and otherwise that are familiar, in the most direct sense of the word. People talk of so-and-so looking like one parent or another but that's because we know what we're searching for."

She was silent a moment, pensive. Then, "I've always been intrigued by the old idea, Plato's, wasn't it? That we're only half-beings, that male and female were once one and we spend our lives seeking that missing half." She paused again and said, "And when you do find that one, and then lose her. Or him. Where does that leave you? Forever again abandoned? Or can there be more than one?"

He was the silent one now, studying her. "Go on," he said.

"It seemed to me that no, there couldn't be. After all, if only two particular halves make a certain whole, how could there be? But then I started thinking about the idea of who we are. Of who I am. The I of each of us. There's a constant, of course, but there's also some mutability. Am I ever quite the same person I was yesterday? Or perhaps it works differently. Perhaps we hold too rigidly to the breaking down of time into days and months, even years. When I look back over my life so far I see it as one thing rolling into another, but I also see it as being periods. Cycles of time. Parts of your life that begin at a known, or even not-known-at-the-moment point, and go on for so many years, and then you realize that time has ended. Sometimes that ending just slips away and other times it comes rapid and unexpected."

She stopped. Somewhere during this she'd taken her eyes from him and had been looking off down the river, appearing to watch a barge and tug coupled moving upstream into the distance. When she stopped talking her eyes came back fully upon him just as he was swallowing hard. "There are many ways that can happen, Henry." And she reached and touched his arm. He nodded. She said, "People never fully leave you. Sometimes that's a good thing, Henry. Sometime's it's not."

He managed a smile. "And sometimes it leaves you seeing ghosts."

She smiled. "Yes. Ghosts. They do come, and in many forms. Sometimes walking about Amsterdam I think I spy the young girl who first came here so many years ago and fell in love with the city."

He'd straightened up, replaced his handkerchief and they resumed walking. He said, "And that would be you."

"Oh yes. I was still a schoolgirl. And while it was some years before I returned, it never left my mind. Somehow I knew it was a place to return to and somehow, also, whether by the fortune of events or some other understanding, I didn't return until it was the very best, perhaps the only place to go."

Casually he said, "That part does sound intriguing."

She tapped his arm with her knuckles. "Don't fish. Allow me my schoolgirl."

"A delicious vision, no doubt."

A quick smile and she said, "Actually I was an ugly duckling. Stringbean arms and legs and no bosom to speak of. If I passed for a boy it would've been a scrawny one. Although of course I still had my hair long. And there were the undergarments that would've accentuated what I didn't posses by nature but even then there was a bit of an obstinate streak in me."

"Obstinacy? Or self-determination?"

"Thank you. But I was fifteen. It was the summer before I went to Russia and while I was hardheaded and determined to remain in Europe that attitude failed me when I considered my appearance. I was still with the first chaperone, the British cold-cup-of-tea, but I must give Eugenie credit—she bluntly told me not to concern myself, that time would take care of what time can take care of and for the meanwhile I should attend to my brain. Which I mostly did. Now, look at you—I was trying to tell you a story of a young girl's first visit here and you've got me rummaging around in the drawers of my memory."

"A lovely place." The sun was still streaming over the upper reaches of the city and the cloudless sky held flocks of shale-colored pigeons and above those the white floating spirals of gulls. The bricks were dull blood in the shade although the heat of the day still rose from them.

She paused them both and said, "Are you so certain all those young women you taught were as safe as you make them out to be?"

His chin came up a bit. "Absolutely." His eyes hard upon her, then softened as he said, "Although I've no idea what would've happened if you'd been among them."

"Nothing," she said. "You aren't that kind of man and I was not the woman I am today."

He nodded. "Fair enough. Tell me of your schoolgirl."

She grinned and waved her hand, a dismissal prior to the telling. She resumed walking, their hands still linked. "When the school year ended Eugenie wanted to take me to England for the summer. But because I disliked her bossy ways, I insisted we go to Rome. Which did not please her at all. Oh, God, it was hysterical. Rome in the summertime. Dreadful and stinking and empty as could be. She hauled me relentlessly around to all the sights with an enthusiasm for her duty that was cruelly funny in hindsight. The whole city to me was nothing more than a gorgeous but decayed sewer. Not at all the sort of place a fifteen year old girl would want to be. And of course I wasn't quick enough about such things then to question where all the people were—it still seemed a huge city to that little backwoods girl. And all the alarming black-boxed warnings in the newspapers—the death counts from malaria and other nasty things. It never occurred to me to insist we get out into the countryside, up in the hills and mountains, away from the swamp of Rome. Because I didn't know such places existed until the next year in Lausanne when I told my schoolmates about my summer. And that was when I fired her. Or wrote letters demanding my father do so. Anyway, I'm off track—"

"No, no," he said. "This is wonderful. Keep going."

Lydia glanced and shrugged, grinning. "I pretended to break down and holed up in my room for several days until she feared I was getting sick and then one morning when she brought me cold beef bouillon for breakfast I burst out crying and demanded we leave. I told her I wanted clear bright air and refused to be dragged around her precious England but wanted to be in one place, one place that would satisfy me. Still, it was enough to crumble what pigheadedness remained in her and she suggested here. Anything sounded much better than where I was. So I came to Amsterdam. And was amazed. Oh what a difference it was to come into Amsterdam in midsummer after Rome. We spent that last month here and every day, even when it rained, was spectacular. I do think, I honestly do, that even then I knew it was a special place and that one day I'd return here."

Henry walking alongside, seeing that young girl, a part of him wishing he could've been here to have actually seen her. So he said in echo, "Which eventually you did. And when was that?"

Only then realizing their ambling had not been idle or capricious but directed ever so gently for they stood in the grand square of the Dam before the Royal Palace, behind them the rising wonder of the Hotel Krasnapolsky. The towers of Nieuwe Kerk rose into the evening rose-colored light, the sun still striking down here and warm, the throngs pressing down or out of Kalverstraat—shopping as an evening outing.

"Ah," he said, trying to conceal his surprise. "Home again, home again, jiggety-jig. Am I dropping you off so early? Does the story end before it begins?"

But her face remained solemn. She appeared to be appraising him once more before speaking. Perhaps she just wanted the pause, for then she said, "I'd like you to come up. I seem to be in the mood to talk this evening. If you want."

Somewhere they'd lost each other's hands. Now deeply serious he reached and ran a finger along her jaw and took the finger away. "I wish," he said, "you felt you didn't have to ask me that."

She looked off across the Dam. Then back to him. "The asking," she said, "has nothing to do with you. Shall we go?" And took his hand but did not lead him—they walked side by side to the broad stairs up to the entrance of the hotel. Through the spread doors and across the lobby to the elevators, toward one with the cage open, the boy upon his stool watching them come as if he'd known they were his and his alone the moment they entered the hotel. He cranked the cage shut and without asking began to lift them up toward her floor.

The front sitting room was hot, the large windows overlooking the square and even though the windows were cranked open the air had died as the day did. He followed her down the short hall past the bathroom and the small dayroom which held a soft chair for reading and a secretary for a woman with much personal correspondence, as well as a set of bookshelves that appeared to have been brought in— not a regular feature. And then the spacious bedroom with broad louvered closet doors, another smaller bathroom adjacent, the crisply made bed and nightstands, a pair of lounge chairs with a standing lamp and cigarette table between them and a bank of high narrow windows that were opened to the north side, catching and drawing in cooler air. It wasn't dark in the room but off-white and muted blue cast over into grey shadow and she left the lights off.

"Make yourself comfortable," she said and stepped out of her shoes and lifted her dress over her head, leaving her in stockings and a waist-slip and thin chemise. He contented himself, as he had before, with removing his jacket, collar and tie, rolling up his shirtsleeves and, seated on the far edge of the bed where she was already curled upright with her legs tucked under her, removed his shoes and socks and garters and rolled his trouser legs up two turns before sliding around to face her, crosslegged.

A moment, long, easy, cool in the interior twilight, Henry with his fingers laced in his lap, Lydia resting one palm flat on the bed, the other laid on her covered thigh.

Finally she said, "For so long it seemed I just kept meeting the wrong man. There'd be a spark, an interest, usually mutual and as things went along I'd realize that while my independence was attractive, it was an attraction that included some version of taming me. Domesticity. And Henry, for all my bluster I desire that as much as the next person. Perhaps I made poor choices but the idea of being a challenge for someone to conquer was never what I had in mind. And, not to put too fine a face on it, it's true that being a woman of independent means also invited a certain appraising eye, often from those well-accomplished in appearing quite other than as they actually are. One result of which was I learned to make my way through initial levels of those attractions with a bit of the actress about me—which was perhaps unfair but ultimately justified. And there were a couple of times when everything seemed almost to click into place and then didn't, and I realized I'd gained a bit of a reputation, ill-founded as far as I was concerned but there you have it. And I had my friends, male and female both, who accepted me just as I was. Which can be a great source of relief under such circumstances. And so, slowly but inevitably I just gave up on love, on a single love. I was lonely sometimes but never in want of companions."

She paused and looked at him. "Companions in all the meanings of the word."

"And why not," he offered, as much reassurance as was needed. He said, "Go on."

She smiled. "They say when you stop looking . . ."

"When it's the last thing expected."

"Exactly" Another pause taking Henry in and his eyes bold upon her. She said, "So I met Duncan. Duncan Bryce-Meraux. Not British or French as the name suggests but from an old New Orleans family. Before I met him I knew nothing of that city or its cultural and social levels. Let's just say Duncan was a kindred soul, a black sheep, set loose somewhat the same way I was, to roam the continent and basically get him out of New Orleans. I was twenty-seven, the summer of 1910. He was staying with some friends in an old family home in Normandy. It was a grand house, a chateau really. With a moat. Quite enchanting. I'd met him in Paris and two days later we took the train out and were met at the station by a luxurious automobile. And he insisted on driving and they let him. Turned out later he'd never learned how to drive, he just did it. That was Duncan. Two days later he had me driving the thing. Shining black eyes and a dandy mustache and long almost medieval locks of curly black hair. He was a wonder to be with. Smart as smart can be but with a delightful off-center sense of humor that was a natural part of him, a glibness played straight if you will. Henry, I fell deeply in love. Oh, he was a god and I his goddess. I knew a few of his friends as light acquaintances and others by name and that too seemed right. As if in meeting him I'd also pierced the veils of pretense and social chattering. Those people simply didn't care what anyone thought of them. And what a time we had. It was all so wonderful. Because, whatever we were doing, wherever we were, there were the hours and hours alone, just the two of us. His spontaneity was even greater than mine. We went to Nice and Monte Carlo and then when the heat got too bad he took me to Brittany, to Saint Malo, which I'd never even heard of. When the autumn rains came, one morning he spread a sheaf of tickets on the bed and we were off to Morocco, to a wonderfully run-down ancient house in Tangiers. Where we spent the fall tramping about the bazaars and living like lords on pennies, with a whole crew running the house. And we couldn't talk to them and they couldn't talk to us but everything got done. A magic carpet. The most wonderful savory foods. We didn't drink a drop all winter—he told me we could easily obtain wine or spirits but we'd risk offending the staff. I was intoxicated anyway—it didn't matter. Although he brought home a water-pipe and a thing you cupped between your fingers called a chillum and we smoked hashish. Which is where I learned there are good things in life you just haven't encountered yet. The hashish, oddly, presented no issue for the house boys and the shrouded woman who cooked. As the winter went on I rose more and more out of myself, feeling not so much more free but unleashed—the exact opposite of what I'd felt with other men. I'd wake in the morning with the horns calling the faithful to prayer at dawn and watch him sleep. It was, he was, a miracle and yet what I'd always known would happen. I remember thinking that I was blowing apart, that I could walk off into the desert hills and spin like a dervish and never stop. That he'd brought all that to me.

"Then it grew cold, the wind blowing off the desert, sand coloring the sky, grit between your teeth, in every plate of food. And he was restless—it was time to go. So we returned to Paris, where we stayed a few days while he took care of what he said was business. One evening he took me to dinner with friends, who I understood were business associates in some vague way—a refined gentleman and his wife in their late forties. I met their children who then were sent off to bed before we dined. Although there was one other guest—a young woman, a girl really, in her middle teens or thereabouts who I'd assumed was the children's governess. It struck me as odd that she'd be asked for dinner but she was charming with me, although she ignored Duncan—I only saw that in hindsight. And Monsieur was very solicitous toward me, which seemed to irritate the girl. Oh, she was a pretty one! And Madame, ah Madame. Such a great beauty, one of those women who as age creeps are transformed from beauty into elegance until you can't tell the difference. And she also was attentive, focused on me as if I was indeed the sole purpose of the evening. Duncan was almost lounging, the half-smile of his that indicated he was thoroughly delighted with the proceedings. It was very strange, very casual and yet formal and with a curious atmosphere, not a tension in the air but the feeling was more to me as if there was an inner layer to it all that I didn't fully understand. Of course I thought I did. Both the man and his wife, but, as you'd expect the wife in particular wanted to know all about me. I felt I was being introduced to another level, a different inner circle of Duncan's life. Although Madame seemed to be unable to recall my name and kept referring to me as Duncan's *petite amie*."

She paused here. It was growing dark and she leaned and bent and switched on one of the bedside lamps, a low glow throwing itself up her corner of the room, the shadows not abated but retreated. She turned further and bent to the bottom of the nightstand, her slip rising to show her garters and the swell of her bottom and came up with a bottle of Armagnac and a single glass. Henry sat silent while she poured the glass amber half-full. She'd offer some when she was ready. She wasn't disregarding him but rather drawn fully into herself. He waited, silent. The air cooler, pleasant through the bank of high windows, the high slice of sky now also the charcoal slate of pigeons.

She sipped and set the glass on the table, turning her eyes back to him. And here, finally, quietly, he said, "What happened?"

She lighted a cigarette and blew a small cloud toward him as if to obscure his question. But her voice was tight and keen. "The next day we returned to Normandy to stay with his friends there. I was a silly ass and thought if ever there was going to be a time this rounding of the cycle would prove to be it. I truly thought he was going to ask me to marry him and I'd worked it out in my head. I had no plans to be coy or hard to get. We knew each other, that was how I intended to respond. For two days it was the same old high times and I actually thought everyone else knew, that they were all in on it. Duncan had smuggled in hashish and the second night we all smoked that and drank endlessly out of the cellar and ended up sometime after midnight calling out the stable-boy and mounting up and riding across the starlit fields, splashing in low streams, jumping hedgerows. A mad wild dash. It was cold but we were insensible. The horses plunging beasts in the night, raising us all close to the stars. And then back for a late or early breakfast. Cooked this time by the gang of us in the huge kitchen. And while we were eating, everybody just clumped around with plates and glasses, Duncan led me off into a pantry of some sort where we made wonderful love. I remember coming back out and the faces turned laughing toward us and I thought Yes, they do all know.

"I slept late and woke about noon, alone. I went down through the house and it was very quiet. Not a soul in sight. I found tepid tea in the kitchen and wandered about until I heard my name being called and found Yvor, who owned the house, seated in the library with a book open upside down on his lap. I asked where everyone was, where Duncan was. I still thought something was being concocted, something special. But Yvor shut the book and stood and told me he was growing weary of Duncan, if only the rascal wasn't so charming and then looked at me and told me I wasn't the first and wouldn't be the last. I pulled myself tight and there was suddenly a strange luminosity in the air, as if the remains of the hashish and wine from the night before had surged back into me and very coolly asked if he might explain himself more clearly. He shrugged and asked if I had not met them the other night, the baron and his wife and the baron's little mistress and when I was silent he said Of course there were rumors that Elise enjoyed her husband's conquests in her own particular ways but of course was largely content with Duncan. With his attentions but also his peccadilloes and that he, Yvor, couldn't figure out whether Elise put up with them because they bound Duncan more strongly to her or simply because she found them amusing. The truth, he suspected, was some complex intertwining between the husband and wife and the freedoms they allowed themselves and each other—that there had to be secret balances because while Philippe seemed to change girls as frequently as he wished, Elise had owned Duncan for eight years now, ever since her previous lover had committed suicide. Then Yvor looked at me and said, there was nothing to worry about that with Duncan, was there?

"Henry, have you had the feeling where everything is closing in on you and you can't breathe? That's how I felt. I understood and I didn't understand. Yvor came over and gently put his hands on my shoulders as if to steady me and explained that while everyone, and I knew what he meant by that, was charmed and delighted by Duncan there were also those—and clearly Yvor was among them—who felt pity for him also. And so tolerated him. I think it was then I screamed. A terrible howl from my heart. And I pulled away and raced up the stairs and started throwing things into my trunk and then began to drag it thumping down the stairs and Yvor came and lifted it from me and carried it down. We stopped in the grand hall and I asked where he was. Yvor shrugged and said perhaps Paris but most likely somewhere else. And then I became very cool, a strange floating sensation as if I was watching myself and I asked Yvor if he might drive me to the station. And he said Of course and asked if I needed any other help and I looked at him and said I'd never taken help from a man and never would. He studied me a moment, as if seeing me anew and then I told him if we didn't leave immediately I'd start screaming again and he walked over and lifted something out of my hand, some ceramic I'd picked up without realizing and told me smashing things wouldn't help. So he drove me out—it was one of those beautiful early winter days, the sort of weather that seems to mock one's emotions. Yet it calmed me and I said it was clear I'd been deceived, that Duncan was far, far from the man I'd thought he was. And Yvor said, quietly, his eyes on the road, that Duncan wasn't even the man he thought he was and that one day it would fall down all around him. And so finally I turned to him and asked Why. Yvor raised his driving glove and flicked his fingers, as if tossing away something small or foul and said matter of factly But Duncan has no money, you see? And so enters Elise and her husband. I started to ask something but Yvor was ahead of me and told the story they all knew and had no reason to doubt it unless it was even worse. Ten years before, Duncan was about to be married, in the great cathedral in New Orleans when he stopped at the altar and turned from the priest and his pregnant bride-to-be and announced he would not go through with it. He told it as if it were his great adventure, with the father and brothers of the girl chasing him through the streets with pocket derringers and how he hid in an empty beer barrel until it was night and he was able to slip to the wharves and get passage to France with the honeymoon money in his pocket and once here, once he arrived in Paris he'd wired for more money only to learn that his father had cut him off. Again, Yvor looked at me and then said Perhaps after all it was the life that was meant for him—that we all find not the lives we want but the ones we make. He was very kind at the station and tried to pay for my ticket, offered me money again but I was already gone from there. I thanked him and kissed him gently and wished him well. Then I took the train to Paris and as the afternoon grew dark and night came I realized I only wanted to disappear. So sometime after midnight in the Gare du Nord I bought another ticket. For Amsterdam. That's when I came back here. That's when I knew I'd found my home."

Henry pushed one leg out straight toward her and leaned forward and stretched himself. Finally he said, "That was a while ago."

She said, "I know."

"But you still return to Paris. Did you ever see or hear of him again?"

She looked at Henry and slowly shook her head and then said, "I didn't go back for a while. It wasn't hard. I avoided certain places and saw only old friends. And the next year the war broke out." She took a swallow of the Armagnac and said, "But damn it, Henry. He wasn't going to steal Paris from me as well."

Then she began to cry.

Eighteen

*I*t was the beginning of that terrible summer of 1907, with Robbie eight, just finishing second grade as the spring advanced, the girls in the seventh and eighth grades and the days grown warm and so plans and even some packing for the Lake had begun. The second weekend of May, Henry took the train to Lakemont with Doyle, Dick Pyle and Emery Westmore as was usual, to open the cottages, assess any winter damage and arrange repairs if needed beyond their own modest capabilities. Their wives made routine jokes about getting out from under the domestic yoke for a few days but in fact they were a mild crew—they might drink beer with lunch and continue moderately through the afternoons until time for stronger beverages, and certainly few vegetables were consumed, largely because they mostly chose to cook on the big stone grill or if the weather was wet, they'd go to the railroad hotel in Himrod and enjoy the German cooking of the proprietress who also had a supply of excellent homemade schnapps to compliment the bratwurst or spareribs in sauerkraut or whatever the dish of the day would be. But this involved a hike and then borrowing a horse and buggy from Joseph Jensen so usually they made the best of it, taking down the shutters and sweeping out mouse droppings, priming the pump and inspecting the water lines, checking window screens for rips, the roofs for loose or blown shingles, opening the boathouse and, if the weather was fair to flush the engine for a shakedown run on the *Mary Nan* after the winter. The work was unexceptional but enough of it over a short time so all returned late Sunday evening usually sunburned and with muscles pleasantly sore. Satisfied that all was well with this special corner of their world.

Alice was on the platform awaiting them, striding up and down in agitation. She was direct and spoke to Emery Westmore as if she was an adult, her fear only showing as she flitted her eyes to her father.

"Mother said to meet you. To ask you to come to the house if you could. It's Robbie. He has a sore throat, a runny nose and a cough. And just isn't himself—"

"He's listless?" Emery asked.

She looked at her father and back to the doctor. "Not a word I'd use for him but yes. Mopey."

Henry said, "There's been whooping cough—"

"Or he has a spring cold. Let me go home and get my bag and I'll be along. And tell Olivia that far more children catch colds than get whooping cough."

Polly was wrapped in a sweater on the porch swing against the cool of evening, watching her father striding long-legged, purposeful, catching his eye and the bolt of fear passed between them, even as Henry had tried to not rush beyond his normal stride, Alice keeping up easily, her silence on the walk from the cable car her own fear. The house was closed tight as if for winter and he jogged up the stairs and found his wife in their son's bedroom, the little boy in a flannel nightshirt, a fire burning low in the coal grate.

"See there, now. Father's home." Her eyes all question, peering behind him.

"Hi Daddy." His blond hair in a sweat cowlick, his voice trebly.

Henry sat down on the bed and Robbie sat up and hugged him. "Hullo you little rascal. Caught a cold, did you?" Rubbing the boy's head, feeling the heat. "Well, Doc Westmore's going to be along any minute now and I'll bet you a hot fudge sundae he'll fix you right up."

"I'm sure glad you're home."

"Me too, little man. Me too."

Emery was still in his weekend shirtsleeves and as he walked in the door, led up by Polly, the room seemed to soften, a calm exuding. Henry had seen this with the birth of all three children, as well as on other, less dramatic occasions and for a short time knew all would be well. Emery plopped down on the bed and had Robbie strip off his nightshirt, listened first to his chest and back with a stethoscope, taking the time to let the boy listen to his own heartbeat as Emery quietly held his wrist and took his pulse. He peered close at the boy's eyes and asked him to blink several times, Henry quite sure this was not diagnostic but meant to further calm Robbie. Olivia huddled close, but was silent, waiting. Finally Emery pulled out a wooden tongue depressor and inserted it in the already open mouth and listened and squinted as the boy Ahh-ed for him. Then Emery sat a moment on the side of the bed before turning to Henry and Olivia.

"That's a heckuva sore throat there, buddy. Glad it's not me."

He turned. "I'm quite sure," he addressed Henry and Olivia. "But just to be on the safe side, I'd like to take him downstairs where I can look in his mouth under the brightest light."

So Henry carried the boy, back in his nightshirt, down to the kitchen, where the new electric lights held a cluster of three bulbs over the table, and on Emery's instructions held his son across his chest as the boy tipped his head far back and so Henry was able to see this time the depressor actually lift the tongue, Emery leaning very close, his own mouth and nose turned away but his eyes just above the boy's stretched wide mouth. He probed a bit with the wooden depressor, pushing and lifting the tongue as much as he could. When he was done he turned to the girls clumped against each other in the kitchen door.

Addressing either or both he said, "Take him back to bed. Leave him in the nightshirt but let that fire die and open some windows. I'll bring up some drops soon that'll help him sleep." He turned back to Robbie. "You're a tough little fella. You'll be fine in no time, you listen to your mother and father."

When they were alone in the room Emery drummed his fingers a moment on the table, then caught himself and stood and went to the sink and washed his hands, scrubbing hard. As he did so he addressed the window before him, not the parents at his back. "There are small ulcers on the fraenum linguae under his tongue. It's early but you should assume this will indeed be whooping cough. He's a sturdy boy and should come through just fine—in fact it's best that we caught it this soon. First of all you need to open this house up—fresh air and sunshine are the two best treatments we know of. Beyond that, it depends to a certain extent on the course it takes but you should prepare now, even if, as we all hope and there's every reason to believe, this will prove a mild case. And we start there. Even if it is mild, you must resist the temptation to believe he's cured before it has time to run its course. And by that I mean not hoping to hurry things, even, or especially, if he seems much improved."

He paused. Then said, "You must understand I'm talking about months. And also that there's every possibility his case may become more complicated than I've laid out so far."

Olivia said, "Children die from this." Her voice sucking at the words, as if she could retract them.

Emery stood. He bent, rummaged, and came up with a small stoppered phial. He said, "Place two drops of this on his tongue tonight. It will help him sleep. But no more and none in the morning. I'll be by early, around eight. Yes. Children die of whooping cough. But children die of many things. We all survived at least some of those. If not most. And even now I'm seeing a plan. There is, you know, a best way to deal with this illness. And you're fortunate to be well situated for it. Allow me the night but let me tell you this now: While it most certainly won't be the summer you planned or hoped for I couldn't imagine a better situation for a positive prognosis, for a full recovery."

"Oh my boy." Olivia turned her upper body, her face into Henry's shoulder.

Henry said, "So we douse the fire and open all the windows? Is that what you're saying?"

Emery walked over and placed a hand on their shoulders. "Just let the fire die on its own. And open a few windows but make sure he has ample covers. It won't help for him to go from one extreme to another. And I'll be here first thing in the morning, although you can call me on the telephone anytime you need tonight. Don't worry about disturbing me. But Olivia. Look at me."

She did.

"Your son will be fine. We might have a fight on our hands but we'll prevail."

She was frenzied, spread around, throughout the room. "How can you know," she cried.

He snapped shut his bag, stepped forward again and kissed her forehead. "You have to trust Robbie," he said. "The way I do."

There passed a couple of quiet weeks with the boy bed-bound and certainly ill but not of great alarm. After consultation with Emery Westmore, Alice and Polly were allowed to continue school, although their contact with their brother was limited and during this time, Emery sat with Olivia and Henry and discussed what lay ahead—all knew to expect anywhere from a month to three of greater illness, or, most hopefully, only an exaggerated form of the coughing and sore throat the boy already had. But it was Emery who finally disclosed what had been obvious to him from the first. There would be no summer at the lake. The house on campus, once the students departed, was as ideal a location, of isolation, as could be hoped for. He would be allowed to spend a great deal of time in the beneficial sun, as much in fact as he was able. Neither of the girls had contracted the disease nor had Henry ever had it although Olivia had survived so young she barely recalled it.

"The problem," Emery explained. "Is that we just don't know when or even if it ceases to be infectious. Anecdotal evidence suggests that as long as the cough persists the pathogen continues to be released into the air. As you know the whoop usually infects young children, so you, Henry, are probably safe, although I've seen a few cases in the elderly and infirm." He paused and peered at Henry.

"You're not feeling infirm, I hope?"

"Emery, please don't joke."

"Olivia, first, I wasn't completely joking. Both Henry and the girls must be watched closely. And as importantly, you're all going to need to keep a sense of humor about you. For Robbie's sake and your own."

"I don't need a cane, yet," Henry said.

"You're both driving me mad," Olivia said.

Emery leaned forward, his elbows on his knees. He looked directly at Olivia and said, "You knew enough to be worried, when you only suspected. And I'm going to tell you now, even with the milder cases, you're about to enter a frightening time. The cough will only get worse, far worse, before it gets better. There will be days and nights where you will want to slam your ahead against the wall for want of anything that will bring him relief. And he may experience convulsive episodes. You'll want me to do something and there won't be much I can do. We fear using any opiate tinctures because while they may bring some relief to the spasms, it's uncertain if they also may weaken the natural resiliency of the lung's walls. Which is going to be the great battle. His lungs will have to support themselves, even as they'll want to collapse from the spasmodic cough. If convulsions occur he'll be further weakened. I'm not trying to frighten you. But you must gird yourselves, both of you. I'll be here every minute I can be. And you may reach me at any time. But you must understand. There's little I can offer. Unless the convulsions become terribly severe, but that's rare and we'll cross that bridge if we come to it. Now, do you have any questions?"

After the long moment of stunned silence, Henry finally ventured. "One. Would you tell the girls about the summer? They're at that temperamental age."

Emery smiled. "Very good, Henry. Stay game."

"I don't think it's a bit funny," Olivia said.

"Actually," Emery said. "If you prefer, they are your daughters after all. But Henry may have a point. The seriousness will be undeniable coming from me."

In the end, Henry called the girls in and left them with their mother and the doctor, closing the double parlor doors before he took a glass of lemonade up to Robbie. The windows were open but the shades were partway down, the room softened in the late spring light. The boy was asleep. Henry placed the glass on the bedside table and stood looking down at the little boy, suddenly so frail, fragile, the small ribs of his naked chest rising and falling with his fluttering breaths. Henry pulled up the sheet and stood a long time watching him, his own heart thunderous, unwilling to make any prayer at all, fearful of asking for anything. Fearful it seemed, of calling attention to the boy.

He was puttering in the kitchen when he heard the parlor doors open and came out into the hall. Alice had been crying and she looked at him, biting her lip as she also went up the stairs, going, he knew, as he had done, to her brother's room. Polly saw her father, her face a twisted mask.

"It's not fair," she blurted.

He stepped, raising his hand to smack her, something he'd never done. She froze and he did too. Emery and Olivia vague figures down the hall.

His voice tight as wire. "I'm ashamed," he said. "The world does not, and never will, revolve around you, Miss Polly. Now to your room. No books." He dropped his hand.

It was the summer the girls learned tennis. With the campus empty and the rest of Elmira largely off limits, Alice and Polly began at Olivia's suggestion—she herself had never played the game but Henry was able to obtain basic instructions with helpful photographs from the instructor of Women's Gymnastics. At first they were half-hearted, near lackadaisical over this imposed poor imitation of summer expectations but as the summer went on, as Robbie got worse, they took to the courts daily and it soon became clear that some sort of struggle, some mêlée greater than the game had been joined. They were smart enough, and worried for their brother and thus also their parents, to leave the rivalry outside, away from the house. Girls becoming women, Olivia explained and Henry understood that they battled as much themselves as each other—the other a convenient extrapolation of frustrations, questions, fears, anxieties, as well as concrete and somewhat safe persons to rub against, to bounce themselves off of.

There was the added benefit of physical exertion, thus a peace that otherwise would've been harder to obtain within the house.

After discussing it with Olivia he also gave each of them a copy of *Anna Karenina* and sat back, awaiting their questions. Alice's only comment was she'd never throw herself under a train, while Polly was quiet, although he found her studying him, as if she'd learned as much about her father as about herself. He went through several silent wrestling days, dearly wanting to give each Chaucer but finally didn't. They were too young still, Tolstoy had been enough so far but mostly he couldn't promise himself that he could give them sufficient time. Robbie was taking all he had. No. He was giving Robbie all he had and that was not enough, never enough.

The nights, afternoons, the long pre-dawns when Robbie sat up in bed with the ripping cough unrelenting, over and over, sucking air only to have it blown back out, the bathing sweat soaking his sheets so they were changed under him two or three or four times a day, sometimes in a single night, his pushing away the cool damp towels, the ice-pack that Henry had spent twenty minutes hacking ice from the block to fill and then screw on the top, only to have Robbie refuse it. Despite the sweat he wasn't hot. He simply couldn't breathe. He lost weight which seemed an impossibility and yet daily his limbs and chest became thinner, even, it seemed, his skin was a flimsy taut membrane containing him. Emery was in and out and to Olivia, infuriatingly calm. Henry also wanted more but understood there was no more. The doctor's presence and reassurances that this was to be expected, that it was nothing out of the ordinary for whooping cough, was not only all he had to offer but also there was a reserve, a sense of strength and expectation of greater needs to draw upon that the doctor was quietly trying to impart.

Then in mid-July the convulsions began. The coughing didn't let up but seemed if possible to be worse. Henry quickly came to look back upon the weeks just passed as the easy time. "Don't hold him down," Westmore said. "However much you want to, however much you think you can stop them just by hugging him, holding him. It only makes the cough worse and doesn't help the convulsions. Just always have someone each side of the bed, add more pillows so he doesn't strike the headboard or the wall, talk to him. Talk to him. The sound of your voices may be the best thing, the only anchor that might break through and offer some comfort and produce a relaxing effect. No one knows for sure. But talk to him. It doesn't matter, if you're exhausted and can't think of any more stories to tell or encouragements to offer, make something up. Tell him stories of your own childhoods. Have Alice or Polly sit in the corner by his bed table and read favorite books. They can read them over and over."

The day the convulsions stopped the rest of them were all too exhausted to even realize it. A bit past nine that night Alice came down from spooning in the dense beef broth that the housekeeper made from roasted bones and marrow and delivered every other day, along with food for the rest of them and came into the parlor where Polly was sprawled sleeping on the sofa and Henry and Olivia sat stuporous in armchairs side by side and Alice stood in the door and said, "He's sleeping. And except for the cough fits, I don't believe he's been shaking even once all day. Has he?"

After mother and father tiptoed upstairs and stood watching their little boy for an uncountable time, Henry went back downstairs and waited patiently, his first very small glass of rye in hand in over a month while the Elmira switchboard connected to Watkins Glen which then connected to Dundee and then on to Lakemont and finally the Westmore's cottage. He had literally no idea or care of the time. Emery answered on the third ring, the doctor's voice indistinguishable from sleep or wakefulness. Henry explained, with a quivering barely held excitement and also in the back of his mind the malevolent fear that he might be calling too soon.

Emery said, "That's just grand. Don't panic if they recur but I'd say the worst is over. I'll be down on the first train in the morning."

Somehow it was not the full response Henry had hoped for. But it would do.

Two weeks later, with Emery's blessings and to the relief of them all Henry rode the train north to Lakemont, delivering the girls for the final weeks of summer into the care of their grandparents. He had a bad moment there, glancing at his own closed and empty cottage where he just wanted to stay also. Which prompted him to leave for the twenty minute walk up the hill an hour ahead of the next train which meant he had ample time to sit and visit with Joseph Jensen and also to follow Joseph around to the back of the barns and into the big woodshed attached to the rear of the farmhouse where he leaned on the pen and watched the collie bitch snapping and worrying her almost-weaned litter of puppies. Henry was always comfortable around Jensen, the farmer exuding the same weary but alert confidence of the fishing captains of his youth and so found himself riding the train south with an old grape tote on his lap, holding a bed of bright fresh wheat straw and the incessant poking muzzle, the darting slender pink swath of tongue and needle teeth of an eight week old collie puppy.

"You've lost your mind, Henry Dorn," Olivia said, smiling. "Don't think I'll be the one to care for it until Robbie's fully able."

"I'd not give up the pleasure," he said. "Now let's sneak upstairs and see what the young master has to say."

Robbie gazed silent and wide-eyed into the crate held at bed level. He looked up at his father. "Is it a baby goat?"

"No, no. Look again."

A pause. The puppy was whining and trying to climb from the crate and licking Robbie's uncertain fingers.

"A puppy? Is it mine? Can I have him?"

"He's a collie pup from Jensen's. Up at the lake. And yes, my boy, he's all yours." And Henry tilted the crate slowly and the puppy bounded onto the bed and onto the boy. Who shrieked and grabbed the puppy who responded by wriggling wildly and peeing on the bed. Henry quickly set the crate down and reached for the pup when Olivia took his arm.

She said, "Get them down on the floor. It can't hurt for a few minutes. And Lord knows, we have plenty of clean sheets."

"I'll get fencing and put up a little yard out under the hickory first thing in the morning."

She smiled. "That would be a good idea for both of them." She shook her head. "Now and then, Henry, you do amaze me."

He smiled back, the scrambling pup back up in his arms. "That often?"

"Oh, often enough."

"Bobo," Robbie said. "I'm going to name him Bobo. Give him back. He's mine."

Two weeks later a telegram arrived from Nova Scotia. George Dorn had died without warning the day before. The service was to be in three days. Below that blunt message was pasted a single name. Fred.

There was no question of taking the family. He packed a single strapped suitcase and left that evening, taking locals to Geneva and east to Albany where he caught the express to Boston in time for the morning steamer to Yarmouth where again he got lucky and got the last steamer out for Freeport. Crossing the Gulf of Maine he realized he was so tired, had begun the trip with such haste, his focus the entire way upon his next destination and the connections to be made, that he'd barely registered what he was going toward. Now in the last light of high summer, waiting on the rail, straining for the first glimpse of home, most likely the strobic flash of the Brier Island light, trying to calculate if he was arriving the evening before the funeral, or if there lay a day between, when he was struck with a vivid image of his uncle, as the last he'd seen him, seven summers ago but somehow then unchanged from earlier memories; the lined reddened face, the heavy walrus mustache iron-grey, the whiter hair that flowed back from his forehead and behind his ears, the simple captain's hat, black wool felt with a leather visor, free of any trim, his red suspenders up over the denim work shirt he wore summers, along with canvas duck trousers —fisherman's gear, always. And realized that, despite the fact he knew well enough where and what he was headed toward, until this moment and without thinking of it, had somehow expected the man to meet his boat. Nor would he again receive the several letters a year written in the man's old-fashioned spidery hand with quill nibs. George, the oldest of them all, was gone.

There was no one on that late steamer that recognized him, nor any he knew by sight. And since no one in Freeport knew when to expect him there was nobody to meet him at the wharf. He stood off to the side, waiting with his suitcase for the small crowd to disperse. Finally, when all were gone but the gang of men unloading freight, he made his way slowly up the shell road and sat in the gathering darkness for a time on a bench outside a netting shed. He was in a strange state, and now that he was here, in no hurry to announce himself to anyone. His mother, he knew, would be up long past the slow northern dusk. He fully expected her house would be the center of activity anyway, as like it or not she served as family matriarch. He smiled briefly. She liked it all right but would never reveal so.

It was a clan grown thin. A thinning that, now Henry thought of it, had been gaining for some time. Henry expected his mother had asserted her role as matriarch and George would be laid out at her house, the family homeplace. Although Fred was the apparent one in charge he was four years younger than George and they had lived all of Henry's life and a good long bit before as bachelors together. The two had been young men, boys by modern standards, Henry supposed but George already working the boats as bait cutter and Fred already behind the counter in their father's store, the one their great-grandfather had founded with money from the Indies molasses trade, which at the time completed the great triangle of the raw goods for rum to the Indies, while the Yankee captains were whaling or slaving and the Island captains brought home all the goods not available from the Boston states. Each in their way involved in trades either illicit or frowned upon within their communities but each narrowly compromising by providing a more locally acceptable slice of the triangle. And then, with both boys in their teens, Henry's grandmother found herself pregnant at the formidable age of forty-three. He guessed (or did he know—had there been stories floated down in his own childhood?) that Martha and Holland Dorn had taken some ribbing over this late arrival, Samuel, Henry's father. It was not only her age, as women often continued to reproduce into middle age and often died of it during that time, but more that such a long time separated the two older sons and this child. Surely, the phrase came to him, with all its implications, a love child. Or perhaps, perhaps this notion dawned more slowly, and later, as young Samuel was not only different but tolerated as such by a father who'd never hesitated with the belt upon the older boys. Legend had it (from George, Henry thought, somehow, sometime from George) that it had been Martha who'd recognized and abetted the boy's feminine pursuit of drawing, of flattening any sheet of butcher paper or brown wrapping paper that came into the house, of saving, scrounging for pencil stubs beneath that high clerk's desk in the store and sharpening them with his penknife to the finest tip, it had been Martha who, whether in consult with her husband or not had ordered the blocks of drawing paper, blocks of a hundred sheets that had to be razored carefully apart from their gum borders, as well as nibs, pen holders, India inks, a full box of squares of dried watercolor pigments and assortment of brushes, up from

Boston. The stories, bits of allusion that perhaps sitting in the funereal dusk of what would always and never again be home, finally came clear, or again floated up from some hidden recess of his mind, came vivid as if he was scampering along after his own father and grandfather, Holland Dorn with his full patrician beard and stern face, this from the one daguerreotype framed forever above the counter of the mercantile, this older man out with his so very young son, perhaps not following but actively leading him down along the mudflats at low tide and also over to the tidal pools on the Fundy shore under the great basalt cliffs and columns or the more benign, slower southern side toward Saint Catherine's Bay, yes, Henry thought, not following but leading, pausing to squat in his boots, or wade into the shallow pools, to show his young curious son all the things that were, if known by name, largely regarded by others as mere trash mostly, oddities but worthless at best. The baby crabs, minnows of all sorts that Holland could name, the quick spurt of a clam from the mud, but also the puffin nests, the views out to the passing whales, the spring and fall migrations of thousands of birds, mostly sea birds; duck and geese in all possibilities, mergansers and brants, scaups and scoters, widgeon, teal and the grand cormorants. As well as the migrations of otherwise inland birds, woodcock, warblers of all sorts, even the sudden bursts of flocks of robins arriving in the spring. A man who knew everything about where he lived, who could name every wildflower, every grass or shrub others called weeds, who knew all the trees and their uses as well. And who also must've sat silent some or many mornings, evenings or noontime hours while his young son took all this in, perhaps sometimes side by side, others, certainly, the older man waiting patient as the boy labored over his sketches. Some rare communication stirring between them. And some great ease and comfort, extended, Henry knew now, not from one to the other but between both.

The early September Sunday forenoon when Martha and Holland had taken their fancy matched team of bays up-Island to Tiverton for a revival—no great tented affair but rather a minister of Maritime renown who'd come to preach a long afternoon service, which as the handbills and advertisements in the Digby newspaper promised to offer blessings uncountable to the faithful, hope for those who wavered and the absolute guarantee of a great and awesome illumination for the doubters, downtrodden, drunkards and strays (*You know who you be! Look but inward and honestly is rewarded by the Lord almighty!*) Samuel stayed home, faithful enough in his regular church attendance to once again be allowed this privilege. He was ten. Returning from Tiverton the disaster was later easily enough discerned— a clap of thunder, a bolt of lightning nearby spooked the hot-blooded and bored team, so they exploded in a heartbeat beyond control, veering off the road and then back on, the sandy track and ditch catching and overturning the carriage. Martha was thrown clear and broke her neck against a roadside birch while Holland had the lines wrapped around his wrists, determined to control his horses when the carriage overturned and the pole and eveners, the entire front rigging tore free and so he hit the road in rapture with the now terrified horses. When they finally came to a blowing foam-flecked stop outside their stable behind the house, his hands were suffocated blue from the bound-tight lines, the back of his head laid open where he'd struck upon a spiny outcropping of granite in the road so his brain emerged coated with sand and grime, his body bruised and clothes shredded nearly off him from the four miles of twisting turning battering last run for home.

It was Sam who found him, who'd heard the snorting farting terrified horses bringing their burden home.

George was fishing, captain of a seventeen-member-crew schooner, sending out pairs of men in the dories to longline for cod. It was brutal work from before dawn till well past dusk, often working blind in fog. George was a fine captain, never wanting for crew. Fred sent out a high-rigged fast-sailing racing boat, a wealthy man's toy that didn't belong to him although the two-man crew went without question to find George and deliver the news. It was George Dorn's final stint as captain of anything. Over the years he found many reasons to go down to the boats, to go to sea for a day or three. But never again as captain.

Once back ashore he and Fred, with young Sam between them, buried their parents. And each in his way put aside assumptions for themselves. They had a child, a brother, a boy neither of whom quite knew what to do with, to raise.

And now George was dead.

A few stars were out. Venus bright beaming low above the last sheen of sunset. A bare spattering of others coming against the dome to the north and east. Henry's neck and shoulders ached, as if he'd been holding them in place for hours and hours.

Around the bay lights burned in windows. He stood and stretched, hefted his suitcase and began the slow walk toward his mother's house. Not yet visible. His heavy shoes crunched loud and uneven, lurching him along the road. Even with the twilight he could see the white shell dust settling onto his shoes. Across the high tide of the bay he could make out the pale white-shingled, gable-hipped roof of his uncles' house. A single light pale in one window, there.

Euphemia was magnificent. Henry stepped inside the door to a houseful of people and she was immediately before him, as if she'd been watching that door. She held his upper arms and leaned up tiptoe to kiss him, then said, "How is dear Robert? As well as you report or still a worry?"

"He's coming along quite well, now. Oh, Mother. I'm glad to see you. I feel badly we're not all here."

She kept her grip on his arms but pulled her head back slightly. "You did what could be done. And Henry, you'll learn things aren't everything they could be, here. Or hoped for. But that's the way of life, isn't it? Come now, meet everyone you already know."

The funeral was the following day, and the grand wake had been held the night before at the Community Hall, so this evening the large kitchen was spread with food and filled with family and several dozen of the closer friends, old fishermen and their wives or widows. They spilled into the day room—the less formal large sitting room off the other side of the kitchen. The parlor door was closed though from time to time one or another would slip through the door for their final viewing, their final visit. Old stories told a final time, confessions made, debts recounted, never to be repaid. Henry looked long toward that door but waited. When he was to enter he'd want the house quiet, to spend as long as he wished, to be alone with the body.

Meanwhile the faces and names came. He'd pumped Nelson Thurber's hand before hugging Lucy, his sister grown old and plump while Nelson seemed awkward, a quality Henry didn't recall. And then Eva and her husband Roger Curtis, Roger with the fisherman's flushed leather skin and oversized hands, his eyes bold and direct, his voice soft as a girl's. They'd married when Henry was studying for his doctorate at Yale and so while he'd met them when he'd brought the family seven years ago, as well as through Euphemia's frequent updates, he felt momentarily uneasy, as if greeting strangers he'd met once on a train. There was a gaggle of children he couldn't keep straight, although he remembered Lucy's oldest girl from the fight she'd had with Polly on that visit, a fight that lasted only minutes but which later Henry realized had made a lasting scar—the couple of times Olivia had nudged Henry about another trip it had been Polly who broke her father's dithering resistance with her firm pledge that they all could go if they pleased but she was remaining right there in New York. "Certainly Grandpa and Ma'am Franks would take me in." It was enough for Henry.

The old men and more than a few of the older ladies made their way to him, wrapping hard horny hands about his, or feathering up to press dry powdery lips to his cheek as they leaned in close and mostly said versions of the same thing. All understandable enough, given the missed evening yesterday when surely the stories flowed but also his essential strangeness. They knew him by name. A handful recalled how he'd delivered coal as a boy, to cellars or galleys and even then there was a reach, an effort to place him among them. As the memory, the shade, he'd become. Those few who mentioned his life, his modest accomplishments, did so with the wary false cheer of someone not sure they've got it quite right. Information learned from Euphemia and so both trusted and uncertain.

Abruptly, a cup of tea in hand, he realized Fred was absent. For a moment considered the possibility that he'd be in the parlor, the keeper of his brother's corpse this final night. And then knew it was not so. If for no other reason that if Fred was in there, one of those visitors would've informed him of his nephew's arrival and thus brought him out, however briefly, to greet him.

He surveyed the room and chose the obvious candidate and slowly made his way until he was side by side with Nelson Thurber. Who, while Henry doubted was full-partner must have advanced considerably within the family enterprise. It seemed Nelson watched his progress warily.

"Nelson," he said, his voice resuming Island cadence. "I'd bet a dime to a dollar you know the workings even better than him, by now. Where is the old fella, anyway?"

Nelson frowned and studied Henry, his thin parched lips worked a mild unaware twist. Finally he said, "You talking about Fred?"

"Course I am."

Nelson looked Henry up and down. Even with his long journey and the dust now settled on his once-polished shoes and the cuffs of his trousers, still better dressed than anyone else in the room. By certain lights. Henry wasn't sure of this inspection.

"Fred's to home," Nelson said. "On account of me. You'd care to follow me outside, I've a little bottle. Don't know about you but I could use a tipple bout now."

They went out the backdoor of the kitchen, the women ignoring their passage and even most of the men, although more than a few eyes came up and followed them.

Nelson had a half-pint of pale rum. They exchanged it twice and then Nelson spat in the yard, the big cabbage roses heavy in bloom, a murky presence of scent and heft off to their sides. He said, "My dad and I built me a dory. And I rebuilt as many lobster pots as I could find or scrape together. So that's what I do now. Like a old man, I run my pots were I can row to em." He paused and said, "It holds us together. Lucy's a hand at the garden, learned that from her mother, I guess. We got the house. We're fine. Happier, someways."

"You and Fred fell out."

"Shit." Nelson passed the bottle back. "I was doing right well. But like George, there, I got along better with the captains and such. Knew their needs and when to press, when to hold off. And toward the end there, George couldn't do a thing for me. He was upset bad by it. I could tell. But it was blood, ya know. And whatever else bound them two. But towards the end, the last couple years, Fred and me was at it like cats and dogs. And then," he glanced up at the stars and took the bottle from Henry, pulled and said, "Then two years ago I come in one morning and Fred handed me a envelope. I opened her up and it was a list, an account, of all I owed him. Which was the coal provided, the fish we ate, the things that come with the job. I said, 'What's this?' and he said, 'You're done.' Well, I got a little lathered right then, I admit. Couple days later, after I pulled my pride back outa my boots, I went down to the docks to talk to the captains. And not a one of them would take me on. Because each a them done business, had to do business with Dorn Brothers. And I paid Fred that money. It wiped out everything we had but I done it. So here I am, lobstering for what cash there is, fishing and scalloping to fill the table. All them years, all them years come to nothing cept for useless information crowds my skull. And Lucy and the kids. I got them. Nobody can take them from me."

"Jesus, Nelson," Henry said, accepting the bottle again. "I'm sorry as can be. What the hell set Fred off?"

"I know right well. When the century turned I went to Fred and told him. I said we got to get the refrigeration onto the boats, the big ones, the schooners and steamers we was starting to use. He looked at me and told me We got a ice house and all them holds are well set up. The men know how to ice down their catch. We know how to handle it when it comes in. When we ever lost a catch of fish, he asked me. I told him, You gonna wait until that happens, going out further and longer each time now? He said when he wanted my advice he'd ask. Then two summers ago there was one a them summer gales, come right at the wrong time. Time it was passed and over and the boats all got back in they was every one of them empty but stinking to high heaven. I don't know how many thousands of dollars was dumped in the sea. But it was considerable. Not so long after that was when he give me that envelope. And that, as the old ladies say, was that."

Much later, when the house was cleared but for his mother, after she and he had sat and talked of Lucy and Nelson and Fred, Euphemia so tired and not willing to condone nor condemn any of parties involved, playing her hand as she saw it, and Henry knowing it was a weak one not to be pushed, after he finally gathered his suitcase and was shown to what had been his boyhood room although otherwise unrecognizable with its bright wallpaper and barren bed, after that, when he'd heard her final steps up to her own bedroom and then waited, he went in his socks down through the otherwise dark house and let himself into the parlor where a single lamp burned, trimmed low, on the table at the head of the casket.

The Dorn family plot with its worked-iron fence was in the rear section of the old burying ground, flanked by a pair of twisted cedars and a trailing ancient rose gone wild, the stones, fence and all lit dense and soft by the heavy rain. Fred and Henry were the lead pallbearers, carrying the pine box, smooth as satin, darkening in the rain as if foretelling how the enclosing earth would color it. Nelson was behind Henry, Eva's Roger behind Fred and holding up the rear two captains, sturdy enough although of advanced age. At graveside, the raw mound covered with canvas to keep it dry, Henry stood in his wet clothes, holding an umbrella while his mother held his right arm with both her hands, the rain and tears washing through and plastering her veil, as the minister intoned the committal, the mounds of umbrellas around the grave seeming to Henry like so many small storm clouds come low, this day of rain appropriate to placing this man back in the earth, this man of water. He heard nothing of the minister's words but when all looked up from the final prayer he stood waiting, looking across at Fred who stood alone bareheaded in the rain, head still bowed. Around Henry it seemed people were rocking on the wet ground. Finally, when it was clear his uncle would not or could not, Henry stepped free of his mother and pulled back a corner of the canvas, took up one of the spades and dropped five shovelfuls of dirt on the box, then turned and passed the spade to Nelson, Roger waiting and a great lot also of the fisherman, old and not so old.

When Henry turned again to look across, Fred had disappeared. Then he saw him, cutting cross lots among the graves, a bowed raven shrunken inside himself.

The final gathering was in the neat, clean and spare basement room of the church, where the ladies had laid out cakes and pies, plates of cookies, along with urns of hot tea and coffee. Henry led his mother there, found her a seat among the wooden folding chairs, armed her with a cup of tea and then spoke briefly with the minister, a man he did not know and so had to begin by introducing himself, then thanking the man for all he'd done for the family during this difficult time. Then with a last look about the room, he slipped out, back into the rain.

Fred opened the door as if he'd been waiting, even watching for him. He'd changed into another suit, without a tie and wearing carpet slippers, his hair slicked back thin over his shining dome. He stood in the door rather than stepping back. "Better you'd come often as you should've then only now when he can't know it."

"Of course," Henry said, expecting something like this. "But I had my reasons."

"I expect you do." Fred opened the door and stepped back. "Come in then, and learn how wrong you was. Or leave now and go home thinking you know everything."

They sat in the kitchen, the range throwing heat against the damp of the day. In straight chairs across the table from each other. Fred offered nothing and served himself nothing, although a percolator on the back of the stovetop threw a wispy steam of coffee.

"How are you, Fred?" Henry tried.

"How I am doesn't matter. They're dead now, all of them." His arm lifted to sweep the room, indicating all those he spoke of. "Excepting your mother, even the living. I'd excuse Eva but it's her own children swipe candy from their great-uncle's store and expect to get away with it. Tell you the truth Henry Dorn, it's a sorry lot it's come down to. Some ways I'd say it started with you. Or your father. George not here to defend the both of you, I can tell it how it is, how it was."

Henry waited the pause and then responded. "I'd of returned more often if I'd been able. It's easy to sit in this place and forget the complications of a life you know nothing about."

"I was not hatched yesterday. But that's a good one to start with, this business about the complications of life you know nothing about. Why you bastard, you don't even know the man you just buried."

"I know he was not you."

"Attack me until I'm dead. It don't change a thing. You just stay ignorant, that's all."

"Well, then, Fred Dorn. Tell me what I don't know."

Fred said, "I don't have eternity yet. But I'll tell you what you need to know about my brother."

"I'd welcome that."

"You think."

"I do. I'm curious." Henry's mouth twisted, anger barely contained.

"A man's made the way a man's made," Fred said. "Which does not excuse," he glared at Henry, "failing to take that into account. Or even be the least bit curious. Which you never were. So I'll tell it to

183

you straight. First thing you need to know was when Mother and Father were killed, George was all but set to get married. I don't name names and she's dead now anyways but he walked over the night they died and she told him he couldn't ask her to take on rearing a little boy. More to the point and I guess he heard her, was she couldn't take on a husband now with a little brother, one she already knew to be a particular strange sort. And so I had no choice. He had the most clear head on his shoulders I ever encountered on a man and I'd say that even if he wasn't my brother and even though he and I differed more than agreed. No one much likes me and don't think I don't know it. And that's fine with me, just fine with me. But there wasn't a soul didn't like George. So pretty much for about a dozen years he set his life aside to raise up and then watch over your father. And helped him, helped him more than you can know, though maybe by the time I'm done with you, you can make your guesses.

"Then when your father died and Euphemia brought the litter of you back up here, he offered to marry her. He wasn't after some young thing—he knew her too well to expect that. And when she turned him down he didn't bat a eye but peeled it for what was coming next. Which was you. He never wanted or intended to replace Sam as a father to you. But his eye was on you, always.

"I got to tell you, I had my doubts about you, right along. And seems to me my own doubts paid off. But I humored him. I've gone to church all my life and read the Bible and thought a great deal about it but truth is, Henry Dorn, the only way I understand a damned thing about love came from my brother. I had to sum it up, he loved like Christ. Or as much as a human can.

"When that plan was hatched, the one to send you off, that was George and Euphemia. They strong-armed the minister then, what was his name? It don't matter. And your school teachers, why they all thought it was a fine idea. A course they would. I wasn't going to have any part in it but George come to me so I played along. But this is what you need to know. That man was buried this day, he was the one. It never was the both of us. I knew you weren't coming back and so did he but it meant different things to each of us so I told him, I said, George, I'll play it any way you want. But there's not the first dime coming from me. Course he knew that but thanked me. Because it was important to him that you not think it was all him. But it was."

Fred stood then. Henry couldn't move, pasted in his chair. It was all of it, he told himself—the death, the reach of the summer before that news, the long journey, the burial. And now this angry grief-stricken man. Henry now glad he'd come alone. He couldn't imagine them all there.

Fred came around the table, standing above Henry, the small man in his immaculate suit and ridiculous slippers somehow looming over Henry.

Fred's mouth curled in anger. "He never expected to be repaid. In money or kind. And he wasn't. And if it bothered him he held it in. I never heard a thing but how glad he was for you, what news mostly came from your mother, those few letters I seen came in from you to him. The ones he sent out—I knew what tone they had. And maybe you thought you were doing what he expected, what he hoped. But still, behind it all, was a kind loving old man who deserved better. Not me. I never expected other than what we got. If I brought that upon myself I truly do not give one warm shit. But George. George was different. And either you were too stupid to know that or too selfish to care. In the end it don't matter. Nothing can be changed."

Fred hugged himself, cold in the warming room.

Henry waited, then stood and said, "How could you live with him all those years so close and not know—"

Fred interrupted him. "Someday, Henry Dorn, a sharp stick is going to rip your ass and tear your life apart. Now get out of my house."

It was pouring out and Henry made it back to his mother's house where he found a note on the table about supper at Lucy's with just her family and Eva's. Henry paused, considering, but then left his own note, stole an umbrella from the hall and prayed all the way down to the wharf. Where the big steamer direct to Boston was still tied up. He opened his wallet and bought a private cabin and went on board, the rain still pelting down. He waited until he felt the ship press away to churn about in the Pas and then stripped off his clothes and layered every blanket in the cubby on the bed and crawled in. Shaking and shivering, his teeth chattering, unable to warm. He curled up tight against himself, his heels in his backside, head under the covers.

He was up early, topside as they came into Boston Harbor, the air heavy, humid, hot. The sun a hazed giant splendor behind them, lifting mist. Out there to the east. He didn't regret his cutpurse departure. Not that she'd forgive him, but their weekly letters offered her more opportunity than if he'd seen her face to face. He could and would write to his mother but it wouldn't matter—she'd known where he'd been after the funeral. Of most importance he now understood Fred. That bile of anger had nothing, or very little to do with himself. George, Henry realized, was the only person that Fred fully, without reserve and unconditionally, loved. And while there was no doubt George loved his brother deeply also, his own capacity for love was of a broader range, with boundaries elastic, placid and content.

George Dorn had owned a mighty heart.

Nineteen

One summer afternoon he'd been in his apartment, writing letters to Alice and Polly, one to Doyle and Mary, as well as notes on the backs of picture postcards for his granddaughters. They were the first he'd sent although composing them had proved easier than he'd feared. He made no mention of Lydia, even if she was a silent presence in his descriptions of places he'd been, things he'd seen, and within his final line in all the letters, the same for each—*I'm feeling myself somewhat restored, regaining a hold on life* did not feel to be an act of contrivance so much as one of kind omission. When a knock came at his door, an hotel bellman with a note from Lydia, whom he was already planning to meet for dinner. She'd heard of something that might be interesting that evening and suggested he consider a bit of casual dash for his attire. And then, as if knowing this might confuse him, she'd added, mischievously—*Boat shoes?* He considered this, smiling, knowing it wasn't intended as a joke. After he'd walked down to send the letters and postcards he returned and bathed, then reviewed his wardrobe. Casual dash. Indeed. Besides her own example of careless sensual elegance about all he had to go on were the evenings they'd gone to Le Jas where he'd indeed felt overdressed, almost stuffy but for the quality of his clothes. It was a challenge—he had to pass muster for dinner, wherever that might be. And then it came to him. He'd dress as he wanted and she'd know exactly where to eat before this hinted adventure.

He met her at the Dam, outside the Krasnapolsky at the appointed hour. She looked him up and down. He was wearing his boat shoes, canary trousers, an almost smoky rose shirt, a black tie with muted gold paisley patterns and over that his only sport coat, a soft dark grey drape. He felt foolish but had done his best. It helped but little that she was in an oyster-shell sheath and nude stockings, black heels and a small black turban tipped and pinned in place. But she smiled and kissed his cheeks, then stood back at arm's length and studied him.

"You're missing one thing. Come quick." He caught up her hand as she was off, into the midst of the square where she found a flower stall and left him stranded a moment as she waded through and he took delight in that moment, watching her intent and nimble and then she came forth holding a single dahlia, a crimson so deep as to be near black, which she tucked into his jacket lapel and then as if a magic trick, removed a straight pin from her mouth to hold the bloom in place.

"Where'd you get the pin?"

"I suspected you might need a flower." She then looked over the square toward the looming Koninklijk Palace. "I heard the family is there just now. Shall we drop in?"

"You can't be serious." Somehow suspecting that she very well could be.

She dropped into a stagy British accent and said, "Wot's the matter, luv? Scared of them royals, are ya? It might be yer chance, ya know. That Princess Juliana, she's growin in to quite the fine lit-uhl piece, word 'as it. Might take a shine to ya. She be next up to the throwin. Queen-consort or wot, ya could be."

They ate in one of the old brown bars, his first time in one. They drank the thimbles of gin chilled to a viscous deliberation, the genial bowls of soup and hunks of bread comforting, reassuring, and the variety of pickled fish that came not as condiments but as small helpings, some salty with brine, other hot and fiery, floating in red oil and pepper flakes, others in a light cream, were reward unto themselves.

Every other person within was in working man's clothes—in fact Lydia and one older woman far down the bar were the only women in the room. Glances came their way but Lydia was oblivious to them and Henry easily became so, mildly infatuated with the gin, which Lydia explained to him. "Always straight, very cold and small."

It made sense to him.

They lingered and for a time Lydia struck up a conversation with the old man behind the bar, some version of bartender, waiter and perhaps cook—when they'd ordered their food he'd disappeared for long enough stretches so that more than once one of the old men seated at the bar would go back around and help himself to a refill but always leaving his empty glass beside the new one. Henry could not yet keep up with rapid Dutch, still struggling to make the transition from his scholar's German. But he was happy with the Genever and any vestige of worry over his attire was long gone.

Finally Lydia turned, touched his knee and said, "Are you enjoying yourself?"

"Immensely. You were correct in your note. This is superb. Interesting was not quite the right word." Thinking that the outrageous outfits for this place was simply part of Lydia.

She smiled. "You're right. I do love these places. And they're all over the city, you just have to know what to look for. But Henry. This is the prelude. We're killing time."

It was dark when they went out, although the sky was lit with the final slow threads of twilight. They walked along the pretty Rokin and then she led him closer to the buildings, clearly searching one of those narrow alleys.

"The Nes," she said. "We cross over that way, where all the theatres are. But we don't quite get there. I have to find just the right alley. I know it. I do. At least I will when I see it."

He finally asked the question of the night. "So where exactly are we going?"

She stopped, turned and dug in a small gold chain-mail handbag for her cigarettes. He waited and when she was smoking, she thoughtfully blew off a smoke ring and then another that in the still air sailed through the first. "We're not in the center of the world, Henry. Which I rather like, obviously. But there are interesting things going on in Paris and now in Berlin, I hear. But we're also not, forgive me, in Elmira, New York. So things dribble in here. That jazz club, that's a good place. Very hot. So tonight, tonight we see something else. It could be as good as the jazz or a homemade confection, an imitation of something somewhere else. But either way, as I said, did I say this in my note? It should at least be interesting."

It was small on the outside, with windows painted in blue and black stripes and outside a string of tiny blue electric lights above the black door. The man at the door was muscled and tall with a shaved head and a sleeveless undershirt died blue, baggy oversized black trousers that bunched above his working-man boots. A thin goatee, also blue, sprouted from his chin. He watched them approach with something close to loathing. Then stepped around the head of the line, his face split into a smile.

"Ly-dee! Is that you?"

"Who else, Denis?"

"Ah, love," he said and kissed her hand. "So you came to this. And you brought a friend!"

"Oh, yes, Denis. My dear friend Henry."

"Henri?" A ripple of curiosity flowed over the man's face, Henry watching the blue goatee quiver. Then Denis said, "Ah, Henk! Correct? Henk. The one who has stolen Ly-dee so much from us! Welcome, welcome. Come with me." And extended a muscled arm, almost a jab toward Henry.

Henry shook hands and then all three of them passed back around the waiting people and Denis opened the door and they were inside. Into blackness with a small stage lit by a single hot wide-angle, gas powered footlight. There were no chairs but planks on blocks and two women wearing only tight black short shorts and obvious wigs of shiny black hair circulated with trays holding small glasses in size somewhere between a cordial and a small wine glass, the cups holding an opaque greenish white liquid. Their bare breasts had yellow circles painted around them. Lydia stepped and took two of the glasses and holding them, moved toward a small opening in the middle row of rough seats.

She handed him a glass. "Sip it very slowly," she said.

"What is it?"

"Shhh, love," she said. "It's about to begin."

People came in around them and the seats filled. He sipped the drink, almost medicinal, flowery with herbs, recalling him of the hard licorice drops of his youth. Almost immediately something ashen spread through his limbs and up into his brain and the room shifted and seemed to brighten in his focus. Soon the two women came upon the stage holding baskets over one arm—with the other hand they tossed out slow floating petals of flowers that were the exact color of the flower in his lapel, although these petals were different, how he couldn't tell. At first he thought they might be silk instead of real but then as the women continued and the layers grew the scent also filled the room. A man in blackface came onto the stage wearing a bass drum strapped over his bare chest and began to beat a slow sad tattoo just as Henry realized he was not a minstrel but a naked negro, his face and limbs and torso striped and dotted with white paint, his penis painted white but shrunk tight above his testicles below the brass fittings of the drum. He held mallets and as he stood the force of his beat grew and grew, the mallets blurring in the air and deep within Henry's head. Then the man turned, his back to the audience, the only white paint here on his upper arms, his buttocks tight as he slowed to a ponderous dragging and off-beat striking of the drum. As if he no longer knew how to play but knew he must.

This discordant slowed booming grew, almost too great to bear but impossible to escape. Henry drank a bit more from the fragile glass and within moments the slowed chance rhythm was absolutely perfect.

Girls floated onto the stage. These not the young women of earlier but true girls of twelve or fourteen. Each nude but wrapped in the lightest of gauze, filmy material more tease than covering, their small nipples protrudent, the swell of their buttocks and curve of their waists and legs, the patches between their legs visible. Their motion was constant, fluid but if choreographed Henry could not discern a pattern—more as if each girl had some twining vinelike route to follow independent of the others, their arms swinging up with curved wrists, hands pointed birdlike although there must've been a larger plan as none collided or touched another and then without his predicting or seeing it coming the girls had encircled the drummer—only then did Henry realize the slowed drumbeats had stopped and the sound was duplicated and changed by the stamp of feet in the same discordant pattern, the feet stamping and swishing as brushes through the layered petals upon the stage floor, the girls now pressed together with arms raised, bodies straining upward as if to fly, making a cone of white light around the drummer no longer visible and then slowly the cone came down, down, down, the drummer hidden beneath until the girls no longer girls but some joined diaphanous female creature which just as it seemed could go no lower each again split from the cone and rolled outward, opening as individual petals of a flower, rolling in sinuous controlled backward somersaults to reveal the black man rising again, the drum gone, disappeared, his body cloaked from the neck down in an indigo robe and upon his face a mask of giant yellow eyes above an extending broad black bird's beak, red and blue ostrich feathers rising high above those eyes and the girls now were crawling, hauling themselves with great effort, the legs writhing as if only their arms worked toward the wings of the stage and then the stark white backdrop that Henry had thought was painted brick rose as the bird/man dropped onto the audience floor and ran swiftly through the seats and out the street door, while at the rear of the stage before what Henry thought was a real brick wall, another cacophony began, five men seated, one at an upright piano, one with a banjo, one a mandolin, one with a clarinet and one, outlandishly with a bow and a saw, a shining new metal saw of the sort a carpenter cuts planks with, the saw tip caught against one foot so the saw blade was bent and the man bowed against the blunt edge while maneuvering the tension of the saw by depressing or lifting the handle, the sound a tremulous high-pitched endless wavering sigh of sound, not unpleasant to the ears and blending with the very fast ragtime the other men were pounding out—those men dressed in the bowler hats and checkered three-piece suits of decades before and then all began to sing and he realized they were playing breakneck versions of minstrel songs, singing in high pitched voices, the banjo flailing furiously, the quavering saw growing ever higher and higher and then the young girls were back, now in high leather boots, bright yellow riding breeches and buttoned black velvet vests, all now with long hair down as they began a stylized romp, flitting and swinging each other by the elbows, boots stamping hard to meet the thumping rhythm of the piano in elaborate parody of a country dance Henry thought and then the two older women, still in their shorts and wigs, came out with riding crops and began to swat at the girls and, fairly enough, Henry thought, the musicians as well. . . .

Outside the anonymous cabaret or whatever it was Henry had waited off to the side while Lydia briefly mingled. He was in a curious condition, intoxicated, yet certainly not drunk but rather as if some element of what he'd just witnessed yet infused him. Reverberations of the saw jangled waves in his mind and also his vision. There seemed an unusual luminescence about not only the people but the fittings and structures of the buildings around him. Then Lydia retrieved him and they walked along the Nes, slowly entering a greater throng from the larger theatres with illuminated marquees. The night was warm, their passage through it languid, careless. They were holding hands, the connection just right, needed it seemed as both wandered a bit in their walking. Untethered he could image a sudden and embarrassing lurch but any closer, arms around each other, could be equally disastrous.

"What did you think?"

"What *was* that?"

"Umm." She tipped her face toward him, the yellow electric lights throwing shadows of color over her face. "A good effort, I'd suppose. A bit raw but that may not only have been part of the charm, but intentional. It lacked a bit of the spectacle but that might've been the point. Absurdity is difficult to pull off because too much loses the point and yet too little feels strained. Oh! But I wanted to know what you thought."

"My question," he said, knowing his tone was arched from his uncertainty but unable to refrain or redirect himself tonight. "My question, although not without interest in the performance or spectacle we just witnessed, but my question was what exactly was that beverage?"

"Absinthe. I should've warned you. Are you not familiar with it? No, of course you're not. I'm sorry. Are you all right? It can overwhelm a bit."

"No, I'm quite fine. Better now I suppose. Do you consume it regularly?"

"I've had it before. Like most things, it has its time and place."

"I'd certainly say that was one of them."

"Precisely. But I do apologize. I should have warned you. I'm naughty, I suppose. Perhaps I should have absconded with one of those crops, for later."

"Lydia."

She looked at him, the bright sprite. "Every backside can do with a good tender warming from time to time. If you haven't tried it, don't condemn the idea. But, Henry, what did you think?"

After a bit of walking he said, "It was very strange. Somewhat like a dream where things are vivid and make full sense while they're occurring but when you wake the order of it all is a bit confused. And the sense drains away."

194

"Quite good," she said. "Certainly something of what they were trying to achieve. Pressing boundaries, that sort of thing. I saw quite a bit of it in Paris last winter. Some much more sophisticated, of course. But then there's the bitchy part, as well. People form factions, take sides, apply names to different ideas and soon the raw gist is lost and it all becomes a failure or success of a philosophy. Which makes for wonderful arguments but hurts the work, eventually."

"So you consider it art?"

She looked at him. "Until it becomes pure commerce, yes. Didn't it shake you up and make you think about things a bit differently? Of course it did. Now, what do you say? How about a coffee?"

"That's an excellent idea."

"And then," she paused. "I have another idea."

"Jesus," he said. "Lydia."

"That's my name," she said, laughing.

An hour later he sat in a stuffed chair, looking down on the nighttime fever of the Dam. He had a glass of wine draped down in one hand, the bottle on a lamp-lit table across the bed, waiting for her to come from the bath. His shoes and jacket were off, his tie rolled into a jacket pocket, his shirt opened a couple of buttons down his chest. The dahlia from his lapel lay on the sideboard dresser, near black in the shadow, the door to the bath and dressing room ajar, the scent of soaps swimming in the air. The coffee and then the wine helped regain himself and he was calm, easy, relaxed. Waiting for the woman to come from her bath. He again recalled the nudity of the young girls and thought But we are born sexual, without it we'd be nothing at all. He tasted the wine, a dense dark slow velvet in his mouth and throat.

She came naked and rosy from the bath and stood before him, then slowly turned so her back, her spine and shoulderblades like wings under her skin dropping down to the sudden white of her buttocks and then her thighs and legs. He stood and held her shoulders, his face a moment in the damp hair at her nape, then turned her toward him.

Twenty

*T*he Morozov compositions were both solo cello suites and although Henry had doubted him, the Russian had made a shrewd choice—the array of notes on the staff at first glance seemed bewildering when he gave them to Henry—once back in the apartment he realized the time signatures were simple and both pieces were in D major, which Henry had more or less mastered rehearsing his scales. The first piece was called simply *Exile* but it turned out to be the second, *Elegy*, that captivated him, something in the structure, the tempo and the sonorous lovely ringing notes. He thought, as he had before, learn one at a time until you plateau, then take up the other, knowing that then when he returned to the first his plateau would be gone and he'd press on with the tortured process until, if not mastery, at least another, cleaner, version broke through. And so his afternoons and evenings became elegiac although not melancholy—the beauty of the music was restful and his progress most satisfying. And he spent much time, the most time perhaps since he'd acquired the instrument, content in his rooms, pressing his focus upon the cello and the cello responded and gave Henry long periods of beauty and peace, not thoughtless but with his thought tempered and balanced from the earlier swings of disposition and flits of uncertainty.

At least for that time he slept easier.

He caught himself, one evening while his ear were still aswirl with a near-perfect version of the *Elegy*, supping on cheese and bread, a window-ledge chilled glass of Genever, while the teakettle whistled on the gas ring, wondering if the Russian's story was true, thinking that a man of his professed accomplishments would most certainly have not only found something better than an itinerant impoverished hiding place but also for a moment thinking that if these two pieces were what he was capable of, music clearly by name written after leaving the Soviet Union of Republics, if Morozov was close to what he claimed to be. Or to have been. What other works might he be capable of?

He glanced over at the sketch of cod and below that the desk with its stacks of paper, the odd fragments of notes he'd compiled but nothing more. Certainly not the months-old prepassage vague notion that once in this strange place he would be lit by some fire previously unknown and thus from his pen would swarm words into worlds and so transform him from teacher to something closer to what he revered. If only a minor effort. But instead, nothing. He poured hot water over the dark dense smoky tea Lydia had introduced him to and left it to steep. And lifted the cello, wiped the back of the neck with the soft chamois and sat and played the *Elegy* once more. And then drank his cup of tea.

So on an early winter night he sat in a strange city halfway around the world and gently buffed his cello, his tears falling slow and lightly, momentarily blotching the finish until he polished them off, crying for the first time in months, alone and sad and lonely and missing his wife who would never come again and missing the miracle of a woman who had come into and then now out of his life and also, inexplicably, for the man who had brought the cello to life for him. Who had conferred that late possibility upon Henry and insisted on perseverance. To the point of offering up his own works in what Henry knew was a last best effort to keep him, this modest beginner, filled with hope.

Twenty-one

One evening in late August Lydia had retired early and alone, citing a headache and fatigue. Henry, wending his way thoughtfully slow in the evening made limpid with the first cool touch of late summer tilting toward autumn, considered with mild amazement the simple fact that it had been over two months since he'd been separated from her for more than a few hours and only a handful of nights and those early on. And so cast back over the past few days and cautiously allowed that now in hindsight perhaps she'd been a bit less engaged, mildly distracted at random, inauspicious times. He made his way along what he considered his lovely canal and climbed those three flights, let himself in and opened the windows both in front and the two small ones in the bedroom that looked out over a dormer ledge of the building next door, where several times he and Lydia had spotted what they first thought was a neighborhood cat but when Lydia had tried to seduce it with a tidbit of cheese it had fled and later they saw it with the remains of a pigeon, a feral cat. But it would sit and watch them, grooming itself with its tongue as long as neither approached the window.

As he sat too, now, alone and wanting nothing, full from a good dinner and not interested in tea or a drink, the smack of comprehension coming upon him not as a single large wave but a rapid succession. Constant companions who rapidly and without guile became more than that despite resistance from both, an inescapable lovely

magnetism that he utterly trusted, and trusted even more as her stories slowly had come forth—a woman who had embraced solitude
on a deeply personal level, her guard against further damage, for despite her independence, and face-into-the-wind take on life, wariness
was as much a part of her as a necessity. And how she moved through
the world, unattached and yet surrounded by and surrounding herself with an array of people she clearly valued but would only let so
close. Henry, pausing, wondered how many of those people considered Lydia a dear close friend and guessed the number was considerably more than her own tally. Although he now understood her tally
was marked in a book unlike that of others. Which brought him neatly
to the contradiction central to not only his knowledge of her but his
experience, not only of herself but himself as well.

They were inseparable. And if he'd failed to consider the meaning of this condition, the ramification upon not only his heart but
hers, he understood that also. She hadn't encouraged him to edge
sideways a bit at a time back into life but allowed him, without his
even knowing it, to partake fully. And he forgave himself. It had been
simply the most wonderful time, the summer swift and fleet as if the
years had dropped away from him. A gift, lovely, pure and true.

What he'd missed was how she might view all this. Especially the
lengthening time. Which, beyond the pleasure and those murmured
endearments of passion, the constant touch, the ease of reaching down
or across a table for her hand, he'd offered nothing. Because he was
content and enchanted. As she appeared to be but then again, the
question. What was he offering her?

It was a short argument, neither won nor lost but nevertheless
revealed what was called for, and then a palpable exhilaration—he
would strike out now, just past dusk, surely she must be awake, wrestling no doubt with her own version of this same question. But then
stopped himself. Let her have the night. Most importantly, let him
give her the night, so when he went to her in the morning she'd accept his gravitas, his sincerity and the depth of his intent.

In bed a light wash of guilt over Olivia came to him, that he could find new love so effortlessly, so quickly it still seemed in some ways, a literal lifetime in others and then she came to him. No specter but the direct voice of long knowledge. A younger woman, she might say. You rascal! But he knew she would want this for him, knew his essential nature so well as to know he was not a man to live alone. And Lydia was not so much younger, well beyond the point where those few years made any great difference.

In the morning he rose and bathed and as slowly as he could made his way to the Dam, one hand in his trouser pocket, his jacket pushed back as he fingered her key. Up the broad busy steps of the Kras and through the grand foyer to the elevators and waited with silent glowing satisfaction as the elevator boy rode him up to her fifth floor. Then down the narrow hallway with the rococo plaster ceiling to her door. Where he stopped, the key in his pocket stilled. There, hanging by a braided silk cord over her doorknob the small placard in Dutch, French and English. Please Do Not Disturb. She'd never done this before, even when they'd stayed up most of the night and intended to sleep past noon—the hotel staff knew Lydia Pearce would call down when she was ready for coffee and breakfast—the beginning of her day. The maids would be alerted only after she'd left for the afternoon. So there could only be one person this message was intended for.

The heave of mistrust. Was she alone? And then profound disappointment in himself—perhaps she truly was sick. But no, as he was even then backing quietly on the thick carpet down the hall. The message, the exact message was superbly clear: She was very serious and wanted him, trusted him, to know that.

Because he didn't know what else to do he wandered among the shops along the north side of the big square and picked up his usual newspapers and found a bakery with a handful of mostly empty tables and settled in with coffee and almond-paste pastries. The air was cool off the cobbles from the night but the morning sun was up enough to warm him. He scanned the papers which might as well have been printed in Sanskrit, even the *Tribune*. But it was fine sitting and the coffee was rich and strong and as he watched the flow and flurry of human activity grow on the square as the day truly came on he felt more and more he was in the right place at exactly the right time, on a mission imperative and fundamental to his life. There were no further refinements to be made, no bother to go over what he must say, what needed finally to be said. He was waiting. For how long he didn't know, or what the signal that the wait had ended might be. But Henry Dorn had thrown himself over to the fates if not God and so was certain all that was required was vigilance and staunchness.

A little later, scattering people and heedless, three trucks rolled in and made a small semicircle across the Dam from where he sat. More men then he'd thought possible swarmed out of the cabs and pulled tarpaulins off two of the trucks, revealing steel and wooden trusses in several assemblages of like size. The men were dark—Spanish or Mediterranean, in rough trousers and sleeveless undershirts stained with sweat and grease and they began unloading the trucks, arranging the multisided pieces in groups. Then in teams with heavy wrenches and hammers they went to work and began to construct large V-shaped segments, the steel trusses making the legs of the V and the wide tops joined with lightly arched wooden connectors, the men swarming fast and without extraneous motions, handrolled cigarettes clamped between their teeth and as they worked he could hear their short barked calls to one another and whatever language was being spoken was far different than any he might have even a passing knowledge of. Finally the Vs were laid out in a circle about the square, the bottoms all pointed in. He bought another coffee and paid his bill, leaving his unread papers, and moved a bit closer to the trucks to watch. Where the speech was even more strange and he realized these were gypsies. Then the tarpaulin was pulled partway back on the final truck and the men worked with cleated planks and block and tackle to gently bring to the ground a large single-stroke engine on a massive carriage and this they moved to just off center of the circle. Back under the final tarpaulin was a mound of curious rounded large objects. The men then began to work together fastening the constructed Vs together in sections and he began to see the outline as parts of a giant wheel. And began to know what he was witnessing.

As the sections were joined they also began to rise, lifted with much heavier ropes the thickness of a man's arm and giant blocks the size of a torso and as the giant wheel took shape up against the sky some of the workers scampered along those high edges to meet and guide the two edges into place, to fasten the struts that bridged the twin wheels to one large one. It might have taken an hour, a bit more, but there looming against the sky was the skeleton of a Ferris wheel. Then back on the ground the men worked again and suddenly there was a popping backfire as the engine came to life, a pause for it to settle and the men, now with most off to the side, lounging and smoking and passing small clay bottles among them, while closer to the wheel were two groups, most clearly the operators and the mechanics, as both moved back and forth making adjustments and then, finally, some peering up, others intent on the drive mechanism, one man pulled back a lever. There was a grinding as the engine labored and the wheel remained still and then slowly, ever so slowly, the contraption began to revolve. Sometimes halting and other times pitching forward and around too quickly as the mechanics darted in and out about the engine and the drive and twisted or loosened connections, one man crouched by the side of the engine, a cap tilted back on his head, his face ever skyward as his hands worked to gain control over the thrust and momentum of the engine and then, almost a miracle, the giant wheel began to revolve in a stately sedate fashion. The man with the lever halted the progress completely and then started it up again several times until the whole operation was as smooth and consistent as any orbit could be.

Finally the engine was idled back most all the way, the man who was clearly the crew boss if not the owner of the contraption took a seat up on the deck of one of the empty trucks and lit a cigar while all the rest but the operator swarmed to pull back the final tarpaulin and lifted down four by four the big wicker baskets and carried them over to mount them within the frame of the wheel. The baskets all had panel doors with a strap latch on the outside and all were mounted so the doors faced the operator. And so, bit by climbing bit, the empty baskets swaying gently as they rose, the Ferris wheel was completed.

And Henry Dorn had the most wonderful idea.

Intent as he'd been with this construction periodically he'd glanced up, not only at her window below the ranks of European flags flying along the face of the hotel, but also the steps and entry. So he'd seen when the shades on her windows had gone up and still he waited. And so also saw when she finally, late morning, ventured out and paused at the top of the steps, in an ice-blue summer dress, her hair buffeted by a breeze he couldn't feel, a full whipping helmet atop and above her head, and saw her glance around, looking not quite toward him. And he knew she'd spied him from her windows sometime earlier. So slowly, his eyes never leaving her face, he made his way across the Dam toward her, waiting to see when she'd sense his coming. His feet striking the cobbles unevenly, his brain afire. And then as he lifted a foot for the first step up, she turned a quiver of a turn and her eyes lit upon him.

"You're glowing this morning."

"Am I?" Her eyes seemed to flicker, then held fast. "Was that you crept up to my door earlier then scurried away?"

"I didn't scurry. And you had that sign on your doorknob."

"Did you think that was intended for you?"

"I assumed it was intended for everyone. Have you had breakfast?"

She made a tossed-away gesture. "A bit. How're you, Henry?" And laid a hand upon his arm.

"Well enough. I spent a good part of last evening thinking."

She cocked her head, a gentle study. "And did you reach conclusions?"

He smiled. "A dose of introspection that was a bit overdue, I believe."

She smiled also, without her usual vibrancy but with a serious-ness that led him to believe he was ever more than before on the right track. "And would you care to share that?"

"I would. But Lydia—"

"I have my own, you know."

"I wouldn't expect otherwise. We seem to've reached a serious moment, and about time—well, that's one conclusion drawn." He'd taken her hand and was leading her down the steps and out into the Dam, she leaning gently against him as was her wont. He went on. "But sitting out here, an idea came to me, something that would be just the right thing, a perfect prelude to this discussion."

"Is that so?" And he heard the rise, that lilt of curiosity and expectation.

"Indeed." And with a small elaborate flourish he indicated the Ferris wheel.

"You're joking."

"Not at all. And Lydia?"

"Henry?" Her eyes narrowed a bit, reassessing him. Or revealing some unease—he didn't know which but knew he was correct and pressed on, turning to stand before her, taking both her hands in his.

"Watching the men construct this, I have to admit it took me a little while to even see what it was, because at first it was all just so many pieces laid out on the ground, watching them put it together and then realizing what it was, I thought, much as I've been think-ing, Yes, what you need is right in front of you. And I know what we need to talk about but what could serve us better then to ride those slow revolutions? Because, because, Lydia, it's so much of what you've revealed to me. But knowing this takes nothing from it, does it? In fact, armed with such knowledge, wouldn't it be the most perfect bridge between where we were yesterday and where we're going today? I'm right you know. A small blessing is what it is." He paused and finished, "Oh, Lydia, isn't that what we've given each other?"

"Henry, I'm not sure—"

"No," he interrupted. "You know I'm right. Now come along."

There was a short queue of children loading excitedly into the baskets, nothing, he thought, like the crush that would no doubt soon appear. The alignment of events was impeccable, bolstering his notion that it was a day of portents and he gently placed a hand against the small of her back.

Lydia was red-flushed as she settled on the seat beside him. She squeezed his arm. "You," she said.

The basket pressed them together, rocking gently as it ascended backwards so the great buildings of the Dam rose around them. And then those precious few moments when they were stopped, the basket swaying at the very top of the wheel and in the glassine morning the city spread out far as they could see, the spires of the churches and the peaks of ancient watchtowers and beneath these the dim haze of the lower levels—the vast concentric rings spreading out toward the horizon smudge, here and there the canals visible but mostly the leaf-lined bands of green of the trees and the four- and five- and six-story buildings, all as a joined plain far below, as if the city had not grown and extended by the usual enlargement of convenience but of necessity. As if the plans for this had been laid within that first small village thousands of years ago beside the intrepid bold flooding sea and the occupants had followed less a plan of men than one of the land, the only plan acceptable to that destroying sea. Because there had been no other way to build this city. And out of all this had come a considerable, near unfathomable beauty.

And so Henry Dorn was riding a Ferris wheel in the middle of Amsterdam side by side with a woman he loved. In a soft fusion of heat and light that took away all doubt of the grown man's delight in riding this miraculous contraption with this woman that would, he knew, be with him all of his days. Let this day unfold. Let it burn itself, scorch itself into his memory, become a fusion of his being. The wheel had lifted them high above themselves.

He put his arm over her shoulders and drew her close but suddenly shy and yet committed he kept his gaze forward as he spoke.

"Lydia, where do I begin? I'm nervous and you know, I've never been nervous with you before and that's as fine a place to begin as I can see. We're comfortable and we've been comfortable since the beginning. The only hesitations I've had with you were bits of a guilt that had no place, that in fact I realized last night that my wife if she were able would be amused by—rather than honoring her with those bits of guilt I was failing to pay attention to you. So, yes, I've gone fairly head over heels and had a most wonderful damned time doing so and in the simplest sense of things that's what I want to continue doing. But there's something great, something vast that I've failed to take into account. We're not children, Lydia, but for two and a half months I've been living as if we were. Oh, which is a roundabout way of saying that it seems to me, if I were in your place, I'd be rightfully wondering Where is this all going? What exactly does this man think of me, expect of me?" He looked at her. "Shall I go on?"

Her raised face seemed drained, pale but her eyes were large and just loud enough to be heard above the grinding and swoop of the wheel she said, "Yes. Please."

"Are you all right?"

She pursed her mouth tight and nodded.

"I'd think you must be wondering if perhaps you're a ladder that allows me to climb fully back to life again and once there, where does that leave you? I'd think you must be wondering what intentions or ideas I might have regarding you and the future. Your future, my future. Our future. Most simply put, not just where are we going but what might that we, be?"

"Henry," she said, a mild plea he heard as her own nervousness.

"No," he said. "I'm into it now and not going to stop. If I'm wrong I'll learn that soon enough but let me finish. You told me yourself you'd stopped trusting love long ago, you'd closed a door for yourself. And I think it's been opened back up and you don't know how or why you should trust that, or me with that. And I've been heedless, even as you've told and even if you didn't intend to tell me what I've now finally heard. But I'm right and I know I am. Lydia, if you want to get married this afternoon we'll do it. If you want to wait a year or six months or if you'd prefer a formal engagement or if you want only these, words, this acknowledgement, until you want more or if you never want more than this, I just want you to know. That I love you. That I love you and want to spend the rest of my life with you—"

"Henry."

"And that whatever that means, however you wish it to be, is how I also want it to be. It's been a long time and I've only done this once before and don't expect to ever do it again. But it's clear to me that the time has come."

And she was suddenly pulling away as he turned to face her, the words already out of his mouth, "For us to . . ." and stopped. She was sweating and green and looked wretched, leaning against the side of the basket.

"My God," he said. "What's wrong? Is it that awful?"

"I'm going to be sick," she said. And then was.

He cleaned her up best he could and put his jacket around her shoulders and got her back to her rooms in the hotel. Where he waited, nervous and worried, as she shut herself in the bathroom and bathed. She refused his insistence to call a doctor. She came out wrapped in a towel and climbed into bed, asking him to close the curtains. He did so and once again pressed her to let him bring a doctor.

She smiled, a wan effort and said, "No, no. I eat like a horse and can hold my drink with anyone but time to time this happens to me. Please." Her smile thinly held. "I knew I wasn't fully recovered but wanted to see you. And have to say, but for that damned Ferris wheel, you were very charming, Henry."

"I wasn't trying to charm."

She rested her head back fully into the pillows. "I know that," she finally replied. "Now, if you can bear it, come give my forehead a kiss and let me rest. I'll see you later, probably late afternoon. And if I don't feel better by then, I'll send a boy around with a note."

"If you aren't better by then, you really should see a doctor."

"I'll be better. I will. I'll bet you dinner."

He bent and ignored her forehead and kissed her on the lips. "I'm going to worry about you."

"I'll be fine. I just need a little more rest. And Henry?"

"Lydia?"

"I do love you too, you know."

Midafternoon, much sooner than he'd hoped or expected, brought a tentative knock on his door. Since leaving her, he'd gone over and over the events of the morning, trying to recall exactly what he'd said and as the day went on it seemed more and more that he'd made a mess of things. Even her final profession seemed in recall to be kindness more than full confession. Of course, he reminded himself, she was sick. And then the knock and his heart raced as he lifted from the chair where he'd been unable to read, thinking it certainly was a boy from the hotel, with either a message imploring him to stay away or that she'd had a doctor in or even been taken to hospital, and crossing in sock-feet he had a moment when he found himself hoping it was either of the last rather than the first.

But there she was, dressed for the pleasant afternoon beyond his windows, her face bright and glowing, all the health in the world restored to her.

"Oh my dear," he said. "I was so worried. Are you all right?"

She leaned up and kissed him. "I'm so sorry, Henry. Yes, I'm feeling much better. And I was worried about you, also. Such a gruesome thing. You were so kind."

"Are you sure you're well? Should you be out? Have you eaten?"

She touched his cheek and said, "I had tea and toast with a poached egg some time ago and it's sitting quite nicely. In fact, I've got quite an appetite again but am going to starve it for a bit. Hold out for a decent dinner."

"Well, then," he said, suddenly awkward. "Would you like to come in?"

She said, "Henry, you were quite magnificent this morning. You were quite correct in much of what you had to say—so right that in another man I'd think you'd been calculating that moment a long time. And I know you weren't. But I'm all fluttery with it and so walking over I tried to decide how to respond and still be true to both of us."

After a moment he said, "And?"

"You like boats, don't you? At least, I know you've spent a great deal of time about them."

He cocked his head, no choice but to smile even in his gathering confusion and he replied, "Not about them so much as upon them. But what are you getting at?"

"Very simple. I made a detour and engaged a man with a small powerboat for the afternoon. I thought we might tour the city that way. It's delightful and something we haven't done, although it has crossed my mind, all at the wrong times and then forgotten."

He interrupted. "Do you truly think that's such a good idea?"

"I'm perfectly fine now. Remember this isn't the raging ocean I'm speaking of but a slow steady glide along the canals. And then I'd like very much to have dinner with you and the rest of the evening as well."

He took his time and then said, "What you're saying . . ."

She nodded but also took one of his hands between hers and pressed it. "I want very much to be with you. And I'm not ruling anything out but what I don't want is for you to expect me to respond to everything you said this morning. All I know is I'm not ready now." Then she stopped and looked down and rubbed her fingers together, a wringing gesture. Her face came back up. "I ask too much, don't I?"

"No," he said. "You don't." Then smiled and said, "So where is this boat?"

Twenty-two

*H*e'd gone around to Morozov's in mid December for his regular Tuesday lesson in high spirits, the compositions Morozov had given him the week before had proven to be a wonderful remedy for his Merk plateau. It was a pleasantly crisp clear early winter day.

The door was not just locked as usual but outside door and jamb were joined by a heavy old strap hinge, with an equally heavy padlock through the eye. Not Morozov's doing, but the action of an angry landlord discovering his tenant has fled, Henry frowning, wondering just how much in arrears Morozov might've been. Then he thought of the letter the cellist had received from his wife, the uncertain but undeniable excitement the Russian had allowed himself, the hope that his initial reactions to the revolution would be proven wrong. And then it came—the man was trying to make it to that new home in the Ukraine in time for Christmas, the Orthodox Christmas that fell in January, more than a month away. And so the Russian's reasoning was clear—the faster he responded to the no-doubt sanctioned letter from his wife the fewer potential delays he might face.

At least, Henry hoped that was what had happened. He'd never elaborated on them, but the cellist had also hinted at other, darker fears. For a moment he wondered what he might do and then realized he could do nothing at all.

He stood a moment, as always the wheeling gulls, their sickle cries, familiar and this afternoon discomforting. Morozov had, he guessed, already determined his own course the week before and the gift of his music was his encouragement, his urging to Henry to continue, to make his own way. There would be other cello and violin teachers in Amsterdam. It was up to him.

So he trudged home. And was halfway there when the full force of the date came to him. Self-absorbed and just barely conscious that he was facing a solitary and melancholy Christmas himself, he'd overlooked his family. And knew also that just like the weekly letters that arrived, all but the last unanswered from his mother, as well as the less frequent but still considerable cheery news-filled letters from Alice and Polly, scrawled notes from granddaughters slipped in on the same onionskin postal paper and finally the two brief but kind letters from Doyle over the course of the long autumn, just as he knew those had found their way to him, he guessed that any day now he would find slips directing him to the main postal office near the Centraal Station in order to pick up parcels, packages, perhaps modest in size given the price of such things but certainly with thoughtful riches and reminders tucked within.

Aloud, just as a wagon of fish, great frozen slabs with the open eyes of ocean depths passed around him, he said, "We'll see about that, won't we?"

Next morning he was up early, bathed and shaved with the frustratingly capricious cold water through the hot spigot and then off to the American Express office. Certain he still had enough time for train delivery and because he didn't know Chicago or Utica as he did Elmira, he dictated telegram orders to a handful of establishments there, with his selections and instructions for how each order was to be split and shipped, then a telegram to First Elmira asking them to authorize these payments, knowing, cheered, that this telegram was likely unnecessary but wanting everything to proceed as smoothly as possible. Especially with his granddaughters, his directives were made in trust—trust that he would be known and understood and all energy possible would be expended upon his vague but stated requests. For his mother he sent a separate telegram to the import company in Boston, instructing that two one pound tins of Hu-Kwa tea be sent to her. Probably, given her habit of drying used tea and brewing again with triple density from old leaves, amounting to something like a five year supply. He wished he could add a note asking her to, just this once, forego that propensity but it was enough to know she would love the tea.

He arranged to have the confirming telegrams delivered to his apartment and then walked home through a stinging wet snow in a graceful state of mind. That evening he went out, not to one of his usual brown bars but to a restaurant he'd last been in with Lydia. It didn't matter this night that he was dining alone. He was expansive and peacefully exuberant and had a fine three-course dinner and almost all of a bottle of wine. For much of the time he was enchanted by the couple at the table next to his, a man and woman slightly younger than himself but his source of delight was the full-sized poodle, a ginger-haired dog with a close cropped coat who sat erect and intensely alert but never moving between the couple who were leaned over the table in their own absorbed conversation although without apparent forethought, one or the other would pluck something from their plate and hold it down, open-handed, for the dog. Who lifted the morsel from the offered fingers as delicately as if the dog's tongue was a surgical instrument. Finishing a dessert of apples and crusted caramelized brown sugar, he wished Lydia could've seen the dog.

As so often, he couldn't sleep. After much turning and fretting and stretching he rose and poured himself a cold Genever from the windowsill and read a bit. Old words. The Keats he would've recited to Lydia on the suddenly long-ago afternoon.

> *But when the melancholy fit shall fall*
> *Sudden from heaven like a weeping cloud,*
> *That fosters the droop-headed flowers all,*
> *And hides the green hill in an April shroud;*
> *Then glut thy sorrow on a morning rose,*

Or on the rainbow of the salt sand-wave,
Or on the wealth of globed peonies;
Or if thy mistress some rich anger shows,
Emprison her soft hand and let her rave,
And feed deep, deep upon her peerless eyes.

In the morning, for the first time, he walked over to the Hotel Krasnapolsky. He wended his way through the grand lobby, crystal-lit, marble columned, with thick Persian rugs, past seas of women and men as well in winter furs, somehow an altogether different place than he'd known in the summer and fall until he came to the concierge and, overcoming his gruffness, asked if Lydia Pearce happened to be in, or, if not, did the hotel have a forwarding address for her.

The man, in his green uniform with bits of gold and red braid, handsome in the way of hotel employees, looked up and smiled. "Mr. Dorn. So very nice to see you, sir. No, I'm afraid Miss Pearce is not with us just now. Let me check," and made a small show of leafing through a heavily embossed notebook. "No, sir. I'm sorry. We don't show a return date for her. And she's never left her itinerary with us, or even if she did, I'm sure you'd understand that would be confidential. Although she does always return to us! I'm sorry but it's Professor Dorn, isn't it? Forgive me. Is there any other assistance I can provide this morning, sir?"

Henry mouthed polite inanities and fled.

Back to his apartment. Barren, cold even with the heat hissing and the stark brittle light falling through the windows, nothing monkish about it but rather a decrepitude of spirit and soul. His pathetic short shelf of books. The sheaf of unread scribblings, not even notes, certainly not the scholarly or creative project he'd vainly and silently hoped would come to him. The ridiculous cello. Even his father's sketch—so long cherished as memento or paternal talisman but now starkly revealed as only a piece of fine amateur draftsmanship. Carried everywhere throughout his adult life as if in someway his father might, through the son, enjoy the greater fruits of success, or at least the world. Only to wash up here, a place, Henry had to admit that almost certainly would've served his father better than it had himself.

He dug through the trash and found yesterday's *Tribune*. It was December 12th. And he realized there was no reason why not, in fact all reasonable possibility that if he got cracking, he could get a boat and ride the rough North Atlantic and make it in time for Christmas. There was plenty of time to walk over to the Amsterdam office of the Holland American Line and find out what opportunities he had. As long as he could get a berth alone, he told himself, he didn't care how he traveled—steerage or some base equivalent would be fine. In that frenzy of thought he pulled out his big hooped steamer trunk and opened it for the first time in months. At the bottom were a couple of starched white dress shirts, still in their papers from the Elmira cleaners. He'd never bothered, in those first days, to unpack them— two others already hung in the narrow closet, many times washed and pressed. Well, good. One less thing to bother with. If he took some care they should serve him just fine for the voyage. He imagined the boat, decked out for Christmas no doubt, festive and cheerful. Taking him home.

Which was when he sank back on his heels, his hands resting flat on the light dust of the floor. Which was, exactly, where? Neither Polly nor Alice had mentioned any plans of making the journeys, long, and much longer, to spend the holidays with Mary and Doyle. They were close but Henry realized his absence was a deterrence—how many explanations had been offered his own granddaughters about where their grandfather was, and why. And when he might return. And even if he went to Elmira anyway, what then? After the holidays. Travel to Utica and then Chicago for, between the respective husbands' work and the granddaughters back in school, what would at first be a welcome visit but so soon after the holidays very quickly intrusive, plain and simple, denials aside. He could practically hear both Alice and then Polly finding the right time, some late but not too late evening to catch him alone so conveniently and question him about his plans. He rose from his squat, his knees biting protest, wiping his dusty hands on his trousers. But now, just now, beyond his family, spread and scattered and thin, what would he be returning to? Boiled down, as Olivia used to say, where was home?

The cottage. But only for summers. For now, perhaps forever. Unless some grand project of writing overcame him he couldn't see himself in hermetic existence there, taking the train to Elmira far too often to alleviate his loneliness. And beyond that he had no idea.

And so he remained. Waiting for Lydia. Difficult as it had been to accept, he'd told himself he understood and would grant her the patience she'd so clearly needed and the absolute lack of any sense of time had not bothered him. But now, now alone, barren and brutally alone, he finally asked the question. The one not allowed. But how long? When did continued absence and silence become the answer itself?

He walked across the apartment and stood before the windows. Above the frozen canal, above the buildings, high skiffs of clouds sailed the dense late-afternoon blue. Below, the small patch of city spread. Outward to a place he knew. That he among thousands knew and yet he knew alone. There was time, he told himself. If he stretched far enough back, the reason in entirety, he'd come here. Those letters for that life he'd always more or less envisioned, those could be written and sent just after the first of the year. A good time, he knew. A time when others who looked ahead in life and practice would be considering their options, their needs and vacancies, for next fall, next year. Meanwhile he could, for the first time ever he realized, read Chaucer for nothing at all but pleasure. Perhaps, he told himself, depending how things worked out, he could take a springtime trip to England, to Canterbury. And the idea quickened him—not just Canterbury but the width and breadth of the isle, the island of words, of literature.

Meanwhile, with purpose restored, he was not abandoning hope. Abandoning Lydia.

But between now and then there was one thing he had to do. An homage to be made.

He pulled the overhead chain for the light, needed at this sudden falling-dark time of year. Unstrapped the canvas case and lifted out the cello. He took his time, buffing it with the soft chamois, especially the rounded underside of the neck where his striving hand always left a smear of anxious perspiration. Then extended the end pin and tuned, plucking the richly vibrant strings and gently twisting the pegs which once seemed so cumbersome for tuning. He tightened the bow, ran a quick coat of rosin upon it and then bent again, holding the cello safely and easily upright between his spread legs, placing the sheet music on the dented perfect old stand. He read through in his mind the opening bars and then slipped back to the first bar and lifted the bow. About to bring it down in the gentle rising riding swoop of the opening measure of Morozov's somber and tearfully lovely cello suite, *Exile.*

Twenty-three

Next morning after their splendid peaceful canal tour and equally easy dinner and night, they left the hotel midmorning, Lydia with a quiet determination that alerted Henry she was finally ready to respond to his declarations but with a gentleness in her usual bold stride that hinted at something else, as well. They paused at the flower stalls where on impulse she bought a great bundle of sunflowers, red and yellow and black, and all colors in between. She handed it to him, telling him it was for his apartment. That he needed to keep flowers. The first she'd bought him long since gone.

They walked until she led him along another narrow alley, this time entering into a small garden courtyard, with some of the largest and oldest trees he'd seen in Amsterdam, along with hedges and flanks and ranks of flowers; in beds, climbing the walls, on trellises, and covering several arbors. They sat on a bench beneath one of these, the brilliant cone of sunflowers set beside him. Butterflies drifted on fluttering wings.

"The truest beauty," he said.

She watched for a moment, pensive. "It's not something you can grab for, is it?"

"No," he said softly. "Even watchful, you can sometimes miss it." Then impulsively he went on. "We both seem to have moved forward. On that search, for true beauty, new beauty, new love. So surprising how that happens."

"This place here, this garden, it took someone, likely many people over the years, to construct it. And yet it's not grand or intended to be. In ways, it's the childhood garden that an adult would create. Children are happy with daisies in a field. Adults demand more."

"Sometimes too much."

"Yes," she said. "Then it ceases to be a pleasure and becomes an artifice."

He touched her arm, the thin dark hairs growing there and she wrapped her fingers in his. "But isn't there also a place for form? For boundaries of a sort? They don't always have to break down into squabbles. Take this garden—we agree I think that it's a formal evocation of some elemental, you suggested the childish, but elemental works just as well—it's a formal creation not duplicating anything real so much as something dreamed. And so holds a perfection of its own. A sonnet. A sonnet in landscape. And the sonnet is a pure thing that has indeed changed over the years but always has its central essential meter and line, even to varying degrees, subjects."

He stopped. Her eyes wide and snapping bright, delighted upon him.

"Do I amuse you?" he asked, smiling.

"Of course." She smiled also. "Sonnets. Oh how they tortured me in school! Shakespeare and his Dark Lady. But it was a pleasant torture." She paused and said, "Henry, is there a sonnet you had in mind? When you were speaking so passionately I thought I could see one just behind your eyes, perhaps wanting to break out altogether. Will you recite for me?"

"Are you acquainted with John Keats?"

"I'm not that old. But I know his work. Do you have a favorite? Will you recite it for me?"

He stood, his head bowed under the bower. "No," he said. "Suddenly I feel foolish."

She stood and turned away and walked to the end of the arbor and studied some blue and white blossoms vined there. She reached a finger and drew a flower to her nose. He followed her, waiting, silent. Then she said, "Henry?"

"Yes," he said, and she turned. Her face struggling to be composed, stricken.

"Much of what you said yesterday mirrors my own thoughts . . . my love . . . for you . . . And when you spoke of how I might feel . . . of my concerns . . . that was extraordinary. No one has ever done that before—"

"Lydia—"

"Please, love. Allow me. To say this. It's not something I wish to do but have to do. For many reasons. Some of which you know and some which you can't . . . Things I have to work out on my own. Things that, and you have to trust me, are better if I work out alone—"

"I can't imagine anything you can't tell me."

"Henry, please. This is difficult enough."

"I'm sorry."

"There's nothing to apologize for. It doesn't make me happy to tell you this, but as I said, my soul demands it."

"You're frightening me, Lydia."

"Oh, love," she said and collapsed against him. He held her, trembling, the trembling running through both, then bent and whispered her name in her hair and she lifted her mouth and they kissed—as if to halt everything that was unstoppable.

Then she pulled away. And placed her hands above his elbows and stepped back to hold him at arm's length, to make this small distance definitive.

She said, "I'm going to Paris, Henry."

Blankly he said, "What? For how long? I'll come if you want . . ."

She dug into her shoulder purse and pulled out a cigarette and lighter, dropping the lighter which he bent to retrieve and saw the cigarette was broken by her struggle to get it free and she tossed that off and got another and he struck the wheel. She exhaled smoke and plucked the lighter from his fingers and returned it to her bag. And as she blew smoke again, tipping her mouth so the smoke went past, above his head, he saw composure settle back upon her. He felt he was witnessing death once again. The strange numbness as if he was elevated slightly above and to the side of himself.

"I don't know how long. Several weeks at least, quite possibly a couple of months. Because I have to figure out what all this means and I can't do that when I'm around you. Which you should consider a good thing. And there are parts that are just mine. At least for now. It's been so delightful, so damned wonderful but it can't continue as it's been and you know that. It's not only who I am but who you are as well. Who we are together. It scares me and exhilarates me and Henry I'm not twenty years old as you pointed out yesterday and this is what I need to do. So I'm going to Paris. To sort myself out, you can say. And if you know me as well as I think you do, you'll understand. But there's also this—I think it's something you need as well. Even if you think you don't."

"I don't," he said.

Softly she said, "But I must."

"I can't talk you out of it, can I. That's clear. Oh, Lydia. My chest aches."

"Mine does too, Henry."

"So," he paused. "When are you leaving?"

She pressed her fingers against her eyes and took them away. Just above a cracking whisper she said, "Seven fifteen. The seven-fifteen."

Stunned speechless he gazed at her. She held his gaze, a terrible tremble in the air between them. Finally he said, "Seven fifteen? In the morning?"

And something shrouded her as she drew herself upright. "No, love," she said. "This evening."

Then moved and held him, holding each other, silent, both knowing that for now they'd moved irreversibly beyond words.

Last thing, as he was ready to walk her back to her hotel, he caught himself and for the shortest of moments let free her hand as he retrieved the sunflowers.

He'd let them sit in their big jar until the water first went green and then daily dropped its level until the water was gone, the greenery long since rotted back, until even the rotted ends of the stems had dried in the jar and the flowerheads had lost most of their petals but for the few that remained, dried themselves by luck or chance holding on. And weeks more before he'd finally dumped those in the trash and washed out the jar and put it high upon a shelf.

Twenty-four

*H*e was coming in from errands, primarily picking up laundry but also a small sack of Christmas treats, fresh dates, a pastry with almond paste, a small tin of candied orange slices, and it had come to him to ask about and determine where he might go to church on Christmas Eve, not certain he would but knowing it would be preferable to sitting alone, this while out among the crowds where suddenly Father Christmases were appearing and it seemed people were more brightly colored, the skaters along the brushed-clean canals more exuberant, even the older men and women in their stately glides and then, there, just inside the entryway at the foot of the stairs, jutting from the mailbox numbered three was an envelope of unmistakable blue. If other women traveled with their own stationery, there was but one he knew.

He had to set down his grocery sack and cotton laundry bag to lift it free. Again, he recognized the raggedy penmanship but was most struck by the lack of a return address, although the Paris postmark and stamp fit his expectation. He stood holding it, nigh giddy but shaking, the letter trembling in his fingers. She'd written. There had never been a promise of a letter, his expectation and hope simply of her arrival. Suddenly that lack of a return address was ominous as if contained within were her final words—a decision had been reached. He slipped it into his overcoat pocket and made his way up the stairs.

Once inside he set the envelope on his writing table and with slowed deliberate motions put his laundry away and his abruptly meager treats on a shelf above the counter, next to his tin of coffee and the hard bread and butter dish. He took up the letter again, dug his penknife from the fob pocket of his vest and opened the small blade. He paused one last time and told himself regardless of her words, he'd continue with his plans for the remainder of the winter and spring. He'd grown excited about the idea of England and reminded himself when that time came, whatever was within the letter would be far behind him. And neatly slit the top and lifted out the single folded sheet, opened it and read.

My dear Henry,

I hope this letter finds you still in Amsterdam. If not, then you'll have made the decision you deem best.

I've carefully and slowly considered my condition and situation regarding you, and feel that ample time has passed for you to have done the same. I've examined my emotions and thought carefully and, I admit, cautiously about you, our summer together and the declarations you made at the time. All of which was unlike anything I'd experienced before and remains so. And thus, on many fronts, I believe the time has come for us to reunite, even if that reunion results in an inevitable final parting of ways.

I trust that if you're reading this, you also will have come to your own conclusions concerning the possibilities for the future, and that you will remain firm in your convictions when we meet again. This is most important to me and hopefully is to you also, prior to my return, prior to our meeting again face to face.

I'll arrive in Amsterdam some time on the afternoon of 16 December. There is some sort of rail strike, as it seems there always is these days, and so the timetables and schedules mean nothing. And because I don't know if you'll even receive this, let alone what time I may arrive, I ask that you not attempt to meet me at the station. What I think best is for me to take a taxicab directly to your apartment.

If I don't find you there I'll proceed as usual to my suite at the Krasnapolsky. Where I'll settle in for the winter. And dear Henry, if this letter should chase you to some far end of the earth, only pause to read it and remember for a moment what we gave each other and then let life proceed apace. Life, Henry, I've learned is relentless and wonderful and you showed and gave me much of this understanding. Part of which is that we are always falling forward into the future. If you're not there, don't return for me. Because, my love, you won't find me.

Lydia

He set the letter down. She was coming back. She was returning, here, directly to him. Tomorrow afternoon. He kept reaching out to touch the unfolded blue paper upon his desk, as if his fingers might learn more somehow than the words seared into his brain. It was everything he'd hoped for and frighteningly, improbably, real. He didn't know what this meant and then did and then didn't. Her words so careful, clear and precise. Certainly Lydia had arrived at conclusions. And what had he done, beyond miss her terribly and wish her there at impossible times and plug along with some version of life? How had he resolved her? How had he come to terms with her inarguable declarations and decisions on that final September day when she already had her ticket, was already packed and met him for a walk and then the last bittersweet exchange at the flower stalls on Nieuwmarkt? Had he in fact done what she'd hoped for him?

He heated the last of the morning's coffee and drank the bitter brew. And thought, Yes, I think I have. Not following any course but my own. Including her if she'd have him.

I'm still here, aren't I? With plans stretching ahead. And she was returning. And so whatever was to come to pass, whatever hesitations she still held or not, whatever choices they might make together, he was now, surely, entering a new phase of his life. And to do so meant allowing what was already gone from the old life, finally go.

But it was never so easy. Even as he stood, his fingers resting on the open page of her letter and the array of work and errands and preparations needing to be accomplished in the twenty-four hours ahead, he also in more than a year and a half allowed through once again that final awful question, the one he'd done his best to seal and allow to be buried with the two caskets on that day two Mays ago. What guilt, what responsibility did he bear? Far too much and none at all was what he'd told himself on that raining day as his wife and son were lowered into the ground.

Now he had to admit it was not so simple at all, and never would be. He'd spoken with no one about it, not because it was unanswerable but because he'd feared the answer. The one time he'd skirted close had been with Doyle but Doyle's response, in its grace, munificence and heartfelt compassion had stopped him, had made him afraid not of what he wished to reveal and how he might then be judged but of the damage it might cause others. Some things must be borne alone. Never forgiven, no scar of flesh or time thick enough to cover or forget.

Twenty-five

*I*t had been the Saturday afternoon two weeks before the accident. Olivia was out for the afternoon, playing mah-jongg with three other friends. A recent but avid recreation that Henry, who disliked board games and such, could genially listen to descriptions of the subtleties and strategies over dinner and was in fact pleased Olivia had broken free once again of the house and family, after the cloistered past few years with Robert home, thinking, knowing, it was a good thing. Her enthusiasm was all the confirmation needed.

So he was alone in the house. Finishing off his notes on his senior students' final papers for his often contentious but always interesting seminar on Blake, Milton, and Emerson, an unusual trio that he nevertheless was able to stitch together in a fashion that prompted some of the more intriguing thinking and intellectual agility from the girls. When down the hall he heard his son rise and haltingly make his way to the bathroom, the cane employed mornings or very late at night a frustrating counterpoint to the thin touch of feet, as Robert held the cane before him in both hands and labored silent behind it. Along with the mild steady low stream of cursing. Then the bathroom door shut and it was quiet in the house but it was as if Henry was in the bathroom with his son, watching the loose-belted robe swung carelessly open as Robert dug into the cabinet and pulled down the small wooden box that held his syringe, rubber tourniquet, alcohol and gauze pads. Except in the waste basket under the sink Henry had

226

never seen the ampoules of morphine, and those the crushed-neck remains, but guessed his son kept them more safely in his room. A troll guarding his treasure. Then after a sufficient time, Henry heard the bath begin to fill. Between injecting and the time it took to fill the bath there must be sufficient time for the drug to take effect. In order for his son to lower himself into the bath. Once there, Henry knew he'd stay until the water had grown almost cool.

It wasn't as if he'd been waiting. But right then in his small office under the eaves he suddenly knew not only what he had to do, but that it was the right thing, at the right time. So he went downstairs and dumped out the old coffee, filled the percolator and set it on the heat, a small kindness, one of many, he realized. And repaired to the parlor off the dining room to await his son. Leaving doors open along the way so he'd not only see Robert in the kitchen but most importantly so when he hailed his son, Robert would have no escape.

Henry sat in a padded armchair facing the kitchen, his right leg lifted over his left knee, both hands cupped on the right knee, a position he'd long ago learned to use with students, both commanding and relaxed. In charge of the situation. He listened as he heard his son moving overhead, dressing, and then the slow descent of the stairs. The cane set away now. Robert was dressed for golf. He glanced at his father and busied himself with the coffee.

"Good afternoon, Robert. I see you're set for a bit of recreation at the Club. It's a fine day. But join me while you have your coffee. I'd like to talk."

"Can it wait? I'm not really awake yet." Those blue eyes cutting over his father, then peering down at his coffee, the blond sheaf dropping to his forehead.

"No. Come in. You've had plenty of sleep, your usual bath, and a bit of a chat over your coffee will round things out. Besides, your mother's out of the house and what I have to say is just for us men. So come and sit."

Robert carried the cup and saucer with both hands, shaking slightly as he made his way in, then lowered himself to perch on the edge of the damask sofa at a slight angle to his father. Henry readjusted to correct the angle and studied his son. Robert balanced the saucer on one knee, holding it with a thumb and finger, the same way his grandmother Euphemia would a cup of tea. His head cocked, tipped back, defensive and dreamy at once.

"So how are you, Robert? How's the spring coming along for you?"

Robert sipped and the cup clattered lightly against the saucer as he set it down. When he spoke his voice was low, his eyes out on some spot of carpet between them. "Well, Dad. I'm glad you asked. It seems I'm miraculously cured. I played three sets of tennis yesterday afternoon, then practically galloped through nineteen holes of golf. I apologize for missing dinner with you and Mother but ate dinner at the Club with this girl I'd met, pretty well polishing off the steamship of beef single-handedly and then the girl, Myra is her name, perhaps you'll meet her sometime, and then she and I just tore up the dancefloor until the band closed down for the night. After that we drove up the old road past Twain's summerhouse where we employed a blanket to astonishing effect. Yes, it was a fine day altogether and one that, once this little chat is out of the way, I greatly hope to repeat again today."

Henry almost smiled. He wasn't angry, was determined not to grow so. Despite the acid dripping from Robert's tongue, Henry thought there was a gameness there—something he hoped this afternoon would turn. So evenly he said, "Irony is a fine thing but demands a light touch. Or it becomes sarcasm. And sarcasm is a weak shield."

"I see. And you intend to pierce that shield, is that it?"

It would be too easy, Henry thought. He said, "No, Robbie. I want to talk about your plans, your future. It's time, wouldn't you agree?"

"I think you want to talk about your plans for me."

"They're not mine to make."

"So I guess that ends this discussion."

"No it does not. And Robert, it has not yet turned into a discussion. That implies a rational back and forth between two people. As far as I'm concerned, we're just getting started and have yet to reach that goal of discussion."

"So you do have plans for me?"

Henry said, "Robert, what do you intend to do with the rest of your life?"

"What's this? Time to kick me out? Too messy for you?"

Henry sat silent.

Robert finished the coffee, glanced toward the kitchen and Henry almost offered to refill the cup, then did not. His son could easily do so if he wanted. Instead Robert reached, his hands shaking a bit less, and set the cup and saucer on the three-legged round table beside him. Henry still waited.

Finally Robert said, "I don't know what you expect of me. Half the time I can barely walk, and when I can, when my leg's limbered up enough I can go thirty or forty feet, a hundred if the air's clear before I start wheezing and fighting for breath. Do you think I'm happy? Do you think I enjoy living like this?"

"To be blunt, Robert, I think you've grown comfortable with it and perhaps a bit soft because of it. I'm not suggesting you become a sprinter or jockey for God's sake. Or that you take up farming. But you have a brain, a mind. What infirmity precludes you from employing that, pray tell?"

"How well could you work if your lungs ached and your knee felt there were hot pincers gripping it?"

"I'd find a way. How can you expect your brain to function if you're doped up all the time?"

"You don't know what you're talking about. You can't imagine what it's like."

"I can imagine it all too well. You've been an excellent specimen for study these past four—Jesus, five years. What I can't imagine is where your pride went, your sense of yourself. Is it all sucked down into the morphine or is that only a cover, a trick that masks some deeper weakness or fear?"

"Fuck you. I'd like to see you go through what I did and how well you'd manage."

"I suppose a good part of that would be if I had to take care of myself or could simply rely upon others. We've meant well, Robert, your mother and I, but I'm beginning to see we've done you harm, that we've not helped you at all."

Robert stood. He was pale, visibly perspiring and shaky but up. He said, "Very well. I shall not stay where I'm not wanted. There are places I can go—"

Then Henry was up. "Sit down. Now, goddamnit. You are going nowhere until we've talked this through. You shall not make inferences that aren't correct or are self-serving. And while we're at it, you'll hear me through and then as time demands you'll come to me again, as many times as you need, to talk through your intentions. But you're not leaving this house. I said to sit down! There. And one more thing. You will not discuss this with your mother. She's protected you, as a mother should, but the time has come Robert for you to stop hiding beneath her apron. And I shall not allow it. How will I stop you, you might ask? Very simply, Robert. I don't have to stop you. You'll stop yourself. Because you're a grown man and it's time. And you know it. Listen sport, before I was half your age I knew men who'd lost fingers, arms, legs, not to mention the many who lost their lives, not in a war but simply trying to make a living. Fishing. Not bobbers in a creek but small boats out on a huge angry sea, a sea teeming with fish, with food, with money, but also a sea that seemed to have a terrible hunger for men. Your Uncle Gilbert died that way. I lost my first job because a man had been too badly mangled to work the boats anymore. But he had to make a living and I didn't. Simple as that. Or the old man, you remember him, who sat legless on a little dolly at the telegram station, with arms stumped at the elbows, both of them. And he'd hold the goddammed telegram in his teeth and push himself along the sidewalks to make the delivery. Do you think he was without pain? Did you, as a boy, ever follow him, as boys did, and call for him to go faster, faster? If you didn't, I'm proud of you. But think now how that was for him. Did he ever turn and curse those boys, spit at them? No. He simply went on. Doing his job."

He stopped a moment, looking down at his son, the part in his hair. Henry walked back and forth and then took Robert's cup to the kitchen, refilled it, and poured one for himself. He brought them back and set them side by side on the table. Robert had swung his head sideways to watch him. Henry resumed walking. He dearly wished he could sit but knew he had to keep his son bolted firmly in place.

He said, "By the end of June I want you to have made a plan for yourself. Not something vague but concrete, with steps in motion. I expect you don't want my advice but I'm going to give it: Go back to school. Cornell will take you back in a heartbeat and I see two benefits in that. The first, obviously, will be that you'll be drawn out of this selfish malaise you've descended into. And, as importantly, while you'll have to maintain a schedule, which will be good for you, you'll have at least a year to determine what course of study, of what life, you wish to engage upon."

"I'm too old to start that all over."

"Nonsense. If anything, your experiences should serve you well. There's adjustment of course but even as a freshman there is. You'll be a step up in the game, once you determine to play it."

It was quiet. The sun had shifted far enough to the west so the first bars of light were dropping through the windows, small rectangles on the carpet.

Henry sank back into his chair. They were getting somewhere, at last.

Robert said, "What if I just can't do that?"

Henry thought a moment and then said, "If you decide you can't, that it just won't work for you, then the obvious thing is to talk to your grandfather. You know he wouldn't simply create a position for you. But he has fingers in many pies and he'd find a beginning for you, and knowing Grandpa Franks, it would be the sort of thing where he was already mapping out a good route for you. It's nothing to be ashamed of—he'd do that because, just like Mother and me, he loves you and wants to see you get on with life." Henry paused and then said, "But I do hope you consider carefully going back to school. In the end, if you were to apply yourself and take it seriously, it would offer you the best chance at forming a life that you yourself controlled. And that's important, isn't it, Robbie?"

Then Robert stood, walked close and loomed over his father. He said, "That's nice, Dad. It's really thoughtful of you. I especially liked the hard-luck fishing stories. But what it comes down to, really, is you're done with me. No. I don't blame you. I'm sort of tired of myself as well. And also it was thoughtful of you to close Mother out of this conversation. Excuse me. Dialogue. She has, it's true, spoiled me. Perhaps all my life now that I think about it, now that you've enlightened me. Funny. When I was a boy she was the one who understood me. I was always afraid of you. But I shouldn't have been, should I? You were always right there for me, weren't you? I just was too young to see it. There wasn't anything to fear, was there. I must've had a bad dream. That's it, a bad dream. Gosh, Dad, isn't it strange how those things can just overtake you and you don't even know that it's not true? That in fact your father doesn't know what to do with you, is scared of you and so you end up scared of him? Astonishing, really. It doesn't matter that Alice and Polly adored you and for as long as I can remember excused you to me, tried to explain you to me. As if I would get it. But I do. I do now. Fuck all. You used to call me your little man. Love and endearment, no doubt was how you saw that. For me all it ever meant was I was less than you. But hey? I have to agree with you. You want me out and you know what? I have to get out. So I will. By the summer. And, Dad? It just relieves me no end to know I can come and talk to you about that, about how it's going in the meanwhile. It really does. And also, yes, set your mind at rest. I won't bother Mother about any of this. Not a word."

Robert then lurched sideways and regained himself. "No," he continued. "Mum's the word."

Henry stood then and harder than intended poked an index finger in his son's chest. "That's the dope, Robbie. Your morning morphine has kicked in. You have to quit that. You have to. Where're you getting it, anyway? All I have to do is call Emery Westmore and this whole town will be shut down for you. Don't you understand?"

Robert stepped back and coughed, those lungs harsh in their need for air. Then he looked at his father and said, "You're a goddamned idiot. You and Westmore can't do a damned thing. I've got a medical history, papers, a record. I'm sorry to tell you this, Dad. But there are some things you just can't control. Including me."

Then he coughed again and bent over a bit. Henry stepped closer and Robert came up swiftly and punched his father first in the stomach and then as he crumpled forward, a hard right that boxed his ear, sent stars through his head as he fell back roughly against the chair.

Robbie was also bent, breathing hard as Henry began to recover. As he pulled himself upright into the chair he saw his horrified son looking down at him. Then the boy was gone, clumping hard through into the kitchen cursing there as he looked for his keys, his wallet. Both, Henry knew, beside the toaster. He forced himself to stand and croaked, "Rob. Robbie, wait."

Then heard the backdoor slam and so pressed himself out into the kitchen, his air coming back into him as he went, the unmistakable heaving of vomit licking the back of his throat. He swallowed against it and went out the back door and down into the peastone just as the roadster growled to life and backed around, then quieted as Robert shifted and Henry called as loud as he ever had his son's name. Robert's face in full panic, looked at him, then popped the clutch and the car went fast out the drive, gravel chucked up behind. Henry staggered down the steps and off into the still-dead grass to the beds along the shed where heavy clumps of almost-blooming daffodils were stalwart and here he bent and vomited into them.

After Henry collected himself he washed his face and brushed his teeth and tongue, then went to the kitchen and washed and put away the coffee cups, cleaning up. When Olivia came in later that afternoon he was back in his upstairs office, the door closed, ostensibly working but slowly mending himself, realizing that of course their conversation had to have been explosive. Robert's blurted confession of his feelings, his perceptions of his father were difficult for Henry, but ultimately he thought it was best they were out now between them. Henry would ignore them and hold to his course in the weeks and months, perhaps even, he knew, years ahead. Having the wind knocked out of him and his head boxed were also, he thought, a reaction that eventually would work in his favor. Again, to be ignored, not mentioned. He understood most boys have some moment when they feel the urge to try to better their father, although in this house physical violence had never been used, except for the occasional swat to the rear when all three children were youngsters. But Robert had also learned and seen far too much outside of this house. And sadly, while no longer a boy, still was not yet a man. Perhaps this afternoon would begin to make him one.

His failure to appear for the evening meal went unremarked, had happened far too many times so that any comment had become touchy ground and so he and Olivia had long since made a truce over that issue.

But then, with Olivia in bed, her reading light already off, as Henry stretched his arm to turn the switch on his own, she said, "You know, Henry, I know you doubted my judgment about Robbie. About being patient with him."

Very slowly, while trying not to appear so, he turned the switch and lay back against the pillow. Cautiously, he said, "Yes?"

"He just seems more upbeat recently. I can't pin it down but there's something in the way he carries himself, as if he's coming to terms with where life has led him. I do so hope so. For you know, I believe that's his first step forward. The rest will come naturally enough, don't you think?"

"Perhaps," Henry said. "Perhaps you're right." Then he leaned and kissed her goodnight. She was shortly asleep but he lay some time.

Twenty-six

N ow—overwhelmed at the prospect of Lydia's return, realizing that while he'd hoped for it and missed her dearly, he had no idea how they might go forward in life, that he'd not allowed what until moments ago had seemed a dangerous fantasy but now felt like a dereliction on his part—he took matters firmly in hand. From the closet he dug out the broom, mop, mop bucket and box of soap flakes. When he took the apartment it had come with the services of a weekly cleaning lady but he'd determined to take care of himself—that and he wanted no interruptions, scheduled or not. The landlady had taken great pains to make clear there would be no reduction in the rent, too much effort Henry thought, until the woman presented him with the necessary tools and then he understood she doubted a man was capable of the work involved. It had all seemed rather easy before Lydia departed—a quick sweep and wipe of the counters. In fact, the mop was yet new, the soap flakes unopened.

So he went to work. Work necessary but also the best antidote for mindless worry. And the work proved more labor than he'd expected, the mopping especially pressed upon his back as he bent scrubbing up old layers of dirt invisible after he'd swept. For only the two rooms, large as they were, he had to change the mop water four times. His arms ached and by the time he emptied the final bucket of reasonably clean water into the bath it was sharply painful to straighten fully upright. He was flushed and in the perverse nature of such things the radiator had been clanking and hissing all afternoon, warm enough so he cracked a window. At least the floors dried quickly.

Then he had to work on his knees on the hard tile to clean the squat bathtub and sink, now all with cold water and since he had no rags but dishtowels he tore two in half and made hard use of them. Finally it was done. His shirtfront and trousers were sopping and smudged where he'd wiped dirty hands. And along with those, the linens on the bed had not been among what he'd carried home from the laundry. He looked at his watch and guessed if he changed quickly he could make it back across the square to the laundry and they'd be clean and pressed, the linens beautifully starched and folded by mid-afternoon. So off he went, feeling both tired and accomplished. The outside air was refreshing after the noxious smarting perfume of the soap flakes.

He was a smiling man, full of cheer and mission. The first over-whelming rush of questions and concerns had been answered, not conclusively but as much as could be expected until she arrived, by the long-learned lesson of hard labor. Even as he grimaced, thinking it had been obviously a bit too long since he'd employed this maxim. But the first surge of panic was gone. If, as her letter certainly implied, she desired to make a life with him, he was no closer to knowing the practicalities of such a life. And if she happened to have a plan, it would immediately appeal or, and he knew this was true, they would discuss the range of options until they found a mutually agreeable ground. So this was what he knew: She was coming directly to his apartment and perhaps they'd spend a short time together there as they determined the way forward. Perhaps, if they were to remain in Amsterdam, something he saw as a distinct possibility, they'd search together for more spacious and comfortable but private accommo-dations. He was not the sort to live out of an hotel suite and she knew that. Neither would he be kept. And while he had no idea of her true wealth he knew it far outstripped his own modest but not inconsid-erable savings, which included the inheritance from Uncle George all those years ago—money that no doubt further fueled Fred's animosity but that also had never been touched, the interest accruing essentially what he sent his mother each month. Anyway, it wasn't a question of money so much as how they chose to live and he trusted Lydia knew him well enough not to expect him to live in the fashion she did. On the other hand, while he was still hoping to press for the trip throughout England come spring, he couldn't envision Lydia being the peripatetic visiting scholar's wife. Or perhaps she'd surprise him.

Perhaps they'd surprise each other.

Most certainly, huffing now with the laundry, the steamed windows in sight, they'd surprise each other. And after all, wasn't that their story writ both small and large?

He was smiling like a fool when he passed over his second laundry of the day, filled out the slips and pocketed the stubs. The air inside the laundry so dense and wet he wondered how people stood it, and then was back out into the evening, the sudden winter dusk.

What was clearly out of the question, at least for the immediate future, was any return to Elmira. Or for that matter, he was confident, her home in Vermont. Although there would come a time, and in the not too great distance when she'd meet his daughters and granddaughters. And Mary and Doyle. This paused him a moment before the rising bulk of the Waag, the ancient bricks immutable as the black shadow climbed to obliterate their dusky rose. A short stay at the cottage at the Lake next summer would introduce her to all, and she to them. He'd never seen her with children but she charmed everyone he'd ever witnessed and was more than capable of the Lake. Alice and Polly would be the most difficult and he understood that. But they, the three women, would find their way. He knew and loved and trusted all enough to be sure of that. And stopped again. Perhaps it was more that they, those women, knew and loved him enough to carry through what by then was inevitable. Women understood life itself far more straightforwardly than men. The nuts and bolts, he thought. No, he corrected. The underpinning. What keeps us going.

He ate supper at the old bar where he was a usual, if not regular. To be regular invokes being known and while he was expected he was not, and never would be known. His routine soup, this evening of white beans and sliced sausages in a thick broth with onions and leeks. Several cold Genevers, a couple more than most nights but he already doubted he'd sleep this night but was stoking hope with the food and alcohol. And then was suddenly drooping, alarmingly tired.

He actually bounced against the stairwell twice going up. Then in his apartment stood, gazing at the windows, their arcs and prisms of light, pulling himself to focus on his writing desk, knowing he needed to make a list, the things to be done in the morning. The stocking of foods and wine and everything else that was spilling over in his mind, all the small delicious things he wanted to present Lydia with. And there! A present! He must have something for her. Something simple and beautiful and thoughtful. Not a ring. But, he was momentarily brilliant, a gift that was gorgeous and vast with love and that, above all, said, I'm not a ring but could be and want to be and should be if you'll allow me to be.

Sometime during the night he woke, his head magnificently clear. He was wide awake but free of concerns or worries. It seemed he was floating on the bed, cushioned buoyant between the sheets, warm as all life and within a willful cocoon of inner peace. Dark still, but daylight was coming.

He woke much later than usual and climbed from bed, alarmed until he caught himself laughing. What was late, anyway? He had a handful of errands, some shopping to do but other than that he had, this day, no timetable. He had most literally no idea when she'd appear. So he decided that he'd get out as soon as he could and take care of all those important things and return here.

And play his cello. Thinking of her hiking up the stairs, his door ajar, walking up the stairs to the strains of the cello. If nothing else he could play scales, slowly, and they would resonate out and down the stairs. Both announcing himself and greeting her. If it turned out to be a late train he'd play until his fingers were numb.

So he tidied up a last time and then out he went. Making his way to Kalverstraat. Pausing at the Dam, looking up at her windows in the hotel. Bundled against the cold the summer seemed not so much a dream or place to return to but a wondrous beginning. Then he pressed into the shopping crowds, down the narrow twists and turns of Kalverstraat, intent upon finding the gift first, then working his way back home, toward the familiar, picking up the rest of his notions and dreams as he went.

The gift was not easier than expected but exactly as expected—there, displayed, catching him, inevitable. A modern device of hammered gold, both diminutive and substantial, a necklace with subdued undeniable high craftsmanship evident in each linkage of its parts. Buying it, watching it wrapped in tissue and then in a slender box, he realized it was something he never would've looked at, much less seen for what it was, if not for her.

Then he began the slow maneuver back the way he'd come, done with the holiday push of Kalverstraat—everything else he needed could be found around Nieuwmarkt and so closer to home. Just during the time in the jeweler's the air had softened, warmed somewhat even as the furled clouds hung low and he thought it might snow, both a cheering thought and one worrisome—snow so festive and inviting, intimate and yet too much of it could slow the trains. There wasn't a flake in sight yet and nothing to be done about it anyway except to continue on.

It was a comfortable pleasure that he knew the shops ringing Nieuwmarkt and the nearby streets so well that he could without effort trace out his best possible route, which with the exception of the laundry and one other, final stop, was based not only on convenience but the weight and bulk accrued as he went. So first the butcher for shaved ham and a smoked duck that they could eat cold, or warm in his tiny oven that he could only assume worked—he'd never tested it. But they would eat in this evening, partly because of the uncertainty of her arrival but most purely because he wanted his attention upon only her. On to the fruit and vegetable market where he bought pears from Africa and the delicious blood oranges from Spain, as well as a carton of strawberries from the hothouses. Here also he bought more dates, seeing her in his mind slipping the pits out by pressing with her fingers, then lifting the dense sweet fruits to her mouth.

After this the wine and spirit merchant and going in he paused to hold the door for an older man, bent with his own bags, a man in a heavy black peacoat and black sea captain's cap, who paused as he struggled out, lifting his head to look at Henry and for the strangest of moments it was as if he faced Uncle George—the same weather-lined face and thick white mustache, the same unclouded blue eyes, his hair pushed behind his ears under the cap in white waves nearly down to his shoulders. The man looked at Henry and blinked, then nodded his thanks and went on his way. Henry watched him go and for a moment his heart ached—no ghost this man but an old Dutch sailor which, more or less and several generations removed was what his uncle had been. Inside he wandered the bins, being cautious and wanting to get it just right. He could only manage so many bottles and yet wanted to have everything possibly desired on hand. Which thought, after a few moments stopped him. Whatever he chose would be what was desired. He selected a bottle of Perrier Brut which reminded him he might want to go to the fishmongers for oysters and told himself if that was the case he'd need at least a lemon from the shop just left, as well as an oyster knife at the fishmongers. Then dithered, wondering if they might want more champagne for later, after the meal, after, just possibly after lovemaking. Well, he could only do so much. He searched his brain and then the bins again and came up with two bottles of Gigondas that rang a bell of memory, a Montrachet for the same reason and then, considering it all, went back for that second bottle of Brut after all. Here he was helped by the clerk who packed the bottles sturdily in tied-tight tubes of cardboard before wrapping them in heavy paper, secured with strong sisal twine, so he might carry it one-handed without fear of the package slipping from his clutch.

On then to the bakery for hard bread as well as croissants for breakfast, a slab of unsalted butter and a larger piece of the delicious dense Belgian chocolate he knew she loved. This was a lighter bag but delicate. He arranged himself and stepped back outside.

It was warmer. And a few flakes, small and random twisted down. He paused to take it all in, feeling a little flushed, his heart beating an exuberant tattoo in his chest. He was gaining. He contemplated marching home now and then returning for the rest but he was close to being done and, truth was, once he was inside he wanted only to get everything in order and wait for her. The trains could easily be on time and she might well have caught an early one. There might be no Parisian rail strike at all.

On he went. At the fishmongers he was lucky again. Not only did they carefully wrap and tie the two dozen oysters to carry but had the thick blunt knives for sale, as well as, remarkably, not only lemons but small crocks of freshly made creamed horseradish which he remembered her loving a dab with the shimmering mollusk, already reacting to the acid squirt of lemon just before the shell was lifted and tipped into her waiting mouth.

He was beginning to plod, but it was a pleasant infused plod. And he was almost done. Next on was the tobacconist for the *Herald Tribune* and the faint possibility that it might hold news of any rail strikes. So he also bought yesterday's *Le Monde*. He was getting there, this love-struck camel.

A quick pass by the laundry for his blessedly light sack, which he managed to tuck up under his aching left arm. Something of the mopwork the day before lingering, unworked muscles in cramped complaint. And then out for the rather hearty demanding stroll to the flower shop, at least the closest he'd seen and remembered. The stalls of course were closed. As he trudged toward the farthest corner of the square it occurred to him that if he'd followed Lydia's directive about keeping flowers always in his rooms this might possibly be less of a trek. Live and learn. He smiled. The thin flakes continued, drifting above and within, among the square, the people, making a flimsy coat on the ground.

The flower shop was hot and densely humid. He moved toward the counter and set his packages down, then opened his coat to cool off, his forehead beading with sudden heat and moisture, his shirt beneath his vest soaked. He made a pretense of looking around. There were potted forced tulips and hyacinths and narcissus blooming or about to, which didn't interest him. Similarly there were pots of lilies of all sizes and colors but again not what he wanted. He knew what he wanted even the best hothouse couldn't provide—a bulk of sunflowers. And then thought No—don't reach for the past. So he waited patiently and when his turn came he indicated the glass-fronted coolers behind the counter, laid a ten guilder note down and in his better but still fractured Dutch told her what he wanted. A grand assemblage for my returning love. But with thought. The flowers must balance each other gently. The clerk was young and blond and listened carefully, her bobbed hair swooping toward the corners of her mouth. When he was done she responded, "You desire elegance. A profusion of elegance."

"Yes," he said, delighted and taking it as a sign that his Dutch was not only finally working but truly comprehended. He stood waited as she went behind the misted glass doors, watching as she dipped and swooped and more than once lifted to inspect before rejecting a flower, a stem of them. When she finally came out she held a bundle of blessed magnificence in her arms, which she held across for his inspection and he said, "Yes, yes. Oh, perfect." She trimmed them and wrapped them in paper and held the brilliant cone out to him. He bent and gathered up his mighty arsenal of packages and bundles and then finally took the flowers from the girl. When she placed his considerable change upon the counter he shook his head. "For you," he said. "Merry Christmas."

It was a long trip back up Nieuwmarkt, the Waag a floating marker near where he would turn off the square and make his way the final blocks to home. The snow stung his face although he was warm enough, as if the flakes were tiny reminders of the true definition of the day. In fact the cold speckles were welcome—he was over-burdened and perhaps overdressed, sweating hard and his legs were heavy—so the bright bitter spits against his face seemed almost a force of hope. He was almost done, all he was to accomplish nearly complete.

The Waag, the ancient weighing station when this was the port of entry came upon him looming and welcome and he then was past it, back along the canal that dead-ended at the square and here he turned and followed his own canal, a narrow domestic waterway, the overhanging trees beginning to gather white coats on the topsides of their branches. It was as beautiful a day as he could ask, and unless the snow was much worse to the south and east, nothing to worry about.

He made it into the entryway on his groundfloor. Where in his mailbox waited a clutch of telegrams. Slowly he let his packages down onto the small landing and the first few steep stairs. With a great fear he plucked out the three telegrams only to see they were merely the confirmations of the Christmas orders he'd placed. He tucked them into the same pocket that held the box with her necklace. Again, as the day before, the heat was high in the building. He took a moment and wiped sweat from his forehead, then looked at the handkerchief in his trembling fingers. Get upstairs, he thought. Get upstairs and settle down. He looked about him at the load of goods, the load of love. He could make two trips but all he wanted was to have everything upstairs and then he could stop, put it all away, rest and read the papers and restore himself. So he dug in his pocket for his key, clamped it between his teeth and slowly, thoughtfully, in much the same order he'd purchased it all, gathered up his bundles and proceeded to climb the stairs. He was getting the job done. As he always had.

Outside his door he had to free a hand and so set down the bundle of wines, the oysters, the laundry. He was sweating now into his eyes so his vision was brined and undulating. The door was aquiver. The sack of breads fell from under his arm. He stabbed several times with the key before it sank tight into place. His mostly free left arm was pressed to his chest, holding the precious cone of flowers, as he worked the key back and forth, befuddled by the lock. Then the door, almost as if it chose to, swung open wide. He stepped in, his legs suddenly jellied. The apartment was glittering calm in the light of day. Small hedgerows of snow were forming against the edges of the windows.

Then the swift archer's bolt in his chest and he grasped with both hands and clawed apart the paper cone holding the flowers, his fingers mistaking them for the ripping within his chest, pain and light flooding his body, white and blinding.

Then strangely peacefully prone, watching as the torn flowers floated up, the pinwheel bursts of colors, the perfect gathering of nascent temporal life high above him, thrust up, finding new patterns, new groupings that even as he watched them all made exquisite perfect sense.

There came a small chime as the key stuck the floor. The kaleidoscope flowers reached their apex. He watched their dreaming fall begin. Never to feel their delicate attempt to shroud him.

Jeffrey Lent

Whan that Aprill with his shoures soote
The droghte of March hath perced to the roote,
And bathed every veyne in swich licour
Of which vertu engendred is the flour . . .

Twenty-seven

*I*t had been an uneventful journey. Becoming pretty as she went north and it began to snow. She'd eaten twice and was feeling strong, ready for whatever lay ahead. When the train pulled into the station she was patient, having learned long ago there was no need to rush, that it would speed nothing up. So finally she stepped out onto the platform, a pair of porters behind with her two trunks. They wended their way along toward the main entrance where she knew from experience the first crush of taxicabs would've already departed but soon others would arrive to take their place. Once she paused to pat the pocket of her long coat, touching the package within. Of course still there, Spenser's *Faerie Queen* in an old French vellum and morocco edition. She smiled then. She came out of the station, her coat still open from the heat of the train and the station, her dress stretched tight over the growing pod of her belly. She glanced behind but the porters were close. She turned then, lifted a hand to hail a cab. She knew his location by heart.

Acknowledgments

I want to thank Derek Thurber and Anita Abbot for their diligence and enthusiasm, in assisting with research for this project. Also thanks to Mark Woodhouse of the Gannett-Tripp Library, Elmira College.

Polly Smith, Sayre & Nancy Fulkerson, David Lent, and Ted Marks all gave freely of their time and recollections of Elmira and Glenora, New York, during the time period of this novel; Raymond and Reta Thurber of Freeport, Nova Scotia, for a grand tour, the story of the burnt suit, and outstanding fish chowder; in Amsterdam, Henk van Amsterdam for his lovely apartment, the staff at the Amsterdams Historisch Museum, the staff at the Joods Historisch Museum, my editors at Prometheus (Holland), Hedda Sanders and Job Lisman, translator Peter Abelsen, and in Nijmegan, the staff of the Rijksarcheif Gelderland. Thanks also for support, of varying times, places, and means, to Petra & Rob McCarron, Dick & Sue Walton, John Evans, Richard & Lisa Howorth, Jamie & Kelly Kornegay, Chris & Bonnie Alexander, Andrea Tetrick, Penny McConnel, Gary Schall, Jean Palthey, Mark & Amy Rosalbo, and Donald Hall. For their attentiveness and support, David Forrer and Kim Witherspoon. Deb Seager, for putting up with me. Amy Hundley, for her keen eye, firm insight and gentle humor. And to Morgan Entrekin, whose patience and graciousness went far beyond any expected bounds.